A
DEATH
FOR A
DODO

E. X.
GIROUX

A DEATH
FOR A
DODO

St. Martin's Press
New York

Design by DAWN NILES

Library of Congress Cataloging-in-Publication Data

Giroux, E. X.
    A death for a dodo / E.X. Giroux.
        p.   cm.
    "A Thomas Dunne book."
    ISBN 0-312-08762-4
    I. Title.
PR9199.3.S49D392   1993
813'.54—dc20   92-42573
                                                       CIP

First Edition: February 1993

10 9 8 7 6 5 4 3 2 1

This book is for Garnet and for my sister, Lois Margaret Keyes.

A
DEATH
FOR A
DODO

1

The Hannah Edington Memorial Hospital, affection-
ately known to the locals as HEM, and the Damien
Day Health Home, politely nicknamed Damien Day
but derisively called DODO by the same group, were sepa-
rated by a number of curves in the sea road, a few miles,
and two vastly dissimilar life-styles.

There were some similarities. Both were sprawling
structures built of the local rock, with rear gardens sloping down gradually to where surf foamed against a strip
of shingle and sea grass. But the hospital, located on the
outskirts of the small town of Hundarby, operated on the
National Health Plan and its patients, though adequately
cared for, were not coddled. The clientele of the health
home were drawn from the ranks of the rich and famous
and not only expected but received a continuation of their
lives of ease and luxury.

It was a rare event when a patient of HEM, having
completed surgery, was transported down the winding
road to convalesce in the hallowed halls of DODO. Thus,
on a gray and dreary afternoon in early January as the
tan-and-white ambulance with the logo of HEM pulled

away from the hospital, turned left, and proceeded at a stately pace toward DODO, many avid eyes searched for a sight of the occupant.

Two young and giggly nurses' aides trotting up the driveway, an ancient gentleman walking a borzoi, a curvaceous teacher shepherding a crocodile of small girls from a Hundarby school all strained for a glimpse of a face known to them only from a television screen or the pages of a glossy magazine. All were disappointed. This convalescent was flat on his back on a stretcher, firmly strapped down, his eyes fixed on the flickering shadows across the roof.

Along with Queen Victoria, Robert Forsythe was definitely not amused. Like an animal, he thought, pegged down as though he might try for an escape. Then the corners of his mouth twitched in a tiny smile. Some escape that would be! Hobbling along on the crutches he'd been allowed to use only for the last few days. He wondered whose idea it had been to send him to the Damien Day like a trussed side of beef and momentarily flirted with the thought that it could have been Sandy's suggestion. But that was sheer paranoia. Abigail Sanderson, once his father's legal secretary and now his own, was much too forthright for that underhanded maneuver. Sandy's role in his life was much more important than that of a secretary; she was the closest thing to a mother that he'd ever had, and she knew him as well as any mother could have.

Forsythe's mouth tightened. Although they had never discussed it, he was certain Sandy was aware of his bête noire, the black beast that had terrorized him since he was three years old. Oddly enough, the pretty young mother he had lost then was sometimes clearer in his memory than his father, who had outlived his wife by many years. But his father had been nearly twice his wife's age and had always seemed more like a grandfa-

2

ther than a father to Robert Forsythe. That grandfatherly figure had tried to reassure his young son when the ambulance bore away the most important woman in both their lives. "Don't cry, son," Randolph Forsythe had said, "your mother only has a pain in her side. She's gone to hospital where they'll make it better and then she'll be coming home to us."

The child waited, but neither the hospital nor the staff in it could make his mother better. The last memory Robert had of his mother was when the attendants lifted her into the ambulance and one small hand fluttered a good-bye to him. In that young and agonized mind the child decided that his beloved mother had been killed by the hospital. As he grew older he realized the truth and was able to rationalize that fear of hospitals, but it still lingered and even as a man in his thirties Robert Forsythe was fighting that black beast of terror.

Forsythe had proved adept at sidestepping hospitals. When he was six his father was involved in a car accident and was hospitalized with minor injuries. Miss Sanderson was preparing to take the little boy to visit his father when she noticed Robert's hectic color and checked his temperature. The child was put to bed suffering from what appeared to be flu. His father's release from hospital and Robert's recovery occurred simultaneously.

A few months later his great aunt Rachel broke an ankle and spent three days in hospital. Again Robert was mysteriously ill. But, shortly after his tenth birthday, his luck ran out. This time it was the boy who was sick and the diagnosis was infected tonsils. So Robert entered the hospital with Miss Sanderson by his side and she stayed with him until he was sedated and the operation was performed. When the boy regained consciousness, she was smiling down at him, and she slept on a cot next to his bed, successfully keeping the specter of death at bay.

His luck ran out again when he was in prep school

and this time Miss Sanderson was unable to help. She was visiting a sister in Glasgow when Robert received a knee injury in a hotly contested game of soccer. Without Sandy to ward off his fears, the boy was forced to face them alone, outwardly stoic, inwardly seething with terror. After two weeks of sheer hell, he was released, vowing silently that he would never again enter a hospital.

For slightly more than two decades, he had made good on that promise, until a combination of a deteriorating kneecap and the pleas of the two most important women in his life had forced him to bite the bullet and have the knee operation performed.

So, Forsythe thought, here he was, leaving one hospital and about to enter another. His secretary had made the arrangements and she had assured him that after a brief stay in the Hannah Edington Memorial he would be wafted away to the Damien Day, where he could convalesce in an atmosphere that bore little resemblance to a hospital. He told himself grimly that no matter what the name, no matter how luxurious, a hospital was still a hospital.

He was jerked from his depressing thoughts as the ambulance drew to a smooth stop. The glass pane separating him from the cab was pushed back and the driver stuck his head around it. "Not to worry, sir. Just a security check at the gate."

Security? Ah, yes. From what Sandy had told him about the clientele of the Damien Day, that was no doubt necessary. Security arrived in the person of a wide, ruddy face under a vizored cap taking a thorough look at the patient through the side window and then a deep voice in conversation with the driver. Forsythe must have passed muster, since the ambulance moved away, proceeded a fair distance, and then, once again, came to a smooth stop.

The driver had neglected to close the glass pane and

4

Forsythe heard him call, "If it isn't me old mate! Haven't seen you since you got your notice at HEM."

"See you haven't got the ax yet, Mac."

"Could come any day. Cutting staff back something fierce. Looks like you landed awful soft, Perce. Dressed like you was going out for a golf game."

Perce laughed. "Gotta keep the nobs happy, Mac. Make believe this is a resort. But it pays good and the work ain't that heavy. Wish I wasn't just a temp."

"You know what they say about wishes." Sounds of movement in the cab and a door opening. "Well, Perce, let's get it done."

Shortly afterward, the rear doors opened and the driver and the orderly proceeded to unfasten the straps and lift Forsythe, quickly and competently, into a wheelchair. As careful as they were, pain lanced down Forsythe's left calf and he winced. "Sorry, sir," the orderly said. After pulling out a padded metal shelf attached to the chair, he positioned Forsythe's leg, and accepted the clipboard Mac was extending. While he flipped over pages, the barrister studied his surroundings.

In one instance his secretary had been correct. This place bore no resemblance to any medical facility he had ever seen. It looked like a heritage building the National Trust would be interested in acquiring. Built of the local stone, sand colored and streaked with russet, centuries old, sprawling among gardens nicely kept even in this dreary month, looking like the country home of an aristocratic family . . . the barrister wondered how the devil Reggie Knight, known to millions of rock fans as the Black Knight, had managed to buy it.

As Perce signed the final sheet and handed the clipboard back to the ambulance driver, Forsythe glanced at the orderly. He could see what Mac had meant when he'd mentioned the orderly's clothes. No white jacket and pants for this young man. Perce was wearing casual slacks, a daffodil yellow pullover, and brightly polished, tasseled slip-ons.

The wind from the sea was chill and biting and the barrister gave an involuntary shudder. Both the driver and orderly noticed and no more time was spent on social chitchat. Mac handed over a manila envelope, touched the brim of his cap, and stood back as Perce piloted the wheelchair up a ramp to the magnificent front door. The ancient oak was ornamented with brass studs and a knocker shaped like a peacock with the brass filigree tail proudly spread. The entrance hall behind that door was equally imposing. It was baronial size, pillared, and paneled; the gleaming oak floorboards were spread with silky old rugs.

The woman seated behind a Louis XVI lady's desk was as impressive as her surroundings. An emerald wool dress hugged every curve of a splendid figure, Italian sandals displayed fine legs, and hair the same shade as the peacock knocker fell around her shoulders. Her ripe lips parted, but the voice Forsythe heard came from behind him.

"Ah, Robert. Lovely to see you again. Did the ride tire you?"

Perce turned the chair and Forsythe smiled up at Hielkje Visser. He'd met this woman only once before. He'd gone to an island inn to retrieve Abigail Sanderson when a celebrity murder party had turned real and two people had died horribly. There he'd also met Fran Hornblower, who had acted as the inn's handyman, and Reggie Knight, the Jamaican rock star. Sandy had been shot and wounded by the murderer and Forsythe's attention had been concentrated on her, but he recalled Hielkje as tall and stout and untidy. As he reassured her that the short ambulance ride hadn't unduly tired him, he regarded her with some surprise. The Hielkje Visser of the

Damien Day was much slimmer and more stylish that the distraught woman he'd met in the Jester.

Hielkje returned his smile. "Do wheel Mr. Forsythe into the library, Percival." She led the way into another magnificent room, selected a leather chair from a cluster in the bay window, and indicated to the orderly where to position the wheelchair. Another regal wave of a manicured hand dismissed Perce and she turned to Forsythe. "And what do you think of our health home?"

Forsythe unbuttoned his Burberry and shrugged it off. Under it he was wearing a dark blue exercise suit with white flashes down the pants. The suit had been Sandy's idea and initially he had resisted, but, as usual, his secretary had been correct. The suit was loose and comfortable and warm. "If the rest of this place measures up to the reception areas, Hielkje, it's a veritable palace."

She nodded complacently. "We were fortunate to find it."

Forsythe smothered a grin, wondering what Sandy had thought about the metamorphosis of the jean-clad, hypochondriacal cook from the Jester into this lady of the manor. He glanced toward the entrance hall. "I'd hoped to see Fran Hornblower again and perhaps Reggie."

"Reggie is seldom here. His profession is so time-consuming and of course he trusts Fran and me completely. Fran asked me to tell you she's sorry she can't be here to welcome you but she's having a little time off. You see, January is generally the month we close this place and the entire staff takes its holidays. But this year a few of our clients specifically asked that we accommodate them." Hielkje pursed her full lips. "Really an imposition, Robert. Our work is so demanding we need this month to unwind."

"Did all the staff stay on?"

This time the lip motion was closer to a pout. "Hardly. The lower the rank, the greater the privileges.

We persuaded our chef to stay and Fran and I arranged to take a couple of weeks separately so one of us would be here to supervise, but other than that our present help are all temporary. The hospital in Hundarby is laying off their people so we were able to come up with a skeleton staff. All experienced, I must admit, but none of them accustomed to handling clients of our caliber."

She paused and took a deep breath, apparently savoring the rarified air breathed by the distinguished clientele of the health home named after a singing star's dead brother. "Before Fran left she gave the new people a short training seminar and they're doing fairly well, but I shall be glad to have her back." She patted the lacy jabot at the throat of the turquoise jacket. "My own health, as Abigail may have told you, is delicate and the strain of running this place by myself and catering to the whims of our guests . . ." Her voice trailed off as she glanced at Forsythe, noted the leg extended on the metal rest, and seemed to realize she was pouring out her woes to one of the home's distinguished guests.

The distinguished guest was having his own problem, that of maintaining a serious and concerned expression while inwardly seething with laughter. He remembered Sandy's assessment of Hielkje Visser shortly after the ill-fated murder party at the Jester. *"Bone lazy,"* Sandy had snapped. *"Depending on poor Fran for every last thing. Fran does her own work, most of Hielkje's, and all Hielkje does is whine about her health."*

Forsythe had raised a puzzled brow. *"You said Hielkje had been fired from the Jester."*

"She was. But Reggie Knight—his real name is Day—is planning on opening a rest home in his brother's memory and has asked Fran to manage it. And where Fran goes you can bet your booties Hielkje will tag along. Fran Hornblower is a marvel, can do practically anything she—"

"I know, Sandy. You've raved on and on about her." He

8

grinned. *"But if I remember correctly, one of the little things you once thought Fran had done was double murder."*

Recalling his secretary's irate reaction to that remark, Forsythe let his serious expression slip and his lips curved in a smile.

Hielkje was regarding him coldly. "You find something humorous about my ill health, Robert?"

"Of course not. I was remembering how you and Fran met Sandy."

"I scarcely find that terrible time funny."

"Something good comes from every situation, even a tragic one like that party. Think of it, Hielkje. If you hadn't been on that island, in that inn, you'd probably never have met Reggie and . . ."

"That's true." Her hand absently pleated a fold of the turquoise skirt and she regarded Robert, realizing she found him as impressive now as she had when he'd arrived at the Jester frantic with fear about his secretary's safety. She'd been surprised to see such a young man; his reputation as both barrister and criminologist had indicated a man much older. Forsythe had been wearing impeccable tweeds and had an aura of elegance. Even now, seated in a wheelchair, his long thin frame draped in a shapeless exercise suit, the barrister still retained that quality.

Forsythe was glancing around the library. "How did Reggie come up with this place? I seem to remember Sandy saying that Reggie and Fran had settled on a small rest home near Finchley."

"They did. But it was quite small and really rundown and Reggie soon found it wasn't going to work. Many of Reggie's friends and colleagues thought his rest home would be a wonderful place for them to convalesce from operations and illnesses and they were pleading with him to take them in. At Finchley we simply didn't have the room or facilities for people like that. So Reggie started to

9

look around and came up with . . ." Hielkje waved an expressive hand.

"It must have cost a fortune."

"Not as much as one would think. Reggie is shrewd and has incredible luck. It was what is called a desperation sale. Fitted up as a luxury hotel by a young lordling with more money than brains who then found there's nothing in this area to attract rich tourists. He was more than happy to sell the renovated family manor to the Black Knight." Hielkje threw back her head and laughed. "Much to Reggie's shock he has found this tribute to his brother Damien's memory is a gold mine. There's a waiting list to get in here and you'd be surprised at some of the names."

Forsythe raised his brows. "I feel rather mystified. At being here, I mean. How did a lowly barrister slip in at the head of that illustrious queue?"

She laughed again. "Sheer clout, Robert. Reggie and Fran and I would do anything for Abigail. And it seemed most important to her that you be taken out of hospital as soon as possible." She rose, smoothed her skirt, and placed a hand on the back of his chair. "Now I must see you're settled. By the by, Abigail sent down some clothes for you and your suite is prepared. Flowers have arrived and some gifts. The day nurse will examine the parcels and you mustn't feel insulted. All luggage and parcels are checked."

"Sounds like a prison," he muttered.

"You'd be astounded at what some of our celebrities try to get away with. They come here to recover from their excesses and then make every effort to have forbidden goodies smuggled into them. Like a group of spoiled children!"

She drew the chair to a halt near the Louis XVI desk and the decorative receptionist raised her head. "Gerry, would you ring for Percival, please. Gerry, this is Robert

10

Forsythe. Robert, Gerry Duncan, who is helping us this month. Our regular receptionist is on the Costa Brava and I'm green with envy. Ah, Percival, please take Mr. Forsythe up to Miss Holly. Robert, you'll find Miss Holly most efficient. She's a former matron and she kindly came out of retirement to help us out. I'll see you later, Robert, but now I simply must get some rest. My health, you know, so uncertain.''

As Perce wheeled the chair toward a lift, Forsythe saw the receptionist turning her head to hide a rather snide smile. He had a feeling that Hielkje Visser was doing as much actual work at this health home as she had at the Jester.

The lift proved to be as luxurious as the main floor and when they reached the first floor he found it too was a place of gleaming oak floors, silky Persian rugs, mellow paneling. To the right of the lift was a long polished counter, as in a hotel. Behind it, a door opened into an office. Perce touched a bell and a woman stepped briskly out of the office and reached for the manila envelope.

''Mr. Forsythe? Yes. I'm Miss Holly. Percival, you can return to your duties. Mr. Forsythe, you're in the Primrose Suite.''

''Primrose?''

''This is the Flower Wing. We also have a Bird Wing, an Animal Wing, and a Tree Wing. But at present only this wing is being used.''

Miss Holly's expression was unrevealing, but her icy voice made clear how the former matron felt about the whimsical names given to the various wings. He studied her and rather liked what he saw. She was extremely tall with a heavy build and she held herself as though she'd had military training. She wore a tailored blouse and a tartan skirt, but little imagination was needed to picture her clothed in a white uniform. She stepped out from behind the counter and Forsythe noticed she'd not stuck

11

to the casual dress code with her footwear. Her large feet were shod in white, crepe-soled nurses' shoes.

She swung his chair around and trundled it down a wide, door-lined hall. Each door had a porcelain plate ornamented with hand-painted flowers inset in the panel. He identified a lily and an iris and then Miss Holly swung open a door whose inset plate displayed a cluster of tiny yellow flowers. Forsythe wondered if he was going to have to convalesce in a room like a flower garden, but, much to his relief, the sitting room resembled a reading room in his city club—lined and furnished with wood and leather. Even the oil painting above the mantel ignored the flower name and reflected a seascape similar to the one to be glimpsed through the windows.

"Looks comfortable," he told the nurse. "But why the name?"

She pushed the chair over to the door opening into the bedroom and pointed an expressive finger. Forsythe's first thought was that Sandy had been correct. This room looked nothing like a hospital cubicle. It was larger than the sitting room and the only indication that it was a hospital room was that the ornate tester bed was slightly higher than an ordinary bed.

Waving the nurse aside, he rolled the chair around himself. Over the chiffonier hung another oil, this one a fanciful bed of primroses. The same colors, pale yellow and apple green, were echoed in the curtains, the bedspread, and the chair coverings. The bathroom was brilliant with green-and-yellow tile and gleaming fixtures. In this room there was another hint of the possible physical condition of the suite's occupant. Stout metal bars had been installed in strategic locations.

Forsythe looked around and chuckled. As though to complete the flower theme there were vases and bowls and baskets of cut flowers, two on the chiffonier, one on each bedside table, several massed on a narrow table near the window, even a couple on the tile counter in the bathroom. Roses, carnations, chrysanthemums, but nary a primrose. Miss Holly followed the direction of his eyes. "I don't approve of so many blooms in a patient's . . . guest's room."

"Neither do I. I'll keep the cards and perhaps you can put the flowers elsewhere."

She gave a nod of approval. "Most sensible, Mr. Forsythe. I'll send some down to the reception areas and the rest can go in the patients', guests' lounge."

"You seem to be having problems with whether we're guests or patients."

Her sizable jaw jutted. "I've been a nurse for forty years and it's hard to teach an old dog new tricks. Miss Hornblower begged me to leave my comfortable cottage in Hundarby to take over day shift here. Then she insists I dress like this"—one hand plucked at the tartan skirt— "and that I call the patients 'guests' and pretend I'm something like a cross between a cruise guide and a hostess in a restaurant. I'll tell you this, Mr. Forsythe, I've never seen such a slack medical facility! The people here are even allowed to *smoke*."

"There must be rules. Hielkje told me that my luggage and even gift parcels would be inspected."

"That's true." She was making a circuit of the room, plucking cards from the floral arrangements. "Perhaps I am being a bit unfair. Miss Hornblower does see that the er, the guests abide by some important rules. Diet and alcoholic beverages."

She took the last card from a charming arrangement of yellow daisies and white freesia and handed the cards to the barrister. He read the card from the last bouquet. Ah, Jennifer. Typical of that lovely lass to remember freesia was his favorite flower. He wondered if the Damien Day ran to a Freesia Suite in their Flower Wing.

13

"I think I'll keep that freesia bouquet, Miss Holly. Perhaps in the sitting room."

"As you wish." She picked up the bowl and led the way to the smaller room. "Now, if you'd be kind enough to open those parcels. After that is done I'll give you a booklet with the layout of this wing and also the main floor and the basement area and I'll answer any questions."

The packages were piled on a desk situated near one of the windows. As he picked up a gayly wrapped package, he glanced out. The rear gardens, in a milder season, would be delightful. He glimpsed a rose garden dotted with statuary, an Italian one bordered with dark yews and centered with a rectangular pool, and then a parklike area sloping down until the lawn met the shingle. Surf was foaming against that shingle and gusts from the sea drove sleet before them. Forsythe glanced up at the nurse. "In spring and summer this place must be idyllic."

"I wouldn't know. Now, what is that you have there?"

He handed her the gift that a stenographer in his London chambers had sent him. Mrs. Sutton's consuming interest was in history and she'd selected a tome on the history of the West Indies. He opened the other parcels. Another book, this one on jade, from his partner, Eugene Emory. A box of delicacies from Fortum and Mason from his other partner, Sam Mertz. A small flat wooden box of smoked salmon from a Scottish friend, the MacDougal. Forsythe picked up the last parcel. This was from Abigail Sanderson and was heavy. It was the collected works of William Shakespeare and was a beauty. The book was bound in leather and had brass clasps holding together the gilt-edged pages.

Miss Holly, who had been closely watching, picked up the smoked salmon. "I'll send this down to the

14

kitchen, but you may have some whenever you wish. Everything seems in order here.''

He wheeled his chair around to face her. "Is this really necessary?''

"I'm simply following orders. Miss Hornblower instructed me to use great care in checking guests' belongings. She gave me some examples of what has happened here. People who must be on strict diets smuggle in rich food and alcohol. Why, she told me that one gentleman, a renowned artist, filled his bottle of after-shave lotion with sherry. A lady with severe respiratory troubles had the temerity to stuff her handkerchief case with Russian cigarettes.'' She touched her crisp iron-gray hair. "Shortly I'll be checking your hospital charts, but right now we must discuss a vital matter. Mr. Forsythe, tell me about your bowels.''

2

I t took time to discuss the condition of Forsythe's bowels and more time for the former matron to detail the do's and don'ts of the Damien Day Health Home. When she had finished he was convinced that the regimen was much less slack than she had indicated.

"About crutches," he said. "The last couple of days in hospital I was allowed to use them."

"With a major knee operation one can't spring around like a deer a short time after surgery. It would have been different if this had been a little patch job, but you'd neglected a serious injury for so long that the surgeon had to almost build a new kneecap." She gave him a severe look and continued, "I'll check your chart and if your physician has approved the use of crutches, you may have them in this suite. But in the common areas I must insist you use a chair."

Having partially won his first point, he tried for a second. "I should like a drink."

"Medication, Mr. Forsythe. As I said, I must check your chart."

"I haven't had painkillers for several days." He gave

her his best smile. "And I never take sleeping capsules."

"Good for you." Her lips relaxed in a slight smile. "You *are* a barrister, aren't you? And I would imagine a most successful one, but this place, regardless of how relaxed it may seem, is first and last a medical facility. If, as you claim, you're not taking medication, the orderly will give you a drink before dinner. But that is all you will receive."

He made a last try. Tapping the leather cover of Sandy's gift, he said, " 'A night of good drinking/Is worth a year's thinking.' "

"I too am fond of the Bard." Her smile widened. "That quotation, as you probably know, is not from Shakespeare. This one is. 'O God, that men should put an enemy in their mouths to steal away their brains'!" She opened the door to the hall. "I'll send Percival to assist you, Mr. Forsythe. And that's still *one* drink before dinner."

Just my luck, Forsythe thought glumly, to draw a nurse who's not only a former matron but no doubt the president of a temperance union. He decided to have a try at the orderly who appeared to be a good-natured chap and probably enjoyed a drink himself.

Perce arrived carrying crutches and eager to be of assistance. Soon Forsythe was on his feet—or foot—and with Perce standing guard the barrister managed to hobble into the spacious bathroom and take care of his personal needs. Then, with Perce's help, he changed into a fresh exercise suit, this one maroon with white flashes.

On his own Perce proved to be garrulous and chatted about his previous job at HEM, his wife and two small children, and the town of Hundarby. Come in obliquely, Forsythe thought and asked, "Any good pubs in Hundarby?"

"The Abbot's my pub, sir. Best bitters in town and they make a tasty meat pie." Perce tapped one of the

17

crutches. "Looks like it'll be a time before you get a chance to sample them."

The barrister hobbled over to the chair and allowed Perce to help him get seated and prop up his bad leg. He gave a heavy sigh as he said, "I'd give a lot to down a pint right now, Perce."

Perce busied himself propping up the crutches and picking up the discarded clothing. "Shame, sir, but I guess you'll have to be patient."

Forsythe decided to try the direct approach. "Are you the one who provides the drink before dinner?"

"That would be the orderly on the next shift, sir. Owen is his name. Dour chap and I doubt he'd stretch a point. Be worth his job to do it." Perce hesitated, eyeing Forsythe, who was playing with his wallet. "Like to help you myself but it'd be worth my job too. That Miss Holly's got eyes in the back of her head, she has. Can't slip one thing past that woman!"

Feeling slightly ashamed of himself, Forsythe took a note from the wallet and handed it to the orderly. "Thanks for the sympathy anyway, Perce."

Perce beamed. "Any other way I can help?"

Forsythe picked up the booklet Miss Holly had given him. "It says in here there are three locales for meals."

"That's when the place is running all out, Mr. Forsythe. Right now only this wing is open and they aren't using the dining room on the main floor. When this place is running full out, it must be like a posh summer resort. Theater downstairs for filming movies, big library, game room, and down in the basement there're exercise rooms and saunas. Funny sort of medical facility, but I'm told most of the people who come here aren't what I'd call sick. Just dieting or getting away from too much high living for a time. But to get back to meals—you can have room service and eat right here in your suite or go to the lounge." Perce leaned over and pointed at the diagram of

18

the Flower Wing. "There it is. Cheerful place the lounge is and you can have company while you eat."

"How many patients are here now?"

"Guests, we call them. Only a couple but more are expected soon." He gazed wonderingly down at Forsythe. "Imagine keeping a place like this open for just a handful of people. Boggles the mind, don't it?" He glanced at his watch. "Hey! Nearly four o'clock and I go off duty soon. Want me to send Owen in, sir?"

Forsythe shook his head. If he couldn't bribe the genial Perce to scare up a drink, it would be a waste of effort trying to bribe the dour Owen. I'm acting like a dipsomaniac in for a cure, he told himself, desperate for a drink. Nothing like the denial of something spurring a lust for it. Well, might as well wheel down to the lounge and meet his fellow inmates.

He propelled the chair down the long hall toward what in an ordinary hospital would be called a nurses' station and this time he read all the names of the suites. There proved to be eight of them and they were named after many different flowers but no freesia. As he thought of the flower he thought of Jennifer and pictured her slender supple body, her long coltish legs, the faint scent of honey in her flowing hair. Where was his lovely lass now? Ah, yes, in Saudi Arabia, scripting and directing a documentary on the results of war in that troubled part of the world. How long, he wondered, before we work out how to juggle two such different careers, how to make a home together, have a family? He fought back a feeling of depression and it was a relief to hear his name called.

"Mr. Forsythe?" This nurse looked about Miss Holly's age, sixtyish, but she was shorter, plumper, and had a soft round face and several chins. Her hair was waved back from her brow and was an improbable shade of brown. Her floral dress was fussy and dripped ruffles. "I'm Mrs. Elser and I'm on duty until midnight, when

19

Mrs. Frome takes over. Should you need anything or have questions, please ring for me."

What I really need, Forsythe thought wistfully, is a tall glass of whiskey and soda. He decided not to mention this and Mrs. Elser continued, "I do require your signature in our guest book. If you'll come into the office, please. Would you like me to handle your chair? There's very little space behind this desk."

"Thank you, no, Mrs. Elser. I became rather expert at these chairs in the hospital in Hundarby. Quite often there was nobody around to help me."

"A sad state of affairs." She stood aside and watched him pilot his chair around the corner of the desk and through the doorway into the office. "So many hospitals are laying off and there simply aren't enough personnel left to handle the wards properly." She sighed. "This recession, you know."

"Did you work at the Hundarby hospital?"

"No. Last year I retired and came to make my home with my daughter in Hundarby. Laura is a teacher at a girls' school there. Miss Hornblower heard about me and asked if I would take this position for a month. I was a bit hesitant, but the salary was tempting so here I am. You've met Miss Holly, of course. She too came out of retirement, but all the rest of the nursing staff, the aides and orderlies and Mrs. Frome, who is on night shift, worked at the hospital you just came from." She gave him a cheerful smile. "In fact, if you've been a patient at the Hundarby hospital before, you may recognize familiar faces here."

"This is the first time I've been hospitalized since I was sixteen. The reason I came to the hospital in Hundarby instead of going to one in London is that I wanted to come to the Damien Day to convalesce after surgery."

"Lucky you. Sometimes when I look back in time it seems my entire life has been spent in hospitals. And

20

they can be very depressing places. As often as possible I asked for work in maternity wards, but even there it is often terribly sad."

She sat down at a cluttered desk and started searching through heaps of papers and books. Forsythe glanced around the room. It was windowless but otherwise quite a cheerful place with a chinz-covered sofa, a table piled high with magazines and newspapers, and light cooking arrangements on a shelf in a corner. Tossed on the sofa was a tapestry bag spilling crochet equipment.

Mrs. Elser had finally unearthed a thin ledger with a dark blue cover. "Here we are. I'm afraid I'm a wee bit untidy. When Miss Holly leaves work, this desk is cleaned off, but I soon have it littered with records and my homework—"

"Homework?"

She handed him a textbook. "I'm taking Spanish lessons. I've been widowed for years, since Laura was only a wee girl and I always dreaded the idea of retiring. So hard to adjust after a busy work life. I decided I'd better make plans to fill my time, so I made a list of things I'd always wanted to do and never had time for. Right at the top was learning conversational Spanish and crocheting. Later this year I hope to take a trip to Spain with a dear friend. Now, Mr. Forsythe, don't think I neglect the guests while I conjugate verbs. This shift requires little work that the orderly and the aide can't handle. I should think a nurse is required simply as a precaution. We have a doctor on call and, right at present, there are few patients and none of them are bedridden."

He reached out and placed the Spanish textbook on the corner of the desk. "Perce told me there are only two others in the wing."

"That's correct. Both of them arrived before I came on duty. Several more guests are expected later this week. Which reminds me." She opened the blue ledger and

21

carefully placed a slip of notepaper over the upper part of a page. "If you will sign here and jot down your home address, please."

He signed his name and wrote the Mayfair address of his London flat. As he wrote he thought of his family home in Sussex and wished he could be doing his convalescing there. He had mentioned this to his physician. *"I'd certainly get the best of care, Eric. Mrs. Meeks and Meeks would practically coddle me."*

Eric had shaken his handsome head. *"No wheedling, Robert. You know you'll require physiotheraphy and, although I'll admit Mrs. Meeks is the best cook I know, I doubt expert massage is her strong point. Take your choice—a convalescent home or hospital."*

So here he was, Forsythe thought dismally, still in an institution. While he'd been writing, Mrs. Elser had kept her plump hand on the slip of paper masking the upper part of the page. "Why the secrecy, Mrs. Elser? Am I not supposed to know who else is registered here?"

She gave a trill of laughter. "Dear me, no! But one of our guests wants to play a little game and says it's essential that you not know her identity. When Miss Hornblower engaged me she warned that the guests might become bored and make odd requests. When all the wings are full, I understand the theater and games room and the other amusement facilities are in use and now, of course, they're closed. I heard that quite often they've live performances in the theater. Imagine that!"

"Sounds more like a cruise ship than a convalescent home. I noticed there's a VCR with the TV in my suite."

"And current videos are available in the library as well as a good selection of magazines and books. The *London Times* is delivered with your breakfast tray each morning and"—she broke off and looked at him with glowing eyes—"speaking of videos there's a nice selection of ones starring the Black Knight. When Miss Horn-

22

blower mentioned you, she said you'd met Reggie Knight. I was so excited! Both my daughter Laura and I just *adore* him. What's he like?''

"I only met him briefly, Mrs. Elser, and under rather trying circumstances. He certainly is a handsome chap.'' Her face fell. "I thought maybe you knew him well.'' "My secretary certainly does. They're good friends. Miss Sanderson may be down to visit me and you can ask her about Reggie.''

"I'll make a point of it. Maybe she can get his autograph for Laura and me. But what a silly I am! Talking on and on when I should be telling you about your therapy. You're slated for two sessions a day. One in the forenoon at ten with Geraldo and another at two with Athena. You'll find both are skilled therapists.'' She added wistfully, "Geraldo is Spanish, from Seville I believe, and I should so much like to chat with him, but he works in the mornings and I don't come on duty until four in the afternoon.''

He nodded. "I understand how you feel. My secretary took Spanish lessons too and she eats quite often at a Spanish restaurant, not because she likes the cuisine, but because she's able to practice the language.''

"It seems Miss Sanderson and I will have interests in common.'' Mrs. Elser got to her feet and smoothed ruffles over her bulging hips. "It's been pleasant meeting you, Mr. Forsythe. Laura will be ever so thrilled because she's read a great deal about you. Do let me know if you wish anything, and if you like herb tea, I usually brew up about ten each evening. Owen can get tea for you from the kitchen, but they don't stock herb tea. Now, you'll be wanting to join the other guests in the lounge.'' She led the way back to the desk and pointed down a shorter corridor. "Right down there. Owen will be serving drinks shortly. We don't bother with tea here, Mr. Forsythe,

23

because dinner hour must be early. Don't overtire yourself. If you wish, your dinner can be served in bed."

He smiled up at her. "*Gracias, Señora* Elser."

She pinkened with pleasure and, for a moment,
looked like a girl. A pleasant woman, he thought, rather
feather brained and possibly not as skilled a nurse as
Miss Holly but with a warmer personality.

As he wheeled his chair down the corridor, he wondered who the other guests were and what game was to
be played. The lounge had double doors and both were
propped hospitably open. Beyond that doorway was a
spacious room, already darkening with the shadows of
an early winter evening. He stopped inside the doorway
to allow his eyes to adjust. For moments all he could
discern were the dark bulk of furnishings and the glimmer of fading light against a row of long windows at the
far end of the room. Then there was a rustle of movement
and about a dozen table and floor lamps flashed on.
"Welcome, Robert Forsythe," a deep and silky voice
called. "What do you think of the decor?"

Forsythe had been amazed at the genuine period
pieces in the reception areas and his suite, but the decor
of the lounge dazzled him. Here again were period pieces
but of a much later period. To be exact it was the Art Deco
period of the twenties, complete with all the brilliant
tumult of colors, richness of upholstery, rugs, swags,
outrageous shaping of lamps, clocks, vases of those
years. He decided this was not the rather toned-down
English Art Deco but more the dramatic French one.

"Well?" The voice had a hint of impatience.

"Is this stuff genuine?"

"Who knows? If it's sham, it's damn well done."

"I've never cared for Art Deco."

"I *love* it. It *suits* me."

And it did suit her. She sat in the curve of a gold
satin divan, propped up by tasseled cushions. Behind her

was an amber-colored wall with a windblown, blossom-covered tree painted across it. Painted blossoms scattered onto another wall and the ceiling. At her side was a life-sized, porcelain greyhound, so real the delicate nostrils appeared to be quivering. At her knees was a fanciful low table, teak with the edges bound in ivory.

This setting, the barrister thought, would diminish the average person, cause him or her to fade right away. Not so this woman. Exotic as her surroundings were, she dominated them. She wore a flowing caftan that echoed the rich colors of the rug her slender feet rested on—chrome yellow and purple and plum and pink. He guessed she was tall and she was a big woman with large bones. A high bosom thrust against the brilliant silk, a slight movement pulled that silk taut over ripe hips.

"Do you know me?" she demanded.

Forsythe's eyes moved from the swelling hips to her face. That face was handsome but older than the body, with lines running across the wide brow, other lines radiating from the corners of the eyes, bracketing the mouth, a slight puffiness under the jaw. This lady definitely was no longer in the blush of youth but what eyes, what a mouth!

That mouth moved in a tiny smile and a large, shapely hand touched the high Spanish comb of tortoiseshell inlaid with ivory that pulled her hair away from her face, gathered it on the crown of her head, and then allowed it to sweep in dark red waves to her shoulders.

"Stop staring and answer my question," she said sharply.

He wheeled his chair over until he was facing the vision across the teak-and-ivory table. "The answer is no, I don't know you. If we'd ever met I'd *never* have forgotten *you.*"

"Gallant! I like a chivalrous man. Most men your age—in their thirties—know little about chivalry. Of

25

course, that's not their fault. The ones responsible are stupid women with their insistence on equality."

"You don't approve of sexual equality?"

"There can be no such thing. Men and women are two different species. As different as . . . say lions and bears. Clever women have always done exactly as they wish without howling about equality. And this stupidity has cost my sex all the lovely little perks they once had. But enough of that! I shall call you Robert because I loathe formality."

He grinned. "Particularly between a lioness and a grizzly bear. What shall I call you?"

"Madame X. Until you either guess my name or admit defeat. I'm wondering how astute a detective you actually are."

"My, you do know a great deal about me. Name, age, my hobby of criminology. Strange you don't seem to know I'm actually not a detective but a barrister—"

"Of course I know *that*. I also know your secretary, Miss Abigail Sanderson, is a spinster in her fifties and has assisted you in solving many murder cases. But this isn't important and has no bearing on our game."

"*Your* game. I'm not sure I wish to play, Elsa—"

"Elsa?"

"I must call you something and *Madame X* doesn't fit. *Elsa* does."

"So it does. I too was born free. Don't you at least want to hear about my game?"

Forsythe was having trouble concentrating on anything but the shapely thigh and long leg that had suddenly appeared in a slit in the skirt of the caftan. Forcing reluctant eyes away from that leg, he said, "Very well, tell me about your game."

"I've provided an assortment of clues." One hand waved at a sidetable. Under the light of a Tiffany table lamp various objects had been arranged. All of them, like

26

her Spanish comb, were tortoiseshell and were inset not with ivory but with gold. The barrister stretched out a hand, but couldn't reach them. His companion scooped them up and dumped them in his lap. "Now, for the prize. If, in a reasonable length of time, you are unable to guess my identity, you'll lose and I'll get the prize—"

"And what is the prize?"

The corners of her marvelous mouth twitched up. "If you lose, you must forfeit your pre-prandial drink and sneak it to me."

The barrister felt a stirring of interest. This might be an opportunity to come up with a second drink. "And if I win, I get yours?"

"Scout's honor." She glanced at her dainty watch. "Let the game begin. You have precisely five minutes."

Forsythe lifted the tortoiseshell objects, one by one. A compact, a cigarette case, a lighter. All inset with flowing gold initials. *KK*. He turned each over in turn. No marks on the bottom of any of them. He opened the cigarette case. The inside was lined with gold and filled with Egyptian cigarettes. Snapping it closed, he reached for the compact. It contained a beveled mirror, loose powder, a satin-backed puff again ornamented with gold-colored initials. Nothing there. He flicked the lighter and a tongue of flame sprang up.

"Little trouble detecting, Robert?"

"I've a hunch you're being unfair."

She laughed. Not a tinkling little giggle, but a full-chested, hearty bay. "To get a drink in this damn place I'd resort to any sort of skullduggery. But, best to get back to detecting. Two minutes left and I can practically taste your drink."

He ran his index finger over the initials on the compact. Something brushed his mind. Jennifer . . . a birthday gift. A gift from his secretary to Jennifer. Jennifer will love that, he'd told Miss Sanderson. She'd better,

27

Sandy had retorted, it cost an arm and a leg. A compact just like this one. Gold initials . . . a name. Sandy had mentioned a name. Then he had it. "Kate Kapiche!"

"Blazing blue balls!" Kate Kapiche snarled. "There goes my drink. If you were truly a gentleman, you'd offer it to me anyway."

"If I weren't a thirsty gentleman, I'd consider doing that. By any chance, did you play this game with the other patient?"

"Harry? No use. He's a dodo too."

"An extinct bird?"

"Another meaning. Apparently the locals call this place the DODO, but Harry says the people, like the two of us, who come back here time after time should be called dodos because we must be getting senile. And I agree with him. I simply don't have the willpower to leave all the lovely food and drink alone and every so often my physician gives me the either-or ultimatum and I'm back here again."

Forsythe flicked appreciative eyes over the lovely leg. "You certainly don't look ill."

"There's nothing amiss with the portion of my anatomy that you're leering at. I've hypertension and a cholesterol count that's off the charts. Over Christmas I bolted fatty foods and alcohol until my physician promised a heart attack or stroke if I didn't behave. So I rang up Reggie Knight and begged and he spoke to Fran Hornblower and they agreed to keep this place open this month and take me in. And I'm *suffering*. Gnawing rabbit food and not getting one drop of demon alcohol—"

"Hey! What about the drink I just won?"

She leaned forward, retrieved her pretty trinkets from his lap, and gently patted his bad knee. "Did I say mine was alcoholic? You have just won a Virgin Mary." She sank back against the pile of cushions. "I really didn't expect you to come up with my name. How the devil did you do it?''

"My secretary bought one of your compacts as a present for my fiancée. Sandy was chattering about you and your successes. Beauty salons all over the country and—''

"The world. I've Hair Apparent salons in Europe and Asia and recently I've opened the first of hopefully many in the U.S. In New York, New York. Also I have a thriving business in female goodies. Cosmetics and perfumes and, recently, designer jeans and jewelry. I'm quite a catch. Too bad you already have a fiancée. I'm in the market for another husband and you look a likely lad.''

It was the barrister's turn to laugh. "As well as your business acumen, Sandy mentioned your notorious lack of acumen in picking husbands.''

"Touché! You're now even for the Virgin Mary ploy.'' She touched her full lower lip with a polished oval nail. "My matrimonial record does indicate I pick losers, but it's not accurate. My numerous husbands, with a couple of exceptions, have all been nice men, but I fall in love recklessly, *have* to have the dear man, and fall out of love quickly. Makes quite a turnover and I've been asked why I don't just live with them and not bother with marriages or smelly divorces. That's a hard question to answer. I think it goes back to my early life and my dear old granny. I do hope you don't embarrass easily, Robert, because I'm about to bare intimate details of my youth.''

Robert Forsythe, who rarely bared many details about his own life, intimate or not, made a muffled sound. Before he had time to articulate his distaste for this sort of confession, another voice spoke from directly behind his chair. "It's useless to urge Katie to desist. She's not only a compulsive bride but she's like a flasher, must bare everything to someone who hasn't heard her story before. I'd swear if she didn't have you to tell all to

29

she'd be talking to that thing." A plump hand reached past Forsythe's shoulder and pointed at the porcelain figure of the greyhound.

Kate Kapiche's lips drew back from her teeth in a snarl worthy of the genuine Elsa. "Harry, if you were a woman, you'd be a hundred-percent, brass-plated *bitch!*"

3

The newcomer didn't seem to take offense. He squeezed past Forsythe's chair, sank into one of the gold satin chairs, and offered the plump hand. "Harry Oglethorpe. Please call me Harry."

Forsythe shook the hand. "You probably know my name. Make it Robert. We aren't going to play a game?"

"Not much use. You've probably never heard of me."

"Don't be so modest. I most certainly have. You're the son of Amos St. Carr Oglethorpe and a noted artist in your own right. Portraits?"

"Mainly. Nice going, Robert. With most people I have to stress the 'son of' before they tumble. The *famous* Oglethorpe was my father."

"Must be tiresome."

"On the contrary, I don't mind it at all. I'm a competent painter, but Dad was a genius. You seldom get two genuises in one family in successive generations. Although if my young brother had lived, I'm convinced the world would have seen another Amos St. Carr—"

"You know, Harry, *I* am the one supposed to be doing the flashing," Kate broke in. "I saw him first."

"Katie dear, has it ever crossed your little mind that you're not the only one who likes to talk about herself? Why, even Robert might like to talk about his life."

"Not at all," Forsythe said hastily.

"See?" Kate said. "A born listener. The moment I saw him I knew what he was. Have you any idea, Robert, how rare your species is? Most people are simply bursting to tell all and the rotten part of it is that there are so few like you who are willing to listen."

"Will you get on with it?" Oglethorpe demanded. "I can't tell this born listener about Levi until you work through dear old Granny and your countless husbands. I suppose I should consider it a mercy that you've only one daughter—"

"*Step*daughter." She shifted position and the enticing leg appeared in the slit of the caftan again.

Forsythe tore his eyes away and beamed them at Harry Oglethorpe. Harry was older than Kate Kapiche and his clothing looked contrived, good quality but terribly worn. The cut of the shabby corduroy suit was dated and the shirt cuffs were frayed and yet the flowing silk cravat and polished loafers were not only up to date but looked costly. Oglethorpe was short and a soft paunch billowed over his belt.

Kate reclaimed the barrister's attention by putting a possessive hand on the ankle of his outstretched leg. "As they say, I was born within the sound of the Bow bells and my mum and dad were killed during the Blitz in the Second World War. At the time I was very young and my dad's mum, dear old Granny Muff—"

"Katie, I've always thought you made that name up."

"Not so, Harry. Muff was the real family name. I've had ever so many names since but none of them appealed to me and so I made one up. Oddly enough Kapiche suits

32

me better than . . . But, I'm straying from my story. I'm a Cockney and proud of it—"

"Intermittently," Oglethorpe said. "You went to a lot of trouble to rid yourself of the accent."

"That was Granny's idea. 'Kate,' she told me. 'Never be ashamed of being a London sparrow but you'd better learn to talk nice.' Granny was shrewd, Robert. When my parents were killed, she raised me. She was a flower seller—"

"Katie Kapiche née Muff likes to sound like another Liza Doolittle," Oglethorpe said with a grin. "Actually Granny owned a prosperous flower shop and didn't hang around theaters peddling nosegays from a basket."

The woman gave him a tolerant smile. "If you'd stop interrupting, I could finish and you can bore Robert with your tales about Levi Oglethorpe. Now, where was I?"

While she pondered, Forsythe studied the man. Harry Oglethorpe had a face to match his gross body, wide, ruddy, triple chinned. He was clean shaven but had allowed the rusty colored hair that encircled a high shiny dome to grow until it brushed his corduroy shoulders. The barrister decided this was one artist who worked at looking the part.

Kate started to speak and then looked past the wheelchair and stopped. Forsythe turned his head and spotted a tall, powerfully built man. "Sorry to disturb you, but I can take your drink orders now."

"You're new here too, aren't you?" Kate asked.

"Yes, ma'am."

"What's your name?" Oglethorpe asked.

"Owen, sir. I'll take your drink order and dinner will be served by the aide, Darla McCormick, who is—"

"One moment." Oglethorpe stared up at the orderly's rugged face. "Are you certain that you never worked here before?"

"Never, sir. I worked at the hospital in Hundarby for

a number of years, but there have been layoffs recently and Miss Hornblower asked if I could work here for a month while the regular staff takes its annual holiday.''

"What's your full name, lad?''

The orderly hesitated and then said, "Gareth Owen.''

"Ah! I was right. I never forget a face. You once lived north of Hundarby near a village called Greater Eveline. Katie, surely you remember young Gareth Owen?''

"Vaguely. That was years ago. When you were my landlord, Harry.'' Kate gave the orderly a brilliant smile. "And how are your family—''

"*Kate!*'' Oglethorpe said explosively.

For the first time since Forsythe had wheeled into the lounge, he saw a Kate Kapiche who had lost her composure. A flood of color swept up her throat and over her cheeks and the barrister noticed that Oglethorpe looked flushed and embarrassed too. The artist managed to rally and said, "Nice to see you again, Gareth. I'll have a Perrier with lime and Ms. Kapiche will have a Virgin Mary—''

"I'd prefer a *Bloody* Mary.''

"Don't be difficult, Katie, you know the rules. Robert, what's your pleasure?''

"Glenfiddich, if you have it. Neat and a double, please.''

"Sorry, sir, that will have to be a single.'' Owen unlocked the lavishly painted doors of a cabinet, displaying a well-stocked bar. "Miss Holly's orders, sir.''

Owen's large hands moved quickly and neatly over the bottles. He too looked nothing like the usual hospital attendant. His powerful frame was clothed in a flannel shirt and blue jeans, his huge feet were shod in bright red Reeboks. Quite an ordinary-looking man and yet he'd been the cause of two rather extraordinary people becoming completely nonplussed. A bit of a mystery and Forsythe liked nothing better than unraveling a mystery. Owen was handing drinks around and the barrister accepted his gratefully. He took a long satisfying sip. Owen locked up the drinks cabinet and headed toward the door, passing Mrs. Elser as she entered the lounge. The nurse had freshened her makeup and in one plump hand she clasped the blue-covered guest book.

"Good evening," she chirped. "I've met Ms. Kapiche and Mr. Forsythe, but I missed you, Mr. Oglethorpe. Welcome to the Damien Day Health Home! If you have questions, I'd be most happy to answer them. My name is Nancy Elser and—"

"It would seem that Hielkje Visser didn't explain that I'm what is known as a dodo," Oglethorpe said curtly. "That means I've been here so many times I can recite the rules backward. I probably know how this place runs better than you do."

It was the nurse's turn to blush hotly as she handed the open guest book to the artist. "In that case, Mr. Oglethorpe, you know you must sign this book."

He gave her a nasty look, but he reached in a sagging jacket pocket, pulled out a gold pen, and scrawled a signature. The nurse rewarded him with a warm smile. "Thank you. Ah, here is Darla to lay the dinner table." She waved the aide to her side. Darla was fresh and pretty, looked about sixteen, and was wearing stone-washed jeans and a tight, pink tank top. The tank top displayed a chest development that was much more mature than her face. Oglethorpe was regarding her with interest and he greeted this latest member of the staff with more warmth than he had shown to Mrs. Elser or Owen. Darla obviously didn't return the interest and Forsythe had a hunch that to this girl all three guests must appear genuine dodos. While the aide busied herself at a dumb-waiter, lifting out china, silver, and linen, the nurse took her leave. Mrs. Elser paused by the door, fussed with a

35

ruffle on her sleeve, and called, *"Buenas noches, amigos."*

"Amigos!" Kate snarled. "Where in hell did Fran Hornblower get her?"

"Too familiar for my liking," Oglethorpe agreed. He turned to Forsythe. "This place generally has a much higher standard than that woman." His eyes wandered across the room and then settled on Darla's trim behind as she bent over the dining table near the long windows.

Forsythe opened his mouth to defend Mrs. Elser, whom he'd taken a fancy to, but Kate said with a grin, "Dear Harry, you never change. Eyes glued on any bit of fluff just hitting puberty. Little Darla is more out of place here than Nancy what's-her-name but randy Harry is going to be oh! so nice to her."

Oglethorpe wrenched his eyes from the well-filled jeans and they blazed at Kate. Forsythe said hastily, "You two sound like old friends."

"We've known each other for ever," Kate said airily. "But *friends* is a bit of an exaggeration. Harry, what would you call us?"

He pondered and then said slowly, "I don't think a word has been coined. Something less than *friends* but certainly more than *acquaintances.*"

The barrister turned to Kate. "You mentioned Harry was once your landlord?"

Snapping open her cigarette case, she selected a cigarette. Oglethorpe reached for the tortoiseshell lighter and held a flame to it. Kate patted his fat hand. "Robert smells a mystery. I told you he was a detective."

"Amateur," Forsythe said.

"Amateur or professional makes no difference," Oglethorpe said. "Katie, my lovely purveyor of gossip; with Gareth right in this building I feel it would be a bit . . . indelicate to discuss that tragic—"

"Horse skittles! As Granny Muff would say, you loike a nice bit of 'orror yerself, 'arry Oglethorpe. So you be delicate, Harry, and after I get done telling Robert all about my glorious youth I'll recite the saga of the Owen family.''

Oglethorpe snorted and rubbed a finger over his bulbous nose. ''That I want to hear. Robert, for some things our Katie has a memory like a sieve. I'll wager she can't even remember all her husbands' full names. Why, she didn't even remember *what* happened to Gareth's family.''

''Certainly I did. It was just a shock having Gareth pop up like that. Anyway, it happened ages ago. Meg was only about thirteen and it was shortly before you and Levi went to Paris. About sixteen years?''

''Seventeen.'' Oglethorpe's protruding eyes gazed past Forsythe's shoulder, this time not at the young aide, but perhaps at a past only he could see. ''A different world then, Katie. We were so much younger. You didn't have to keep darting back here for rest and diet; I didn't have to suffer agony from arthritis and gout—''

''Gout?'' Forsythe interrupted.

The artist chuckled. ''You're thinking of the traditional old gentleman seated in much the same position you're in with one foot swathed in layers of padding. My boy, gout can hit any joint and does. Right at present I've a swollen, inflamed left elbow and knee.''

Kate Kapiche was laughing, too. ''You know, Robert, when I was young I sometimes wondered what conversations would be like when one was aging. Now I know. An interminable discussion on aches and pains and medications.''

Without warning, the depression Forsythe had been fighting since he'd entered the hospital in Hundarby struck. He muttered, ''Something like being sentenced to hospital forever. Having other patients showing you their incisions and pouring out their woes for eternity. Living in hell!''

37

Both Kate and Oglethorpe stared at him. "Come now, old boy," Oglethorpe murmured. "Not quite that bad."

Getting to her feet, Kate smoothed the fabulous caftan over fabulous hips. She bent over the wheelchair and dropped a kiss on Forsythe's cheek. She smelled heavenly. "Cheer up! In no time your knee will be mended and you'll be out of here. In the meantime, relax and enjoy. This isn't your usual hospital. Ah, the buxom aide is making gestures at us. I think she's indicating that dinner is served. Not that Harry and I can expect much more than salad and possibly a slice of chicken. Are you on any special diet, Robert?"

"Yes." He waited for her to step aside and then swung the chair dexterously around and wheeled down the long room. "I'm rather badly underweight so I'm on a high caloric diet. They're stuffing me with protein and carbohydrates."

Kate cursed explosively. "And I'm supposed to nibble a lettuce leaf and watch you bolt—"

"Kate!" Oglethorpe snapped. "Stop behaving like a three year old. You know why we're both here. Neither of us has the guts to deny ourselves rich food and—"

"And there speaks the man who tried to smuggle in a pint of Bristol Cream. Robert, you'd never guess where this clumsy oaf hid his forbidden sherry."

"Let me try." Forsythe wheeled his chair into position at the table and gave his plate a look of approval. Obviously the chef of the Damien Day knew his business. "Harry filled an after-shave bottle with sherry."

"*Voila!*" Kate cried. "I told you he was a detective! How did you deduct that, Sherlock?"

"Elementary, my dear Kate. Miss Holly told me about a famous artist who tried to pull that stunt when I arrived today."

Oglethorpe grinned. "Did she also tell you that our

Katie tried to smuggle bars of chocolates in tucked into her tights? Katie was wearing them at the time, but Miss Holly's hawk eyes noticed how bulgy our beauty was and shook her down."

Tossing her hair back, Kate said, "Fill that big mouth of yours with salad." She gave her own plate a disdainful glance. "I will now wiggle my pink nose, flap my long ears, and eat my rabbit food."

Oglethorpe's grin widened. "To say nothing of waggling your fluffy little tail."

Kate glared, Oglethorpe continued to grin, and Forsythe wondered whether they were something less than friends and something more like enemies.

4

The following day Forsythe found that not only did time pass quickly in the Damien Day Health Home but that there was little feeling of being in a hospital. Instead of being roused from sleep in the early morning by the clanking of metal carts in the corridor and the banging of doors, he woke when he wished, rang for the orderly, and was brought first tea and then a delicious breakfast and the morning paper.

After showering and donning an exercise suit, he was wheeled by Perce, cheerful and talkative, to the lift and thence to the basement area. The therapy rooms, decorated in primary colors, were located opposite the lift door. His morning session was presided over by Geraldo Jose Ferdinand Salvero, swarthy and muscular and handsome. Skilled as the Spaniard was, Forsythe found the afternoon session more pleasant, possibly because the physiotherapist, Athena Khalkis, was petite and pretty and possessed of surprisingly powerful arms and hands.

After his session with Athena and when Perce had returned the barrister to his suite, he found Kate Kapiche comfortably ensconced on the leather divan in his sitting room. She was wearing another colorful caftan and, against the clubroom background, resembled a bird of paradise. He promptly told his guest this and she accepted the compliment without false modesty. "That's true, Robert. My old Granny Muff used to say, 'You're a looker, Katie, and that goes a long way, but you'll need more than a big bust and good legs to get on in this world. I'm gonna tell you three things and you'd best abide by them, me girl. Never sit on the seat of a public loo, don't let no man into your knickers 'til he puts that gold band on your wedding finger, and third and last, find some way to make your own money even if you manage to marry a rich nob.'"

Forsythe wheeled his chair over to face her. "And did you abide by Granny Muff's suggestions?"

"More like orders. Indeed I did. By the time I was eighteen I was a hairdresser and when I married my first husband, Roddy Eleven, I was still a virgin—"

"Eleven? Was that actually his name?"

"Not originally. His family name was Hungarian, used half the alphabet, and was hard to pronounce." She blew a perfect smoke ring and regarded it. "Marrying Roddy was a mistake and one danger Granny Muff neglected to warn me about."

The barrister raised an ironical brow. "Roddy wasn't a rich nob?"

"He had bags of money but he was a . . . I can't think of a word to describe him. He was horribly jealous and if I even spoke to another man, he'd beat the living daylights out of me." Kate shivered. "I was a spirited girl and had no intention of being a battered wife, but that man scared me green. As far as Roddy was concerned, our marriage was going to last until death did us part and he was quite candid about whose death that would be if I ever tried to leave him."

"But you eventually did."

41

Leaning forward, she snubbed out her cigarette in a brass ashtray. "Roddy left *me,* thank God. His hobby was racing, cars that is, and his car was wrecked and so was Roddy. You never saw such a merry widow. Roddy left me a nice lot of money and property and a baby daughter from a previous marriage. His first wife had died shortly after the child's birth and I never had courage enough to ask Roddy how. But there I was with Roddy's estate and a stepdaughter to raise. I promptly hired a nanny for the child and opened the first Hair Apparent salon."

"And the rest is, as they say, history."

She nodded and her dark red hair swung around her shoulders. "Salon after salon launched, husband after husband scuttled."

Forsythe reached for his crutches and his companion made a move to help him, but he waved away her hand. After pulling himself up, he hobbled around the room. "I get tired of sitting in that chair, Kate."

"Should you be doing this? What if you lost your balance?"

"I'm careful. As for using crutches, both therapists tell me my leg is healing nicely and it's better if I move around on my own. Keep the rest of my body from getting flabby from lack of exercise. In fact, Athena promised to speak to Miss Holly about letting me use crutches around this wing."

He hobbled over to a window and gazed down at the gardens and the waves crashing against the shingle. Snow was drifting down and had lightly coated the benches and statuary in the garden below him. The dark yews that bordered the Italian garden looked festive with an icing of glistening white.

He felt movement beside him, softness pressing against his arm, and found Kate had joined him. He could smell her perfume and felt that flash of awareness inspired by a woman like her. Regardless of age, he thought, she has

42

that animal magnetism that reaches out to every male within her radius. He had no difficulty understanding Kate Kapiche's appeal, her ability to attract so many men.

"Are you married at present?" he asked.

"No. My last divorce was over two years ago. I may be slowing down." She bent forward and then pointed. A security guard, bundled in a khaki overcoat, was crossing the lawn below them. A sleek Doberman was pacing at his side. They left footprints and dog tracks in the pristine snow. Suddenly the guard bent, scooped up a handful of snow, balled it, and tossed it overhand at one of the yews. The snowball splattered against the trunk and the dog barked and lunged at the tree. The guard hauled back on the leash and patted the animal's bullet-shaped head. Kate smiled. "Reminds me of Meg when she was a little girl. Playing in the snow one Christmas. I helped her to make a snowman. She was such a serious wee thing she seldom smiled, but that day she laughed a lot."

"You were young when you became the child's mother. It must have been difficult."

"Mother?" Kate said the word as though it was in a foreign language. "I fear I was never that. I saw that Meg was looked after and hired a series of nannies and governesses and then selected a boarding school for her when she was old enough. The closest Meg ever had to a mother was my cook, Mrs. Grady. Grady was a childless widow and she loved Meg and Meg thought the world of Grady. If I remember correctly, it was Grady who persuaded me, after Roddy's death, to stop calling the girl Omega and call her Meg. And Meg she's been ever since except at school or work."

Forsythe was tiring and he headed toward one of the leather armchairs. "What dreadful names some parents wish on helpless infants."

"More like parent. The name was Roddy's idea. The full name was Alpha Omega. First and last. Roddy

43

loathed children and he was quite proud of the name. He said Meg was his first child and his last." She added with satisfaction. "He was right, too."

The barrister sank deep into cushioned softness and relaxed. He glanced at the woman still standing at the window, her bold profile outlined against the snow-flecked pane. "Last evening you made a promise, Kate."

"So I did. And you've kept your part and been a good listener to my history like a good little victim. Let me see, shall I tell you about the Owens now or—"

"Now. My curiosity is at the boil."

She shook her head. "Much as I hate to admit it, Harry is right about my memory. It's crystal clear on business details but tends to be fuzzy about anything else. Probably I can give you an outline, but Harry will have to fill in the details. So, following dinner this evening you are invited to join Harry and me in my suite and you can try to solve a crime that occurred many years ago."

Oglethorpe gave Forsythe a warm smile. "At the time I was living in a manor house a short distance from Greater Eveline and, as there was a row of empty tenant houses on the estate, I decided to fix them up and rent them for the summer months. It was rather an isolated area and my young brother Levi and I were living in a large house with only a cook and a couple of maids for company. I decided it would be better for Levi to have more people around—"

"Actually, Robert, what Harry was thinking about was making a return on his investment." Kate winked a long-lashed eye at the barrister. "Granny Muff used to say that them nobs who inherit bags of money are mostly so tight they squeak."

"If you persist in being insulting, Katie, I shall take Robert to my suite and tell him this story without your contributions." Having squelched Kate, Ogle-

44

thorpe turned his attention to Forsythe. "I ended up calling a crew of carpenters in and they threw together cottages to make roomier accommodations and finally I had four premises to rent. In order to assure suitable tenants, I gave first choice to people I knew. Kate and David leased one of my cottages. Katie, which number husband was he?"

"I really don't remember. But David was mad about children and frightfully good with Meg. That spring she was nine and David insisted that we get her out of the city for the summer months. When Harry told us about his rental units, David talked me into taking one. I couldn't leave my business for more than a few days at a time and David was tied up with his practice—he was a physician—so Grady took Meg to the cottage. For the next four summers David and I rented the cottage and that was pretty well the pattern. I'd try to join Grady and Meg for an occasional weekend, but they were there June through August."

Oglethorpe held up a pudgy hand. "There goes that faulty memory of yours again. David was with you for only two summers. The third one you came alone and by the fourth year you had yet another husband."

"Kevin! What a marvelous memory *you* have, darling. We were married the first day of August and were spending part of our honeymoon with Meg and old Grady—"

"Katie, how you run a business I'll never know. It's taking longer to straighten you out than it would to tell the entire story to Robert. Cast your little mind back. You changed your wedding date from May to August because of Mrs. Grady's death. Meg was shattered and you hired a young woman to look after her. A Miss Todd. I've no doubt, my dear Katie, that you were so infatuated with your new bridegroom that you never noticed what a slack, negligent creature you'd picked to look after Meg.

45

But the rest of us noticed. I remember Levi telling me that all Miss Todd seemed to do was loll around eating junk food and watching television while Meg ran wild. We all called the woman Shoddy Toddy.''

Forsythe wheeled his chair closer to the sofa where Kate was sitting. The sofa was purple and beige and a violent green, and the entire sitting room echoed these colors. So did the corner of the bedroom he could glimpse through the doorway. Above the mantel was a painting of a cluster of iris standing proudly at the end of a placid pool. He was profoundly grateful that he had drawn the Primrose Suite and not the Iris. Oglethorpe was glancing around and apparently didn't share the barrister's distaste, since he said, ''Generally I have this suite, Katie.''

She flashed him a smug smile. ''True, darling, but this time I got my bid in first. I happen to like the Iris, too.''

''You know why I like this suite. It faces north and the light is perfect for an artist. You're being a dog in the manger.''

''The word that's tickling your tongue is *bitch* in the manger. There are three other suites facing north and they're standing empty.''

He waved a hand. ''But this suite has the *best* light.''

''You're supposed to be having a complete rest and won't be painting anyway.''

''But I do like to do a bit of sketching.'' He leaned forward and fondled her arm with a pudgy paw. ''You've been after me for some time to do your portrait, dear Katie.''

''Bribe time. I'll consider it. But I'll have to have it in writing.''

''Which explains why you make such an astute businesswoman. No faith in anyone.'' He turned back to Forsythe. ''Excuse our bickering, Robert. I'm badly off track.

Katie does have that effect on one. Can you remember where I was?"

"To be precise—nowhere. All I know is that you had a manor house somewhere near a village where Gareth Owen once lived and you were renting a number of cottages to acquaintances." Forsythe added plaintively, "I don't even know what type of crime was committed."

"Why, murder of course. The most heinous of all crimes. My, what an orderly mind you have, my dear chap. I shall try to emulate you. Now, to fill you in on the suspects—"

"Start with the victim."

"Make that plural. *Victims*. With the exception of Gareth, the entire Owen family. Walter Owen, a crotchety widower in his fifties. Emmy, his oldest child, about eighteen. Two younger daughters in their preteens. Gareth was the second oldest child, around fifteen. Four of them poisoned at one go. Katie, look at Robert's eyes! Positively flashing! My, you do enjoy murder, don't you?"

"I loathe murder," Forsythe told him coldly. "But I like puzzles. I also believe in justice and strongly feel that any person who takes a life must pay."

"A noble sentiment which doesn't apply in this particular case." The artist shook his head and light gleamed on the bald dome. "To date no one has paid for killing four people. You'll no doubt want to question, but first I'll fill you in on the background. Walter Owen had a small farm down the road from my estate and he and his four children ran it. He was reputed to be a miserly old slave driver and even the two younger girls, around nine and seven, had to work hard. Rumor had it that overwork had killed his wife. But his produce was excellent and all of us on the estate got eggs and milk and cream from that farm. The eldest girl, Emmy, usually delivered and she also baked wonderful bread, which we bought, too. She was a nice, quiet child—"

"Emmy, I remember," Kate broke in. "And she certainly wasn't a child physically. She was slow mentally but she had a pretty face, natural blond hair, and a body that had all the boys and their dads drooling. If I remember correctly, Harry, your chin was damp every time you ogled Emmy's buns"—she broke off, gave Oglethorpe an impish smile, and added demurely—"I beg your pardon. I meant loaves."

"Like hell you did!"

"Children, children," Forsythe chided. "Enough bickering. Harry, kindly tell me about the suspects."

Oglethorpe fingered his lowest chin. "This is thirsty work. Katie, are you positive you don't have a bottle hidden away?"

"Miss Holly picked me dry too, Harry. That woman should have been a cop. When I arrived she practically gave me a skin search." She got to her feet and moved over to a polished cabinet. As she passed Forsythe he again smelled her heavenly fragrance. "So . . . my bar runs to healthy juices—orange, apple, tomato. What's your pleasure?"

Oglethorpe accepted a glass of orange juice and cleared his throat. "The suspects. So many you wouldn't believe it. Apparently Walter Owen was loathed by most of the locals and had quarreled with practically every adult in Greater Eveline. Then there was the sole survivor—Gareth Owen. As I mentioned, at the time the boy was about fifteen and rumor had it his father was extremely hard on the boy. It seems people figured if it hadn't been for his three sisters, Gareth would have run off. He was supposed to be devoted to them, particularly Emmy."

"What about the people on your estate?" Forsythe asked.

"We were right on the spot, so to speak, and the police interviewed all of us. Let me see. There was Levi and myself . . . Levi was nineteen, twenty years my junior. I was an early child and our mother was well over forty when my brother was born. I took after our dad and never had any claims to good looks, but Levi was much like our mother, who was quite beautiful. Shortly before my dad's death he had a long talk with me. He'd discerned a tremendous artistic talent in my little brother and he made me promise to raise the boy and nuture that talent. I gave my solemn word that I would. After Dad's death I raised the boy and he was always more of a son than a brother."

Oglethorpe paused, pulled a handkerchief from a jacket pocket, and blew his nose. His eyes looked slightly moist. "Sorry, I still get emotional when I think of Levi. But back to suspects. That summer all my cottages were rented. In all there were fifteen people on the estate. Meg Eleven and Shoddy Toddy were in the first cottage and Kate and her bridegroom Kevin were down that week. In the next cottage were Carolyn and Cliff Chimes and their son. Teddy Chimes was—Katie, how old was the boy?"

The smooth skin between her eyes wrinkled and she said slowly, "He was younger than Levi and John Josephson . . ."

"John was the same age as Levi. I remember them celebrating their birthdays in the same week. Was Teddy around Meg's age?"

"No. He was a few years older. Perhaps around sixteen."

"Anyway, there were Gibson and Barbara Josephson and their boy John. And—Katie, I can't remember who was in the fourth cottage."

"And you call *my* memory spotty. It was rented to that young widow. The one who had twin baby girls. Alice something."

"Right. Alice Constantine. As you can see, Robert, quite a list of suspects."

"Surely the police were able to eliminate some of them with alibis."

"Hardly. Haven't you noticed that foolproof alibis are few and far between? The only suspect who had an alibi was Gareth Owen. As far as the police could narrow down, the introduction of poison into the food occurred between four in the afternoon and six."

Leaning back in his chair, Forsythe templed his fingers and stared down at them. "What was the poison?"

"Arsenic. And that was one of the reasons the police looked so intently at our group. The arsenic came from a gardening shed on my property. I'd purchased it from the chemist in Greater Eveline the previous summer when we'd had an invasion of those pesky red ants, carrying away everything they could reach. So, I brought the poison home and used it myself and I told all the tenants where it was so they could do the same. I recall I also mentioned it in passing to Walter Owen."

"Sounds rather a careless way to handle a deadly poison."

"That's what the inspector in charge said and I couldn't refute it. But the tin was on a high shelf, well out of the reach of young children, and I simply forgot the stuff was there. The only person on the estate who was unaware of the arsenic was Mrs. Constantine. At the time of the ant invasion, I hadn't even met the woman. The police grilled all of us with no result. Not one of us could prove he or she hadn't been lurking around the Owen farmhouse between four and five."

"Not even Kevin and I," Kate said. "And, at the time, we were practically inseparable. But that morning Kevin had to run up to London for some reason and about half past four in the afternoon I went out for a long walk by myself."

"How did the police set the time of the murders?"

Oglethorpe cleared his throat. "By a friend of the Owens, a Mrs. Rita Jarman. Mrs. Jarman detested Walter Owen but liked and pitied his children. That afternoon she walked out from Greater Eveline and arrived at the farmhouse shortly before three o'clock. It seems that Emmy was as good at needlework as she was at baking and the girl was sewing a patchwork quilt for Mrs. Jarman. Mrs. Jarman said she gave the girl as much work as she could because old Walter was so stingy, he seldom bought clothes for his children and if Emmy hadn't picked up money from sewing, the kids would have been in rags. When Mrs. Jarman arrived she found Emmy alone in the house, in the kitchen mixing up a pot of chili con carne. Mrs. Jarman had given the girl the recipe and much to Emmy's surprise her father had liked the dish and requested she serve it that night for supper."

"What surprised Emmy about that?" Forsythe asked.

"Walter was set in his ways and claimed he was a meat-and-potato kind of eater and, as you know, chili is highly spiced. The kitchen range was located right beside a window, wide open that hot day, and the cast iron pot was simmering on the back of the stove. Beside the pot was a wooden spoon on a saucer and it would have been simple for a person to reach in the window, dump the arsenic powder into the pot, and give it a brisk stir.

"But to get back to Mrs. Jarman's testimony. She said Emmy gave her a cup of tea and then took her into the parlor at the front of the house to show her how the quilt was coming. She admired Emmy's work and when they returned to the kitchen, Gareth was coming in from the dooryard. Emmy took one look at him and started to wail. According to Mrs. Jarman, the boy was a mess. His clothes were covered with dirt and he had a bruise on his cheek and a bleeding gash on his chin. While the women

51

cleaned him up, Gareth told them he'd had another argument with his father. Walter had accused the boy of letting his tame rabbit into the kitchen garden and when Gareth denied this, the man had struck him in the face, threw him to the ground, and threatened to put the pet rabbit into a stew pot. Gareth was a big, sturdy lad, but Mrs. Jarman said he was fighting back tears.''

"I can see why Walter Owen wasn't well liked," Forsythe said.

Kate opened her tortoiseshell case and selected a cigarette. "Walter was a proper bastard. Smarmy as could be when he came around collecting for his produce, and violent and mean with his own kids. I can see someone wanting to knock him off.''

"So can I," Oglethorpe agreed. "But to kill his entire family . . . no, I can't understand it. Back to Mrs. Jarman's testimony. She said Emmy was terribly upset about her brother and even more upset when Gareth told them his father had ordered him to walk into Greater Eveline and pick up a fitting for one of the farm machines from the smith. Gareth said it wouldn't be ready and he'd have to wait, which would make him too late for supper. Emmy told him she'd try to put aside some food for him, and Gareth gave a bitter laugh and asked how she'd hide it from their father. Mrs. Jarman realized the boy would probably go to bed without his meal, so she told him they'd walk back to the village together and stop in at the smith's. If the fitting wasn't ready, he was coming home with her and having supper with her family. Emmy was most relieved and grateful. Then the two younger girls, Elsbeth and Annie, came into the kitchen with baskets of eggs they'd gathered and Mrs. Jarman decided they'd better be on their way.''

"And Gareth Owen went with Mrs. Jarman?''

"And stayed with her. Gareth wasn't out of the woman's sight from the time they left the farmhouse until her husband took the boy home, around ten that night.''

Forsythe leaned forward. ''Why couldn't the boy have dropped the poison into the chili before he entered the kitchen? Say when Emmy took Mrs. Jarman into the parlor?''

Kate butted her cigarette. ''I knew you were going to ask that and this time I do remember. From the coroner's inquest. I can still see that poor kid sitting there, his head bowed, those big hands twisting together. Gareth looked so . . . so alone. But to answer your question. Before he and Mrs. Jarman left, Emmy insisted they try the chili to see if the spicing was right and she gave each of them a spoonful. Neither of them had any ill effects. Ergo—the arsenic had to have been dumped into the pot after they tasted it. They left the house at four o'clock and the Owens always ate on the dot of six.''

Oglethorpe patted her shoulder. ''Very good, Katie! You haven't forgotten the gory details at all.''

She bit at her ripe lower lip. ''Only blocked them out. And with good reason, Harry.''

Oglethorpe turned back to the barrister. ''To finish the story. Mrs. Jarman's husband, Carl, then gave his testimony. Carl was a butcher and that evening he got his old van out, stopped at the smith's to pick up the machine part, and drove Gareth home. Carl Jarman testified that he accompanied the boy around the house to the kitchen door because he intended to warn Walter Owen that if he laid hands on the lad again he, Jarman, would be speaking to the village constable. He found the man he was looking for sprawled in the dooryard, his head in a pool of vomit, dead. The two children, Annie and Elsbeth, were in much the same condition in the kitchen, but Emmy's body was up in the loft where the three sisters slept. The police investigated relentlessly, but the murderer was never found. And . . . well, that's about it, Robert.''

"Not quite." Kate jumped up and started pacing up and down. A long leg flashed in a slit in the caftan but Forsythe was intent on what she said. "You forgot to tell him about Emmy.''

"That had no bearing on the murders. Simply dredging up sad old gossip.''

"Sad old fact. Tell Robert.''

Oglethorpe looked at his juice glass, discovered it was empty, and set it on a sidetable. "The postmortem found Emmy Owen was approximately two months pregnant.''

Forsythe jerked forward. "By whom?''

"That was as much a mystery as the identity of the poisoner. Oh, there were rumors. Many of the villagers thought it was incest—either her father or her brother. You see, because Emmy was retarded, her father never allowed her to chum with other young people and kept an awfully tight rein on her. After the inquest I was talking to Carl and Rita Jarman and they said the locals believed that old Walter had got his daughter with child and, in a fit of shame and remorse, had decided to kill off the whole family.''

The barrister nodded. "That sort of thing has happened before, but if Walter was intent on wiping out his family, why did he send Gareth into the village at supper time? From your description of their relationship, it hardly sounds as though he was fond enough of his son to spare his life.''

"He wasn't. According, yet again, to the Jarmans, Walter had hated the boy from the moment he was born. The year of Gareth's birth Walter had hired a man to help out around the farm and there were many who thought Gareth was the farmhand's son.''

"In that case, the whole case against Walter crumbles." Forsythe cocked his head. "You said the police questioned you and your tenants, Harry?"

"Exhaustively. As I think I mentioned, the one place Walter did allow his daughter to go was to my estate. Emmy took dairy products and bread around to the manor and all the cottages. And, counting myself, there were seven males on the estate."

The barrister frowned. "You also said that Walter collected for the items."

Kate bobbed her head. "He was a tightfisted old goat and didn't trust anyone with his money, including his daughter. So Emmy lugged the stuff around and once a week Walter, fawning and tugging the forelock, came looking for his money."

Forsythe glanced at his watch. "Nearly time for Mrs. Elser to make her rounds, so I'd better get back to my suite. One last question. Kate, you said you'd blocked these memories out for a good reason. Why? Shock?"

"Partially, I suppose. It's horrible to have a group of people killed practically on one's doorstep. But I didn't know any of the family that well. I'd only been down to the cottage we leased a few times each summer and had seen Gareth and the two younger girls perhaps a dozen times. I did see more of Emmy and her father, but that was just to take the eggs and stuff and to pay Walter."

"Then why the memory block?"

Her lips quivered. "Because from then on we all seemed . . . hexed. As though something was punishing us—"

"Katie! Stop being ridiculous! You're as superstitious as your old Granny Muff." Oglethorpe added, "By any chance was it dear old Granny who put this stupid notion in your head?"

"Granny did say my marriage to Kevin was unusually short. We were married in August and by October the whole thing had gone sour and I was in the market for a divorce. But Kevin was balky and refused to cooperate. To top everything off I'd fallen madly in love—''

"With Cliff Chimes, as I recall." Oglethorpe shook a baffled head and told Forsythe, "I'll say one thing for our Katie, she doesn't play favorites. She can fall in love with the husband of her best friend as quickly as she can a complete stranger. Carolyn was a one-man woman and Katie here had the poor chap's eyes crossing with frustrated passion. What a bloody mess!"

Kate was pouting and the young gesture looked odd on the aging face. "That wasn't *my* fault. I *never* have affairs and Cliff was well aware of it. But, by the time Kevin agreed to a divorce, I'd met another man and I had to tell Cliff I no longer had any feeling for him." She held up a hand and said quickly, "I know what you're going to say, Harry, and you can damn well shut up. Cliff's suicide had nothing to do with me. Nobody ever dies because of *love*."

"What about Romeo and Juliet?" the artist asked.

She dismissed the famous lovers with an airy wave. "They were hysterical teenagers and Cliff was a mature man."

Kate and Oglethorpe's eyes locked and they seemed intent on staring each other down. Hastily, Forsythe asked, "Was that the end of the hex?"

"No," Kate said. "More like the beginning. In the next few years most of the people on the estate had something horrible happen to them."

Oglethorpe was getting up and a look of pain flickered across his wide face. He winced and bent to rub his leg. "Something horrible is happening right now, Katie. My knee and back are giving me hell. I'm going to draw a hot tub and soak for a time. Then I'm off to bed. Coming, Robert?"

"Yes, I seem to tire so easily. Good night, Kate."

She took Oglethorpe's arm and walked to the door

with the two men. "Harry, darling, don't bite the bullet. Ask Nancy what's-her-name for a painkiller. I'm going to ask for a sleeping capsule. I'm so hungry I'll never get to sleep on my own."

As Forsythe wheeled across the hall to his suite, he was thinking that perhaps more than hunger might keep Kate Kapiche awake that night. In her eyes had flickered an old pain, an old fear. A hex, Forsythe thought, from the shadow of an old crime.

5

Forsythe had scarcely reached his suite when Mrs.
Elser came bustling into the sitting room. She carried
a clipboard and asked questions about his leg, urged
a sleeping capsule which he declined, congratulated him
on his progress, told him she was certain the following
morning Miss Holly would approve the use of crutches to
get around the Flower Wing, and finally took her leave.

He decided not to rely on the orderly to help him
prepare for bed. The sooner I'm independent, he told
himself, the sooner I'm out of here and on my way home;
this is much less disturbing than the hospital in Hundarby, but I still wake in the night, my heart pounding,
convinced something dreadful walks the corridor,
crouches against the door, perhaps bends over the bed.

Giving himself a mental shake, he reached for the
crutches and thankfully pulled himself out of the chair.
When he was washed, clad in pajamas and robe, he hobbled back to the living room, wishing that he could have
a nightcap. He wondered if he should appeal to Mrs. Elser
for a small drink and decided against it. He had a hunch
that even when Miss Holly was absent, her orders were

strictly enforced. The phone rang, startling him. "Robby," Miss Sanderson said.

"Sandy," he said happily.

"I was thinking," she said casually. "I might drive down and spend the weekend with Fran Hornblower. Hielkje and she have a cottage on the grounds of the Damien Day. Fran said it was once a gardener's cottage and Reggie had it renovated for them. It's really quite lovely. We could visit a bit too, Robby. What do you think?"

What I really think, he told her silently, is that you're worried about me being in a blue funk and want to come down and hold my hand. He was sorely tempted, but he was no longer a frightened child. He was a man and it was time he started to act like one. "I think it would be a waste of time, Sandy. Fran is off on holiday and Hielkje is holding the fort."

Miss Sanderson's familiar snort sounded in his ear. "To make a bad pun, holding the fort is not Hielkje's forte. How's she doing?"

"No idea. I spoke with her for a short time yesterday when I arrived here, but haven't seen or heard from her since."

"Probably retreated to her bed with the vapors. But not to worry, Robby. I met Miss Holly, and that lady can run the whole place by herself. How do you like her?"

"Strict, would love to be stricter, and takes an abnormal interest in my bowels. Other than that she runs a mighty neat health home." He sighed heavily. "One of Miss Holly's bugaboos is demon drink. I wish Fran were here now. I might be able to talk her into a nightcap."

There was a pause and then she chuckled. "You don't need Fran. You have me."

He raised his brows. "What do you mean?"

"You're supposed to be a sleuth. Blimey, Robby, how many volumes of Shakespeare do you have now?

Didn't you think it strange I sent you yet another? Talk about coals to Newcastle."

"It's a lovely edition."

"It's a *lovely* bar. Down, boy! Stay where you are. The booze will wait. I'm about to give you something to drink to. Guess who's not only coming to dinner but plans to spend an extended period of time with you in the old manse in Sussex?"

He'd been staring intently at the bookcase where the large, leather-bound volume of Shakespeare sat. Now, his eyes narrowed. "Jennifer rang up before I left the hospital in Hundarby and said she was up to her ears in Riyadh with that documentary she's filming."

Miss Sanderson's laugh resounded in his ear and he could suddenly see her in her flat in London, leaning over that antique desk inherited from her aunt Rose, her long, austere face lighted by laughter, lamplight glinting from the waves of her gray hair, dancing in those cool blue eyes. "Odd how your mind immediately jumps to Jennifer. Your information is out of date. When you spoke with Jennifer she was planning to arrange what I'm going to tell you or, at least, was hoping, but didn't want to disappoint you if it didn't work out—"

"Sandy! Will you get to the point?"

"The point, impatient one, is that she's managed to get another director to take over the filming and is flying back to stay with you in the house in Sussex."

"When?"

"As soon as she can. Perhaps a week."

Forsythe had been balancing on one crutch beside the telephone table, but now he sagged into an armchair and threw the crutch on the floor. "You'd better ring her back, Sandy. I pressed my physician to let me go to Sussex and got a flat no. There's no way I'll be released from this place in a week."

"Trust me, Robby; all arrangements are made. I

spoke with Eric and did a bit of bullying. You must remember Eric's not a celebrity specialist from Harley Street to me, but he's still the grubby little chap I took out for cream teas when I visited your school. Mrs. Meeks helped no end. She has a cousin, now retired, who's a competent therapist and is willing to board in the village and go out to the Sussex house daily to massage you or whatever they do."

By now the barrister was sitting bolt upright, his hazel eyes glowing. "Anyone tell you lately, Sandy, that you qualify for fairy godmother?"

"This is going to cost," she warned. "Mrs. Meeks's cousin doesn't come cheap."

"To get home I'd spend my last pound."

"Right now you're spending mine. This call is costing, so ring off and open your present. Better make a toast to Jennifer."

"And one to Sandy, miracle worker," he said softly, and slid the receiver into its holder.

When the brass clasps were unfastened, the pseudo-book fell into two parts, disclosing a bottle of Laphroaig nestled in green felt and flanked by two crystal glasses. He poured a small nightcap, downed it, and sighed with pleasure. After rinsing out the glass, he sought his bed. Sleep came quickly and that night he slept soundly, undisturbed by imagined evils crouching by his bed.

The Orchid Suite had a sitting room similar to the Primrose—leather and polished wood—and a bedroom and bath echoing the soft tints in the watercolor over the mantel. It was restful and Forsythe found it more to his taste than the garish suite his host coveted and said so.

"It certainly isn't the decor of the Iris that I like," Oglethorpe explained. "As I said last evening, it's the light." He finished pouring chilled Perrier and carried a glass to his guest. "Kind of you to agree to lunch here with me."

"The only reason I hesitated was because of Kate. I don't like to think of her lunching alone."

"Figure our garrulous gal will end up talking to herself, eh? Not to worry. Katie is having company for lunch. Two more guests arrived while you were downstairs being pummeled by Geraldo. Supposed to be a couple more coming later today."

Something about Oglethorpe's expression alerted the barrister. "You have a smug curl to your lips, Harry. Like my ginger cat when she's dragged in a live mouse and is prepared to play with the poor creature. Are we about to play another game like Kate's?"

After squeezing lime into his drink, Oglethorpe put aside the peel. "I don't play games. The two here now are Carolyn Chimes and John Josephson—"

"What?"

"Thought that would interest you. And, later this afternoon, we should be joined by Kate's stepdaughter and Carolyn's son, Teddy Chimes."

"Six," Forsythe muttered. "Six of the people who were on your estate when the Owen family died."

"Counting Gareth Owen, that makes seven."

"I don't believe in coincidences."

"On occasion they do happen, but not this time. The only part of this present situation I didn't arrange is Gareth. I'd no idea he was still in this area and was shocked to find him working in the place I'd selected as a reunion—"

"You arranged to have the other five people here?"

The door opened and Oglethorpe made a silencing gesture. Perce, attired in the flashy yellow pullover, wheeled in a metal cart and proceeded to set up the luncheon table near the windows. Oglethorpe and Forsythe took their places and when the orderly had withdrawn, Forsythe asked, "How did you manage to lure Kate here?"

"I didn't. Late in December Katie rang me up and told me she was going to the Damien Day in January for rest and diet. At the time I was feeling miserable and I decided to join her. Shortly before I left London I had lunch with Carolyn—we still keep in touch—and she was looking like something the cat had dragged in. She confided she'd had a bout of pneumonia and had lost so much weight it was worrying. She also mentioned that recently she'd seen John Josephson for the first time in years and he was ill, too. And that's when I got this fabulous idea for a reunion. I talked both Carolyn and John into checking in here. Then I rang up Meg and Teddy and urged they come down for a couple of days and visit their mothers here." The artist gave his companion a smug smile, delicately removed a bone from his broiled trout, and placed it on a side dish.

Forsythe had no interest in his trout. "Do you think this wise? The way Kate spoke about Carolyn—after all, there was some tragedy surrounding the death of Carolyn's husband, wasn't there?'

"Katie's always felt guilty about Cliff's death, but she won't admit it. Figured he killed himself because she dumped him. But he was an unstable type anyway. Cliff was an actor and a regular Adonis in looks, but he was overly sensitive and frightfully moody. One of the reasons I arranged this reunion is Katie. Generally she hides how she feels, but for years I've known she's afraid . . . well, you heard her."

"The hex?"

"Exactly. Katie's as superstitious as they come."

"She said all of you had suffered tragedies after the murders. Is that true?"

Oglethorpe replaced his fish plate with a salad plate and dribbled oil-and-vinegar dressing over the vegeta-

63

bles. "In the course of almost two decades any group of people are bound to lose some of their families. I lost my young brother and that *was* a tragedy. Not only for me but for the entire art world. As I mentioned, Levi showed the same brilliancy that our father possessed."

The artist lost interest in the salad. He put down his fork and leaned back, staring out of the window at the drifting snow. "In August the Owens were poisoned and by November I'd sold the estate and Levi and I left England. We went to Paris, where I felt Levi would have a better chance to develop his talent and find first-rate teachers."

"Was that the only reason for the move?"

Oglethorpe smiled wryly. "After those people died, neither of us could stand being there. I was depressed and Levi was hit even harder. Every time we passed that farmhouse . . . But we'd only been in Paris for around four months when I lost my brother. Levi died in a boating mishap on the Seine. Levi was my life and I was completely shattered. I couldn't stay on in Paris and I had no desire to return to England, so I roamed the continent like a gypsy, renting a villa here, a flat there. Once in a while I'd come back to London to attend to business affairs and I'd look up Katie and Carolyn and Teddy. Finally, late last fall, I decided to put an end to that vagabond existence and I took a town house in London."

Forsythe had been buttering a piece of bread. Now he pushed the plate away, poured a cup of coffee, and said slowly, "Were you aware that I'd be at the Damien Day when you persuaded your friends to join you here?"

Oglethorpe threw up both plump hands. "Katie was dead on! You really *are* a detective. Guilty, as charged. Fran Hornblower told me you were coming here to convalesce. How did you catch on?"

"You said Kate was one reason you arranged this reunion. There has to be another. You believe that one of the people on your estate killed those people, don't you?"

"I can't find any other answer. It wasn't Gareth and I can't see one of the villagers wiping out three young girls just to kill their father. And the poison did come from a shed on my property. I've had years to wonder which of my friends killed that family, which familiar face hides a cold-blooded beast who would sentence people to die like that. Have you any idea, Robert, what a hideous death is caused by arsenic poisoning?"

"Yes. It's a terrible way to die. You want me to find the killer?"

"I do. I'll help you in any way possible."

The barrister reached for his crutches. "In that case, you'd better introduce me to the two arrivals."

As Oglethorpe and Forsythe entered the Art Deco lounge, the barrister felt a wave of relief emanating from the room's occupants so strong it was almost tangible. Kate Kapiche sat in her favorite spot, on the curve of the golden sofa set before the painted blossomy tree. Flanking her, in the matching pedestal chairs, were a youngish man and a woman of indefinite age.

The man rose to shake hands and Perce, leaving his clearing away at the luncheon table, hastened to carry over extra chairs. As Forsythe sank onto a chair, his eyes were riveted on the woman. Carolyn Chimes was tall and so thin she looked gaunt. She had a beautifully sculpted face and honey-colored hair pulled smoothly back into a French braid. "You . . . you're B. D. Epps!" he blurted.

A smile softened her mouth and she turned to Kate. "There's an example of what I was just telling you about. Character identified so strongly that the public doesn't even know the actor's name. I find, more and more, I'm being identified as that character and not myself. Most of my adult life I've acted, but I much fear that B. D. Epps has ruined Carolyn Chimes's career and I'll never be any-one but B. D. Epps now."

Forsythe smiled. "Some of that may be your own fault. You've done too good a job, made B. D. Epps too much a vital, living person."

"Pardon me for saying this, but you scarcely seem the type to tune into a sitcom on the telly."

"I'll admit I seldom have time for television, but my secretary urged me to watch 'Cor Blimey!' and I find it enthralling. You've the gift of true comedy, of that blend of slapstick humor and pathos. After some of your shows I haven't been able to decide whether the moisture in my eyes was caused by laughter or tears. A rare quality and one that entertains and delights."

Forsythe was not trying to flatter the actress; he meant every word he said. "Cor Blimey!" was a marvel-ous show. The premise was far from fresh and, in other hands, might have seemed forced and trite. Carolyn Chimes portrayed a compulsively ambitious woman, born a Cockney, who was fighting her way up the corpo-rate ladder in a catering business that served the rich. In each show she managed to bungle her way into a final scene of absolute mayhem. Her trademark, a bulging of beautiful blue eyes, a gaping of the mouth, and then a blurted, "Cor blimey! What a flaming cockup!" reduced her audience to gales of laughter.

Kate Kapiche made an impatient gesture and For-sythe's eyes moved in her direction. For once she wasn't wearing a caftan and her full and spectacular figure was shown to great advantage in a lime green *cheong saam*. It had a high-necked, mandarin collar, a fold-over bodice, flowing sleeves, and a long slit in the narrow skirt expos-ing a delicious leg sheathed in green silk. She asked the barrister, "Doesn't it seem strange that here we have Carolyn, a lady from a county family, acting the part of a Cockney lass who keeps pretending to be a county lady?"

Carolyn's smooth blond head turned toward the other woman. "So B. D. Epps is a split personality. Sometimes fiercely proud of being a London sparrow, sometimes terribly ashamed of it. When I agreed to act the part, I had trouble fitting into it. Then I had an inspiration. The character is based on you, Kate darling."

"If that's intended as a compliment, I'd hate to have you decide to insult me." Kate's full lips pursed. "So that's why B. D. Epps is always mavering on about her old auntie Annie. My Granny Muff! Carolyn, I damn well may sue!"

"Better sue the writer, darling. I'm only an actor and read lines."

The feeling of tension, momentarily dispersed by the arrival of Oglethorpe and Forsythe, was back again. Forsythe sought for words to ease the tension, but at the moment a deep and rasping sound tore through the silence. All eyes flashed to John Josephson. His head had fallen back, his mouth was ajar, his eyes were closed. He snored again and Kate snarled, "Another first! I've done many things to men, but putting them to sleep is not one."

Carolyn's light laugh tinkled. "Not to worry, ducks; that happens to be why John is here. Lyme disease. Don't look so alarmed, Harry, it's not contagious. Anyone heard of it?"

Forsythe nodded. "I read an article about it recently. It's caused by a tick bite, isn't it?"

"It is. John lives in the States now and thinks he picked it up on a hiking trip in New England. He came out in a rash, ignored it, and then started to get the other symptoms—"

"Which are?" Harry was leaning forward, intently studying Josephson's sleeping face.

Kate laughed. "You really are a bit of a hypochondriac, Harry. Tell on, Carolyn."

"John said he went from doctor to doctor in the States and was called just what you termed Harry, Kate. A hypochondriac. Then he came to London on a business trip and felt so rotten he checked in with one of the Harley Street boys. John finally got lucky regarding a diagnosis, as this chap's wife was recovering from Lyme disease that she'd picked up on a walking holiday in Germany. When I mentioned the Damien Day, John decided to book in for rest and treatment."

Oglethorpe was still studying the younger man. "He certainly looks ill."

The barrister silently agreed. Josephson was about his height and age, but he was even thinner than the barrister. His skin was the color of pewter and his eyes were sunk into dark hollows. His clothes were similar to those of Perce the orderly, but the pullover and shoes looked like Italian imports; the slacks were cashmere. These expensive clothes hung on his long frame loosely, as if he'd lost a great deal of weight.

As though aware of the barrage of eyes, Josephson stirred, his eyelashes fluttered, and then lifted. He shook his head as though trying to clear it. "Sorry," he muttered.

"Don't be," Kate told him. "Carolyn explained. What a nightmarish disease. Have you any idea about treatment?"

"Actually, once it's diagnosed, Lyme isn't difficult to treat. In my case about a month of intravenous antibiotics. It wasn't really necessary to come here for treatment as I could have had a doctor come to me daily in my hotel. But I'm in such bad shape physically that my physician insists on therapy and special diet—"

"Diet," Kate repeated. "What kind?"

"Designed to put on weight in a hurry. Stuffed with calories."

Kate's eyes flickered toward the other woman. Carolyn was dressed in a long, wide-shouldered jacket over a short skirt. This disguised the upper part of her body, but her face, legs, and neck were painfully thin. "And you, Carolyn? Extra-rich diet, too?"

"I'm afraid so. We always were direct opposites, weren't we?"

Kate's mouth twisted. "Harry, are you aware that you and I are stuck squarely in the midst of a group of people trying to *gain* weight? I really can't stand it! I may end up having my rabbit food served in my suite."

Oglethorpe looked from Carolyn to Josephson. "No fear of Katie deserting us, folks. She must have someone to talk at. Oh, Robert, are *you* deserting us?"

"Not because of diet. I'm due for my session with Athena and I'm cutting it a bit thin."

Josephson pushed back his sweater sleeve, consulted a watch that looked like a Rolex, and jumped up. "Good lord! I slept right through my first treatment and that nurse has a jaw like a hunk of steel."

"And a temperament to match," Oglethorpe told him. "Miss Holly will definitely have at you. When you two are finished, you should both come back here. John, we have a surprise for you."

"Pleasant?"

"More old friends, my boy. Meg Eleven and Carolyn's Teddy are supposed to be driving down to visit their mothers for a couple of days."

"Little Meg and Teddy. I haven't seen either of them since . . . it must have been that summer. I remember Teddy was talking about being an astronaut."

"Teddy grew out of that stage," Carolyn said. "Ended up following family tradition and he's an actor. Doing quite well, too. Almost too well. I've scarcely seen my boy for months. What about your daughter, Kate. Is Meg working in your business?"

"Stepdaughter. I urged her to take a business education and give me a hand, but she had no vocation for it. Meg's a nurse."

"And I'd wager a dedicated one. She was such a serious little thing when I knew her. Pretty?"

"She could be if she worked at it, but she cares nothing about clothes or cosmetics. Would you believe she never even wears perfume? Sometimes I think she'd have made an excellent nun. And she should never have decided on a nursing career. Too thin-skinned. Gets emotionally involved with her patients." Kate snapped her lighter and held the flame to one of her Egyptian cigarettes. She exhaled a thin cloud of smoke that momentarily veiled her eyes. "When she was working at a hospital in Leeds, she lost a number of patients in a short period and cracked up. I persuaded her to give up nursing and now she's a volunteer at some clinic in London. Gives counseling to battered women and that sort of thing."

Forsythe had the crutches in place and was hobbling toward the corridor. Josephson caught up with him. "I'll walk along with you, Robert." He called back, "Harry, be sure to warn Meg and Teddy that if I doze off, they aren't boring me." He slowed his long steps to match Forsythe's laboring gait. "Before I left home I read an article about you and your secretary in *Time*. Interesting."

"England's contemporary Sherlock Holmes?"

"That's the one."

"Don't believe everything you read. That was greatly exaggerated and full of inaccuracies. Sandy hides her actual age and insists the author of that article was out by a decade. The wrong way." Forsythe grinned. "The lady was not amused."

Josephson didn't appear much interested in Miss Sanderson's reaction. Darkly shadowed eyes slid sideways and he said, "The article also mentioned you're an expert on jade."

"A collector. There's a difference."

"What I'm hoping is—oh, oh!"

Miss Holly was at the nurses' desk. Not behind it but standing like a Grenadier guard in front of it, one white shod foot beating an ominous tattoo against the oak floor. Her large features were congealed into an expression that would have made the faces on Mount Rushmore look soft and warm. "Mr. Josephson! You may be a bit confused and best I explain a few things to you. In spite of"—one hand jerked in a semi-circular movement—"your surroundings, you are not in a hotel. You are in a medical facility. We have no objection to you socializing so long as it doesn't interfere with treatment. You were due for your intravenous at precisely half past one. It is now exactly six minutes to two. Where have you been?"

"Asleep."

"Indeed!" Her cold eyes turned to the barrister. "You look rather drawn, Mr. Forsythe. Don't overdo it on those crutches or we shall have a setback." She raised her voice. "Percival! Ah, there you are. Where have *you* been? Sneaking a smoke?"

Perce was piloting a wheelchair down the corridor at a frantic pace. He said breathlessly, "Picking up Mr. Forsythe's chair from the Primrose, matron—"

"Miss Holly. I no longer am a matron and this most certainly is *not* a hospital. You will kindly take Mr. Forsythe down to Miss Khalkis. You've exactly four minutes to get him to the basement. Mr. Josephson, you will come with me and we'll start your i.v."

After the lift door slid closed behind them, Perce sagged against the back of the chair, and muttered, "That woman's a . . . she's a flaming *matron!*"

Forsythe smiled up at him. "You make that sound like a four-letter word."

"In Miss Holly's case, that's what it is. Can't fool that woman. I *was* sneaking a smoke, sir." The orderly's face brightened. "Be a treat to see Miss Khalkis. Enough to make a bloke forget his wedding vows. Guess it's lucky for me wife Owen has the inside track with that filly."

"Owen? Are they engaged?"

"Guess you could call it that, sir. Living together in a nice snug cottage in Hundarby. Owen's nuts about her and it's easy to see why."

The lift door slid back and Perce wheeled the chair across the corridor to the scarlet painted door of the therapy section. Beyond that door was more violent color—orange and electric blue and chrome yellow. Colors intended to cheer the patients and that were inadvertently acting as an exotic background for the dark Mediterranean beauty of Athena Khalkis.

When Perce returned the barrister to the Flower Wing, they found John Josephson perched on a chair near the nurses' desk, idly leafing through a magazine. Propped against the wall near him was a pair of crutches. He threw down the magazine and carried the crutches over to Forsythe.

The barrister struggled to his feet. "Is your treatment finished?"

"Doesn't take that long. Haven't dozed off since Miss Iron Pants took out the needle, so maybe it's working already."

"Seems rather rapid."

"Probably wishful thinking. I get tired of *feeling* tired. How about popping in to my quarters for a while? I laid in a supply of Pepsi."

"Be a nice change from fruit juice. Which way?"

"Suite next to Kate's. If the guys back home ever hear the name of it, I'll never live it down."

"Can't be any worse than mine. The Primrose."

Josephson laughed. "Like to swap? I'm in the Pansy."

The suite with the unlikely name proved by far to be

the most ornate that Forsythe had yet seen. The colors the name conjured up were ignored and it was white and gold, running heavily to velvet and brocade. It bore a remarkable resemblance to an eighteenth-century French boudoir.

"What do you think?" Josephson asked.

"Shades of Madame Pompador." Forsythe crutched over and looked at the oil over the mantel. "Matisse?"

His host shrugged. "Possibly. Wouldn't surprise me if it is." He opened the gilt-and-white door of a cabinet that doubled as a bar and took out a couple of frosty cans from the tiny refrigerator. "Here's the promised Pepsi. I feel as though I should be offering a rare wine, but this is the best I can do." He tore the tab off his can and took a long swallow. "Do be seated, Robert. I'm going to wander around. Every time I sit I seem to doze off."

Forsythe selected a velvet-covered love seat and cautiously lowered his body. It proved to be unexpectedly comfortable. The other man started to pace up and down the room. He paused by a window and looked down at the snow-shrouded grounds. When he spoke, his voice was muffled. "Ever notice how unfair life can be? Think of it. In this huge building, surrounded by every type of luxury, we've five patients, none seriously ill. And coddling them we've three shifts of hospital personnel, three shifts of security guards, a French chef and kitchen staff, therapists, and God knows who else."

Forsythe nodded. "Also a staff of groundsmen."

"That too. Do you know how many homeless people there are where I live?"

"I've no idea where you live."

"La la land. Los Angeles. Thousands of homeless, and that's only one city. Human beings living worse than animals under overpasses of motorways, burrowing into cardboard boxes in alleys. Last winter during a cold snap a body of an elderly man was found in a dumpster. The

73

only remark made by the police was that if the weather had been warmer, they'd have found the body sooner by the smell. The poor old devil died of exposure and starvation. How does that grab you?"

"It makes me feel defensive. As though it's partially my fault. As though I should turn over everything I have to the poor. But we must keep our perspective, John. What all of us in this building own wouldn't even make a dent in world poverty and I think you're well aware of that." Forsythe drained the can and set it on a side table. "You interest me. If you're so repulsed by this lair of the wealthy, why are you here?"

"Would you believe I'd rather be ill among friends than among strangers?"

"No. I don't have the feeling these people are your friends."

"You're quite correct. They're simply a group of people I knew briefly many years ago."

The barrister looked searchingly at the other man. "When you decided to come here for treatment . . . did you know I would be here?"

"Harry Oglethorpe mentioned that to Carolyn and she mentioned it to me. I was interested to hear about you. You see, I've been investing in paintings and fine porcelain as a hedge against inflation." Josephson pointed at the mantel. "That Dresden figurine, the shepherdess, is one I picked up on my way down here. I've been considering buying jade for the same reason but know nothing about it. I thought I might as well pick your brain so I'd know what I was doing."

Forsythe pulled his crutches over and got to his feet. He joined his host near the window and peered out. It was still snowing and mounds were banked up on either side of the driveway. The Pansy Suite overlooked the driveway and the road. At the end of the long driveway, he could see a good-sized gatehouse and the gates. A khaki-uniformed guard was shoveling a path from the gatehouse to the gates. Snow shrouded the evergreens and the bare branches of a huge oak. He ran a fingertip down the double-glazed glass. It was dry to the touch but icy. At his side, Josephson moved restlessly. "Well? Willing to give me some pointers on selecting jade?"

"No."

"Why not?"

"No point in wasting my time or yours. If you wanted information, a man like you would seek expert advice, not check into a place like this to quiz an amateur collector. I've a hunch that you, like Harry, are looking for that amateur criminologist you read about."

"And it looks like I found him." Josephson's lips twisted in a grin. "Is Harry looking back in time, too?"

"Seventeen years back." Forsythe hobbled back to the love seat and sank into its cushioned embrace. "It was August and you were nineteen. Your parents had rented one of Harry's cottages. Were they close friends of Harry?"

"Mother and I barely knew the man. We were fairly well acquainted with Carolyn and Cliff Chimes, but we didn't know Kate Kapiche. Dad was involved in a business with both Kate and Harry. They'd backed him when he was trying to raise loans to expand his factory—"

"What type of factory was that?"

"Small machinery, mainly stuff for home workshops. It wasn't a large concern but it was quite prosperous. At least it was until Dad got delusions of grandeur and decided to expand. Things started to go sour and Harry sensed it, which was why Dad leased one of his cottages. To more or less placate Harry. Funny, you always think artists are unworldly people with no business sense, but not our Harry. Not only is he sharp but he's ruthless. And Dad knew if Harry called his loan in, so would Kate Kapiche."

"So the three of you spent the summer on Harry's estate?"

"Just Mother and I. Dad was up to his neck in business and seldom got down, but Mother and I had been there for June, July, and about a week in August before the Owen family was poisoned. As luck would have it, Dad came down to the estate that very day. He lunched with Mother and me and then in the afternoon went up to the manor to talk with Harry. Levi told me later that they'd had a tearing row. Dad stormed out of Harry's study and disappeared. He didn't come back to our cottage until after six that evening. I remember being surprised that he'd upset Mother. She was always delicate and Dad adored her and did everything possible to shield her from anything worrisome."

Josephson moved over to the fireplace and braced his elbow on the mantel. Tiny beads of sweat glistened on his high forehead and long upper lip. After digging out a handkerchief, he wiped his face and then the palms of his hands. "Perhaps you'd like to direct me . . . ask questions."

"I think it would be best if you continue with your memories, as they occur to you."

"Stream of consciousness, eh?" Josephson took a last swipe at his face and pushed the handkerchief back into a pocket. "I remember I didn't want to go to that cottage to spend the summer. That fall I was going up to Oxford and I hated spending my last months in a dumb cottage in the dumb country. But my father was adamant that I stay with Mother and I had no choice. The only saving grace was Levi Oglethorpe. We were the same age and got along marvelously. If I'd been able to spend more time with him, it would have been a good life, but Harry kept his brother's nose to the grindstone, or in this case, the easel, and I seemed to spend most of the time moping around the estate waiting for Levi to finish his daily stint.

Harry had an old stable behind the manor fixed up as a studio and I tried sneaking in to watch Levi work, but Harry caught me and warned me off.''

Josephson's lips twisted in the wry grin again. "Harry always called Walter Owen a slave driver and he wasn't much better himself. I should imagine he did love his young brother, but most of the time he treated Levi as though he owned him. Anyway, it worked out I had to wait every day for Levi until around four in the afternoon and then we'd take a package of sandwiches and go for a hike or fishing or swimming. There was a good trout stream on the estate and in one place it widened out into quite a decent pool. The only fly in the ointment was Meg Eleven. She was a trying brat and trailed us constantly. The woman who was supposed to be looking after the kid was hopeless and as long as Meg was out of her sight, she was out of Miss Todd's mind—''

"Shoddy Toddy?''

"I see you've been filled in. I suppose I should have felt sorry for Meg, but the truth is I couldn't stand her. I remember one time when Levi and I were skinny-dipping at the pool and there was Meg peering through the bushes, spying on us. If Levi hadn't stopped me, I'd have leaped out of the water and tanned her bottom. Levi was a soft-hearted chap and he did feel sorry for the kid. Once in a while he'd talk to her and a couple of times he shared his lunch with her.''

"Do you mind?'' The barrister had pulled out his pipe and tobacco pouch. His companion shook his head and Forsythe poked dark shreds of tobacco into the carved bowl. "What was Levi like?''

"Harry claimed he was a genius, a reincarnation of their famous father. Perhaps he was. But in every way I could see he was just an ordinary guy of nineteen.'' Josephson paused and then said slowly, "Although he certainly didn't look ordinary. I've a miniature Harry painted that he sent me after Levi's death. Would you like to see it?"

"Very much."

Josephson pushed away from the mantel and stepped into the bedroom. When he returned he was dangling a massive watch on a heavy gold chain. "My grandfather's watch. I had the miniature set into the case."

Forsythe took the watch, ran a fingertip over the engraved case, and snapped it open. The watch face was a beauty, but it was the face looking up at him from the opposite side that engaged his attention.

His companion asked, "What word immediately comes to mind?"

Forsythe didn't hesitate. "Beautiful. An achingly beautiful boy. Idealized?"

"Harry painted that face honestly. That's exactly how Levi Oglethorpe looked. Strange, even with that face and that awesome talent he still was quite an ordinary young fellow."

"Tell me what you remember about the day of the murders."

Josephson slid the watch into a pocket, returned to the hearth rug, and braced an elbow on the mantel shelf. "I remember it as rather a dismal day. The weather was fine but everyone seemed out of sorts. Kate's bridegroom, Kevin, had driven up to London in the morning and she was in a foul mood, snapping at Meg and Shoddy Toddy. She also had an argument with the young widow who was renting one of the cottages. Over her babies. I felt sorry for Mrs. Constantine. The babies were fretful, colicky kids and their mother seemed unable to cope. Quite often she'd hire Emmy Owen to babysit while she got a couple of hours sleep. That day they were wailing like banshees and that's what Kate was irate about. When I walked past the Constantine cottage at four to pick up Levi, I could hear both kids giving tongue.''

"To top it off when I got to the studio I found a note pinned to the door saying Levi wasn't feeling well and was resting. I swore and went back to the manor to see what I could find out. The cook told me that Levi had come in earlier, while my dad was with Harry in his study, and Levi had gone upstairs to borrow some head-ache capsules from his brother. The cook was quite a gossip and told me my dad and Harry had had a flaming row. I asked where Harry was and she said she didn't know. She'd taken his tea up after my dad left but Harry wasn't in his study.

"I was even more irritated. I figured Dad had gone back to our cottage and that he was probably so tense I simply didn't want to be near him. I considered dropping in and chatting with Carolyn and Cliff for a while but that morning Teddy had confided that his mother and dad were having a quarrel. Unusual. Generally they got on swimmingly.''

Josephson's voice trailed off and he put out a finger and touched the skirt of the dainty porcelain shepherdess on the mantel. "Funny, I didn't notice it when I bought it but this figurine looks a lot like Emmy Owen. Blond and blue eyed, slender build but with lush breasts, skin like milk . . .''

"Were you attracted to the girl?''

"At nineteen with all those hormones surging, what red-blooded lad wouldn't be? She was a sexy piece in an innocent sort of way. Woman's body and the mind of a child.''

"Was Emmy badly retarded?''

He shrugged a shoulder. "I'd say only slightly, but then I'm no expert on Emmy Owen. She was retarded enough that I steered clear of her. Teddy Chimes or Harry would be able to tell you more about the girl. Harry spent half his time ogling her and Teddy had a crush on her that could be discerned a mile away. But back to that afternoon. When I left the manor, I wandered down to the swimming pool and peeled off my clothes. First I scouted the area to see if sneaky Meg was spying, but there was no sign of her. Before I started back to the cottage, I ate the food I'd stuck in my haversack and it was well after six when I got home. Dad was just walking up the driveway from the road. He seemed quite calm and we both went in to Mother.''

''Did your father say where he'd been, John?''

''Walking, was all he told Mother and me. Later he told the police that he'd walked down to the church in the village, sat in a pew and meditated for a time, and then wandered around the graveyard. Both Harry and Dad told the same story about the row they'd had, which Levi and the gossipy cook had overheard. Seems Harry had the wind up about the safety of his investment and he also felt responsible for Kate's as he'd persuaded her to put money in Dad's concern. He was all for calling in their loans, but Dad persuaded him to hold off for a while longer. And . . . that's about it, Robert.''

Forsythe was watching the other man intently. ''One point is puzzling me. Why are you here, in a place you don't like, with a group of people you obviously care little about?''

Josephson passed a large hand over his face. He looked incredibly weary. ''Easy question to ask and one hard to answer. I don't feel any desire to avenge the Owens. Except for Emmy and Walter I didn't even see much of the family. Of course all the people on the estate were shocked at what happened, but it didn't really . . . it didn't touch us.

''What touched me happened afterward. That mass murder of a family I hardly knew acted as . . . as a catalyst." He flung out a hand. "I simply can't put it in words."

"Try."

"Very well, but bear with me. If the Owens hadn't died, Harry Oglethorpe wouldn't have sold his estate and taken Levi to Paris. If Levi hadn't gone to Paris, he might still be alive. Harry and Kate Kapiche might have given Dad extensions on their loans. If this had happened, Dad might have been able to avoid bankruptcy. If—"

"Your father went bankrupt?"

"He managed to hang on until late February of the following spring. Then the business folded and he had a heart attack. I was at King's College in Oxford and by the time I reached the hospital, he was gone and then . . . then I lost my mother."

"You lost both parents?"

"Only one to death. I should imagine Mother's last conscious thought was when she realized my dad was dead. Then her mind . . . it simply couldn't bear it and walked away. Until her death in September of last year she was catatonic. As for me—my whole world was swept away. I had no idea how to cope, but, luckily, a cousin of Dad's came to the rescue. He lived in the States, in California, and owned a fleet of those coffee trucks that go around to construction sites. Colin was more like an uncle than a cousin and he took a fancy to me. He was a bachelor and eventually made me his heir. He was the one who arranged for Dad's burial and Mother's commitment. Afterward he took me back to Los Angeles with him. Colin died last year too, but in the meantime we'd built his small business into a large-scale food-service industry—servicing airlines and food machines and industrial cafeterias and so on. Financially I'm in great shape. Emotionally I'm a wreck."

"You never married?"

"Twice. Both flaming failures."

81

"John," Forsythe said carefully. "You can't blame your life, your unhappiness, on a crime that happened years ago."

"That's where you're wrong." Josephson took a deep breath. "I want that bastard. I want the person who poisoned four people and killed my dad and my best friend. I want the beast who drove my mother mad. And I'm willing to pay any price you name to find him. Give me a figure and I'll give you a check."

"Perhaps," the barrister drawled, "you've been abroad too long. There're still a few things and people who can't be bought."

"Meaning this crime is too far in the past and too unimportant to intrigue England's contemporary Sherlock—"

"Meaning criminology is my hobby and I seldom accept fees for this work. Anyway, Harry Oglethorpe beat you to it and I've already told him I'd have a try. But do keep in mind there's little chance I can uncover anything new. It seems the police did a thorough job at the time of the murders and then there's the time element. Many of the people involved are now dead. So . . . don't get your hopes up."

Forsythe reached for his pipe and, after striking four wooden matches, managed to light it. Smoke wreathed around his head. "Harry believes the murders were committed by a person living on his estate. Are you in agreement?"

Josephson ran long fingers through his wiry brown hair. "I've gone over and over the facts and I'm forced to agree. The arsenic that killed them was in a gardening shed behind the manor house and—"

"I understand that, at the time of the ant problem, Harry mentioned the poison and its location to Walter Owen. Owen could have told any of the villagers about it."

"True. But disliking a man like Walter Owen is a mighty weak motive for killing an entire family."

"Which leaves us with the only other possible motive we know of thus far. Emmy was two months pregnant."

Josephson pushed away from the mantel and slumped on a chair. "Which brings us back to the estate. That was the only place Emmy was allowed to go alone. And on that estate there were seven men and boys capable of impregnating the girl. Which means we're looking for a man."

"Not necessarily. For every male there were relations—mothers and wives. Walter Owen sounded like the sort of chap who would cut up rough if his daughter was interfered with."

Josephson gave his twisted grin. "Good old shotgun wedding. And some poor devil stuck with a pretty but dim wife."

"Or, if the chap was already married . . ."

"There's that, too. Old Walter would've milked the situation like he did his cows. Any other thoughts?"

"One. The Jarmans seemed quite friendly with the Owen youngsters."

"So?"

"Carl Jarman was a butcher with a van. Probably drove around making deliveries. Right?"

"Right. I remember him bringing meat orders out to the manor house and our cottages. Come to think of it I saw his old van parked in the driveway of the Owen farmhouse a few times. And you think—"

"Jarman had access to both Emmy Owen and the poison."

"Come off it! Carl Jarman was an old man and a pillar of the church."

"How old?"

"At least fifty. With a bunch of grown kids—" Josephson broke off and snorted a laugh. "Will you *listen* to me? Sounds like I'm still nineteen and anyone over thirty is over the hill. Okay, Carl Jarman is a possibility. Any other candidates?"

Forsythe flipped back a cuff and looked at his watch. "Later, John. Nearly time for the preprandial drinks and I don't want to miss mine." He struggled out of the depths of the love seat. "Coming?"

"No rush for me. All I'll get is fruit juice. Anyway, I want a shower. You go along."

Forsythe positioned the crutches and made for the door. He was opening it when Josephson called to him. He swung around to face the other man. "Robert, you ever consider how easy it would be to murder in a hospital?"

Despite the warmth of the room, Forsythe felt suddenly chilled. "What do you mean?"

"A nice lady in a white uniform with a hypo in her hand. A swab on your arm, a needle prick, and away she goes. Another uniformed woman brings you a little paper cup with two pills in it. She hands you a glass of water and watches you swallow them. A man in a white jacket with a stethoscope dangling from a pocket pulls the curtains around a bed. The other patients in the ward pay no attention to the sounds coming from behind the curtain. The man in the white jacket leaves. Behind the curtain the patient is very quiet. Strangled."

The barrister was unable to respond. The other man's darkly shadowed eyes met his and Josephson made a small gesture of apology. "Sorry, morbid as hell today. Put it down to a tick bite. And I'm terrified of hospitals. Always have been."

A kindred soul, Forsythe thought, and one he certainly didn't need. What he did need was someone who would make light of his own fears, not add to them. He managed a small smile. "Not to worry, John. Miss Holly assures me this place bears no resemblance to a hospital and you must admit there isn't a white uniform in it."

As he hobbled down the corridor toward the nurses' station, he felt as though he'd blundered into a huge spiderweb, the sticky strands had enveloped him and were holding him fast, and a large and venomous spider was scuttling toward his face.

6

Thus far Oglethorpe's reunion hadn't been a raving success. With the exception of Carolyn Chimes, who greeted her son with a warm hug and a kiss, there'd been no indication that this group of people had any feeling for each other.

The last of the Owen family, Gareth, handed drinks around and he had greeted Teddy Chimes's warmth with as stony an expression as he had Meg Eleven's cool indifference. Now, as Darla moved around the oval table serving crab salad to the dieters and an excellent chateaubriand to the others, the diners made stiff conversation. Forsythe ate silently, surreptitiously studying the latest arrivals.

As far as he could remember, Teddy was only three years younger than John Josephson, but he could have passed as the other man's son. Teddy had his mother's pastel coloring, blond hair and pale blue eyes, and her wonderful cheekbones, but he had a chubby build and a softly good-looking face. He was the most likable of the lot, Forsythe decided, good-natured and inoffensive.

Kate Kapiche's stepdaughter was seated beside

Teddy and she justified her stepmother's comments. Meg could have been pretty but made no effort. Her clothes didn't help. She was wearing a twin set, a baggy tweed skirt, and heavy brogues that made her legs look stubbier than they actually were. She was average height and average weight and her hair was black and bright and short and gleamed like metal in the light from the Tiffany lamps. Her nose looked too large for her face and there was a trace of hardness around her mouth. She walked with a boy's bounciness and her hands reminded the barrister of Athena Khalkis's—large square palms and long powerful fingers.

Forsythe's eyes moved in a circuit of the diners. The dodos—Kate and Harry—were devouring their salads and casting envious looks at the bounty of food on their neighbors' plates. Kate had again dressed to rival the Art Deco background. Her tight pantsuit was gold lamé and she'd loosened her dark red hair to fall in rich masses around her face. Ropes of pearls and numerous gold chains dangled past her narrow waist and she wore false eyelashes that looked inches long.

Those eyes moved to the barrister and he frowned back. "Something wrong, Robert?" she asked.

"I could have sworn your eyes were gray and tonight—"

"Emerald green. Contacts. I change eye shades to match my clothes."

Carolyn murmured, "I'd love to see you in pink."

"Or in plaid," Meg said.

Kate made a hissing sound reminiscent of an affronted cat and Oglethorpe raised a fat hand. "Ladies, ladies! Kate actually didn't mean 'match.' She meant complement."

Carolyn smiled. "How lovely of you to translate for her."

In turn Oglethorpe turned a beaming smile on Meg

Eleven. "Do you realize, my dear, this is the first time we've met since—"

"*That* summer. The one we've all tried to forget, Harry."

"You used to call me Uncle Harry and I can remember giving you sweets. You were particularly fond of chocolate mints."

"I used to be a child," Meg said curtly.

Oglethorpe forged gallantly on. "And now you're all grown up and have become a nurse."

"I used to be a nurse, too. I don't know what I am now." Meg glanced across the table. "Good God! John's asleep again."

"The poor devil," Teddy murmured.

"Antibiotics will soon set that right," Meg said. "This constant fatigue is generally accompanied by fever and headaches and stiffness. But I should imagine he's lucky and the disease was caught before permanent damage has been done."

"You seem to know a great deal about Lyme disease," Carolyn said.

"A woman at one of the clinics where I worked had it. She wasn't as fortunate as John and couldn't afford a Harley Street specialist. Lyme wasn't diagnosed in time to prevent facial paralysis and heart arrythmia."

Carolyn arched fine fair brows. "I thought you worked with battered women."

"Battered women have other problems beside brutish husbands. Quite often they have to battle poverty and disease as well as periodically getting beaten to a pulp." She looked scornfully around the table. "But, of course, no one could expect any of you to know anything about ordinary people."

Kate flung her hair away from her face. "Don't start lecturing again, Meg. I'm sick of that nonsense!"

Their eyes locked and Forsythe said, "Too bad

John's asleep, Meg. Earlier he was telling me about the homeless people in Los Angeles. He has an active social conscience and would make a great ally."

Meg's attention shifted to the sleeping man. "Really a wonderful ally. Bemoaning the ills of the world while wearing a designer sweater that cost more than many people make in a—"

"John's no longer asleep," Josephson said curtly. "And that string of pearls you're wearing looks genuine to me."

"They belonged to my father's mother," Meg said defensively.

"Who also always looked as though she'd come out of a jumble sale," Kate said hotly. "You know, darling Meg, even crusaders could make an effort to look attractive occasionally."

"There speaks a woman who knows what she's talking about." Meg was glaring at her stepmother again. "Kate's certainly not a crusader, but she's devoted her entire life to clothes and jewelry and cosmetics. What a bloody waste of time!"

This is shaping up as a great little reunion, Forsythe thought. Oglethorpe was leaning forward, possibly to spread oil on the troubled waters, when Darla approached the table, bearing a dessert tray. Kate lost interest in her stepdaughter and eagerly examined it. On the tray were five servings of chocolate mousse smothered in whipping cream and two bowls of fruit salad. As Darla placed a fruit salad bowl in front of her, Kate snarled, "Blazing blue balls! Can't that excuse for a chef dream up anything but *salad?* Salad for appetizer, salad for entrée, now bloody salad for bloody dessert—"

"Darling," Carolyn chided. "Your Cockney is showing. Please don't kill the poor messenger."

For a moment it looked as though Kate was going to launch her gold-clad body across the table at Carolyn, but then she threw back her head and laughed. "How right you are. Later I'll have words with the salad maker. Ah, and here is Mrs. Elser. Do you by any chance have influence with the chef?"

Mrs. Elser, her face pink, had entered quietly and now stood behind Teddy Chimes's chair, the blue-covered guest book clasped to her ruffled bosom. "I'm afraid not, Ms. Kapiche. Raoul follows the diets laid down by your physicians." She opened the book, cleared her throat, and said, "I see we have four new guests or perhaps I should say two guests and two guests of guests. Confusing but all of you know what I mean. It is my pleasure to welcome the newcomers to the Damien Day Health Home and hope your stay here will be a pleasant experience. Would you be kind enough to sign the guest book?"

The book was passed from John to Carolyn and then handed first to Teddy and then to Meg. Mrs. Elser was glancing around, obviously quite overwhelmed by the guests. Forsythe noticed that she'd dressed for the occasion in quite the fussiest outfit he had yet seen her wear. When she retrieved the book, she looked down the line of sigantures and said, "Mrs. Carolyn Chimes, Ms. Omega Eleven—"

"Miss," Meg corrected.

"Of course. Mr. Theodore Chimes and Mr. John Josephson. I welcome you to—"

The nurse droned on and Forsythe caught only scattered phrases—brewing up, herb tea—and then Kate moved restlessly and, without lowering her voice, said to Oglethorpe. "What absolute drivel! How could Fran Hornblower have wished this . . . this vulgar *welcome wagon* on us?"

The guest book slipped out of Mrs. Elser's dimpled hand and she bent to pick it up. When she straightened she headed toward the door. Her face was crimson and she was blinking back tears. Meg drew her breath in sharply and Oglethorpe looked appalled. Carolyn Chimes came to the rescue. "Mrs. Elser," she called. "Do wait for me. I'm ever so fond of herb tea and would enjoy a cup. Do you suppose you could . . ."

The nurse paused and then turned. She managed to smile through her tears. "I most certainly can. Mrs. Chimes, I can't tell you how proud I am to meet you. 'Cor Blimey!' is my favorite show and my daughter loves it, too. Laura and I never miss an episode. Do you think you could give me your autograph? Laura would be ever so pleased and she . . ."

The door closed, shutting off Mrs. Elser's voice and Kate shrugged a gleaming shoulder. "Don't everybody glare at me like that. I'll make it up to the woman. Notice how Carolyn came to the rescue? Typical. Noblesse oblige. Did you know, Robert, that our Carolyn is the granddaughter of an earl?"

"You certainly can't hold that against Mother," Teddy said. "Anyway, none of her family have spoken to her since she took her first acting role. The whole family are back in the dark ages. Figure anyone connected to the theater is immoral and corrupt."

Meg had ignored her mousse. Now she pushed the plate away. "Your problem," she told her stepmother, "is that you confuse breeding with simple kindness. As you have none of either—"

"Meg!" Oglethorpe said sharply. "That's no way to speak to your mother—"

"*Step*mother. Isn't that what Kate always says? *Step*-daughter."

Oglethorpe took a deep breath. "Katie didn't intend to hurt Mrs. Elser. She speaks without thinking and means no harm."

Meg looked around the table. "Sounds like Mack the Knife acting as character witness for Jack the Ripper."

91

Teddy Chimes grinned and Josephson laughed. "That's *very* good."

Forsythe realized that not only was he getting tired of the infighting but he was extremely tired physically. He reached for his crutches and then envisioned the long walk down two corridors to his suite. He called over Darla and asked her to get his chair, but Meg pushed away from the table and jumped up. "I'll get it."

"I'm in the Primrose," he called.

"I know," she called back.

She wasn't gone long. She helped him into the chair, refused to allow him to wheel it himself, and trundled it briskly down the corridor and past the nurses' station. The desk was deserted but lights were on in the office and Forsythe heard the tinkle of Carolyn's laugh and Mrs. Elser's high, excited voice.

"I'd really prefer wheeling this chair myself, Meg. I'm not a total invalid, you know."

"I know that. But you look dreadfully tired. Is this the first time you've been on crutches?"

"The first full day."

"Remember it can be a strain on the torso and shoulder muscles. Don't overdo it or you'll pay."

"Spoken like Miss Holly."

"I met her when I arrived and I'll accept that as a compliment. She may be lousy at public relations but she's one hell of a good nurse."

"And Nancy Elser?"

"I just met her."

"You just met Miss Holly, too."

"True. My guess is that Mrs. Elser, with a little practice, would be great at public relations. Possibly better than at nursing. I've met her type before. Do a minimum of work, collect their pay, and go home and forget about it."

92

"One way of keeping sane, Meg. I should imagine too much involvement—"

"Leads to a nervous collapse like I had. As usual Kate has told all. Here we are." She nudged the door open and piloted the chair into Forsythe's sitting room. The room was warm and welcoming with the curtains drawn, the lamps glowing, and the gas fire switched on. "Must admit this is a bit of all right. Do you have gold-plated taps in your bathroom too, Robert?"

"Yes. But I should think that was the original owner's doing. The chap who renovated with the idea of running this as a luxury hotel."

"I haven't heard about him. Thought that rock star— what's his name?"

"Knight. Reggie Knight. Also known as the Black Knight."

"That's the one. I thought he put all these luxury touches on this place." She walked over to the hearth and stood, rubbing her hands together as though they were chilled. "Do you feel up to some company for a while?"

"I should welcome it." He glanced up at her. The table lamp at her elbow beamed a circle of light across her face, highlighting her cheekbones and shadowing her eye sockets. "Can you keep a secret or do nurses take vows?"

The corners of her mouth curved up and two shadowed dents appeared in her cheeks. The first time he'd seen this woman smile, the barrister thought, and that smile displayed a set of fine dimples. "Translation," she said. "Robert Forsythe, noted barrister and sometime sleuth, has cunningly smuggled some liquor past Miss Holly and is willing to share if I keep my mouth shut. Where are you hiding your contraband?"

"In the bookcase. Under *S* for Shakespeare. There's a tiny fridge built into that chest near the bedroom door if you fancy ice."

"Probably sounds like heresy with a malt like this

93

one, but I do like ice." She'd unfastened the brass clasps and the leather-covered box lay open. "Ingenious. Your idea?"

"My secretary's. Miss Sanderson has a devious mind."

She made drinks, handed Forsythe a glass, and carried the other, tinkling ice, over to the leather divan. When she'd settled into a corner of it, she took a sip and set her glass on a table. "Mack the Knife told me—"

"Mack—oh, you mean Harry."

"All right, I'll start again. Earlier Harry spoke to me and asked if I'd talk to you about that hideous summer at his estate. Appealed to my dutiful daughterly feelings for Kate. Harry led me to believe that Kate has some kind of hangup about that year that's raising hell with her health. I find that hard to swallow. Kate Kapiche has always been so wrapped up with Kate Kapiche I doubt she'd brood about anything." She leaned forward, ran a fingertip over the misted glass, examined the worm of moisture on her finger, and touched her lips with that fingertip. "You're supposed to be the detective, so ask questions."

"How much do you remember about that time?"

"Very little. For one thing I was a child. For another I was grieving for the only person who ever cared a fig about me. Her name was Grady and she was fat and Irish and far from young and the kindest woman I've ever known. Kate didn't even bother trying to find someone similar to Grady to look after me. She hired a frowsy slut named Todd who wouldn't move off her fat butt even to cook a meal. That summer Shoddy Toddy and I lived on junk food and she got even fatter and my rotten case of acne got even worse. When Kate arrived with her new bridegroom in tow, I thought they'd turf the lazy bitch out on her ear, but Kevin and Kate were so wrapped up in lust they'd have eaten garbage and not noticed.

"Everyone considered me a brat and a pest and I

94

suppose they had good reason." She frowned and the smooth skin between her heavy dark brows wrinkled. "I do remember appealing to Kate, telling her how lonely I was, how much at loose ends. She pointed out that I had television and games and books and ended up giving me a wad of pound notes and telling me to walk into Greater Eveline and buy myself something. Kate never did understand that it was a cry for help, that I was utterly lost without Grady. Finally I started following John Josephson and Harry's young brother around for something to do. John hated that and me and did his best to drive me away, but I stuck like glue."

Forsythe drained his glass. "Did you play with the children on the farm?"

"The Owen brood? No. The only one near my age was Gareth and he was doing a man's work. Any spare time he had was spent with Teddy Chimes. And Annie was only nine and Elsbeth about seven."

"What about Emmy?"

"Emmy was as busy as Gareth."

"I understand she was a pretty girl."

"Ravishing. Hair the color of ripe wheat and a skin that made me wild with envy. Big blue eyes and a dynamite figure. Sad that mentally she was about Annie's age."

"Did you notice any of the men or boys on the estate paying an excessive amount of attention to Emmy Owen?"

"No. Sorry, but I was so wrapped up in my own misery I wasn't noticing much of anything. To be truthful, I don't feel this rooting around in the past is healthy. It's over. Gareth seems to have made a life for himself and I shouldn't think he'd like this. His family has been dead for years. To be blunt I don't think this is anything but an exercise in futility."

"You don't want to know who murdered the Owen family?"

"I don't believe there's any way the truth can be uncovered. Many of the people who were involved are dead. It's possible the murderer is one of them. Babs and Gib Josephson are dead and Levi Oglethorpe, Cliff Chimes, Mrs. Constantine and her twins—"

"Them too?"

"About five years after that ghastly summer. I saw it in the *Times*. A house fire. Alice and both children burned to death."

"What about Kevin . . . I don't believe I've heard his surname."

"Travis. After Kate finally got the divorce from Kevin, he went back to Australia. I've heard nothing about him. Any further questions?"

"I'm curious about Kate's grandmother. Granny Muff. Did she actually exist?"

"Why the interest? She existed all right, but Granny Muff hated the country and never came down to the cottage."

"Curiosity. I've built up a mental picture of a tiny woman like a wren who cheeped like a bird."

"In other words, a London sparrow." Meg's lips curled in something not quite a smile. "Your mental picture is flawed. Kate's dear old Granny was a big fat creature with a voice like a buzz saw. Granny Muff was famous for her pithy sayings. I remember one she made about me when I was about six. Granny said it right in front of me as though I were deaf, but I was quite old enough to understand. 'Katie,' the dear lady said. 'Why don't you get rid of this sniveling brat? Send her to her dad's family to raise. She's costing you far too much in nannies and so on. You don't need her.' I think Kate would have loved to have done just that, but my father was an only child and had no close relatives. Anyway, it

96

was my father's money that Kate was using to fund her new hair salons and if she had put me in an orphanage it wouldn't have looked so great. So Kate was stuck with me and I was stuck with her and Granny Muff. May the old bitch's soul burn in hell!''

Meg got to her feet and set down her glass. ''Sorry I couldn't help more, Robert.'' She moved toward the hall door and Forsythe noticed again that bouncy walk. Over her shoulder, she called, ''Thanks for the drink and don't worry. I promise the boozy Bard of Avon is our secret.''

For a time Forsythe sat staring into the fire. He considered ringing for Gareth Owen and attempting to strike up a conversation with the man, but decided against it. He doubted that Gareth, with that cold, closed expression, would be willing to discuss his family. And Meg had made a valid point. The trail was cold, many of the witnesses were dead, the survivors' memories were quite possibly faulty.

He was struck again with a feeling of depression and futility and he fought against it. It is this damn hospital, he thought. A few days and he would be in his home in Sussex with Jennifer. There'd be warm fires—apple wood and not gas—there'd be Mrs. Meeks's excellent meals, and long evenings for holding and talking and dreaming with Jennifer. This whole period of time would simply fade like a bad dream in the morning light.

At that moment there was a light tap on the door and Mrs. Elser stepped into the room. ''Ah, Mr. Forsythe. Still up, I see. And how are you feeling?''

They discussed his health and Mrs. Elser jotted notes, but her attention seemed to be straying. He wondered if she could be brooding about Kate Kapiche and her rather cruel remark. Hesitantly, he said, ''About Ms. Kapiche. I don't believe she meant what she said at dinner quite the way it sounded.''

''Of course she didn't! She came along to the office

97

after Mrs. Chimes had her tea and apologized to me. Look what Ms. Kapiche gave me as a souvenir." She fished among the ruffles on her skirt, apparently found a pocket, and held up a tortoiseshell compact with flashing gold initials.

From what Forsythe had seen of Kate, he thought this was typical of Granny Muff's little girl. Nasty as hell one moment, sweet and contrite the next. He glanced away from the nurse and his eyes lit on the glass, ice cubes puddling in the bottom, that Meg Eleven had used. Meg had replaced the whiskey bottle in the leather box, but they'd both forgotten about the damning glasses. If Mrs. Elser noticed those glasses, lifted one and smelled it . . . Lord! his whiskey would be confiscated and there'd be no way to replace it.

Hastily, he asked, "What do you think of Carolyn Chimes?"

Her face lit up and she nodded until all her chins were wobbling. "I keep thinking of her as B. D. Epps and she's just as nice and common as . . . well, bangers and mash. No airs at all. Carolyn—she asked me to call her that—says if I bring a camera in tomorrow she'll pose with me for a snap. Wonder if her son would pose with us. I've seen him on telly, you know. Not in a show but in commercials. That one they have about Clene Dreme, the laundry soap. He's the lad in the muddy soccer uniform whose mother mavers on about getting it sparkling clean with Clene Dreme. Ever so good-looking, Mr. Chimes is. Reminds me of Robert Redford when he was a young actor."

Mrs. Elser paused, apparently to collect both her breath and her thoughts. She gave a little giggle and fingered a bright brown curl. "You must think me a silly goose, Mr. Forsythe. Going on like this. But I have to keep pinching myself to see if this is real, if Nancy Elser is actually rubbing elbows with all these famous folk. The only one I can't place is Mr. Josephson. Should I know him? Is he a celebrity?"

"John's a businessman." Her face fell and he hastened to add, "He comes from Los Angeles."

"Hollywood," she breathed. "He probably knows all sorts of famous actors. I must ask him if he knows Paul Newman and Robert Redford. They're my favorites. Laura, now, she likes Nick Nolte and that young chap with the wonderful smile . . . now, *what* is his name?"

The barrister shot a sidelong look at the whiskey glass and wondered how long the woman would rave on. She was still babbling. "Wait until I hand this compact to my daughter and tell her who gave it to me and who else is going to have her picture taken with her old mum. Wonder if I should ask Ms. Kapiche and Mr. Oglethorpe to pose too? I think—but, just listen to me! Talking a mile a minute and forgetting how much you need your rest."

Finally she was gone, leaving a breath of rather pungent perfume behind her. Forsythe toyed with the idea that Kate might have gifted Mrs. Elser with a vial of perfume but decided that any scent bearing the famous Kapiche name would be more subtle.

He also decided that the nurse was indeed a silly goose and badly star struck. He wondered if Miss Holly would succumb to the same wide-eyed excitement and then he grinned. He had a hunch the former matron would prove impervious even to the personal blandishments of Robert Redford. No doubt her only interest would be in the state of his bowels.

As he picked up the whiskey glasses, deposited them in his lap, and wheeled into the bathroom to wash them out, he gave thanks to whatever diety had directed Mrs. Elser's attention to her illustrious guests and away from his illicit Laphroaig.

7

Perce, clad as usual in his yellow pullover, took the order for Forsythe's breakfast, but it was delivered by the man who reminded Mrs. Elser of a young Redford. "Morning," Teddy Chimes said cheerfully. He flipped down the legs of the tray, slipped it across the barrister's knees, and, with a flourish, shook out the napkin and spread it over the other man's chest.

"Well done!" Forsythe told him. "Did you ever work in a hotel?"

"Only in a film and that was as a busboy."

"I understand you also scamper around in soiled soccer uniforms."

"And happy to do it. Commercials pay better than drama and believe me I can use the money. Acting is a precarious living at the best of times." Teddy tilted the coffeepot over two cups, took one, and sank into a chair beside the bed.

Forsythe glanced up from a plate laden with scrambled eggs, rashers of bacon, and tiny pork sausages. "Is that your entire breakfast?"

"Unfortunately, yes. I'm dieting." Teddy patted the

softness under his jaw, the slight roll of flesh over his belt. That roll was quite visible as he was wearing low-slung jeans, a ruffled shirt open to his navel, and a chest laden with gold chains.

Mrs. Elser's going to be over the moon when she sees that outfit, Forsythe thought. "I suppose for a person in your profession extra weight might be a disaster. I understand cameras are merciless and magnify every pound."

"That's what my agent told me." Teddy looked longingly at the creamer, shook his blond head, and took a sip of black coffee, "According to Bert, I'm eating myself out of a career. Mother is so damn lucky. She can eat like a horse and not gain an ounce. I nibble a croissant and start to bulge. And that's a no-no for the roles I specialize in."

Forsythe dabbed ginger marmalade on a triangle of toast. "Which are?"

"Juves. Boy parts. Thirty-three years old and portraying adolescent punks. But it's a living and Bert says if I watch my weight I'll probably be good until I'm fifty."

"Eternal youth. But it would be hard on a wife, if you have one. She'd age while you emulate the fictional Dorian."

Teddy laughed. "No wife, at least not as yet. When I do take the plunge I'll look for a woman mature enough to take a boy-husband in stride. Also one wealthy enough to keep said boy-husband in style." He slid his cup back on the tray and slouched back in the chair. "I suppose, Robert, you're wondering why I'm here. Last evening John cornered me and asked if I'd speak with you privately. Just what is going on? I come here, at Harry's urging, to spend a couple of days with Mother and find most of the survivors of a beastly time in my life gathered in this gilded cage. One nurse—the ruffled Mrs. Elser—is gaga about the patients. Or perhaps the old girl is gaga naturally. The other—Miss Holly—acts as if I'm un-

101

wanted baggage she'd like to get rid of. When I asked Miss Holly this morning where I could get a drink, she responded as though I'd begged for a line of cocaine."

Forsythe choked on a mouthful of toast and his companion was on his feet, pounding his back. "Enough," the barrister sputtered. "You really asked Miss Holly for a *drink?* In the *morning?*"

"Sometimes I do enjoy a Bloody Mary for breakfast. But it's just as well Miss Iron Pants—that's what John calls her—turned me down. A BM is loaded with calories. But speaking of John boy, what do you want to talk about?"

Forsythe was pouring another cup of coffee. He sugared it heavily and poured cream while Teddy watched with longing eyes. "That beastly period of your life that you just mentioned. Both John and Harry seem determined to find who is responsible for murdering the family of Gareth Owen. As you may know, I've had some experience at amateur criminology and they've asked me to look into it. Do you mind?"

Teddy's head shook and a lock of fine blond hair fell forward over his eyes. Impatiently, he brushed it back. "You mean, is it going to upset me? I think not, but I do fail to see any purpose in rehashing the affair. It's over . . . done. But if both John and Harry want this done, I suppose I should cooperate. Now, let me think where to start."

His eyes closed and he looked even younger. Forsythe waited patiently, and finally Teddy said, "I guess on Harry's estate I was probably the one closest to Gareth and his family. Mother and Dad rented one of Harry's cottages and we got down there earlier than the other tenants. It was early in May, a few days after my sixteenth birthday. Both my parents were actors and they were resting, a euphemism meaning out of work, and they thought it would be cheaper living in the country than in our flat in the city. We were short of money but in those days that was far from rare. Mother was only getting bit parts and although Dad made good money, he spent it like water.

"At the start I was pleased to be there. I knew both John and Levi slightly and they were my heroes. I was in prep school and John was going up to Oxford and Levi . . . well, Harry kept saying one day his brother would be famous in the art world. I practically worshipped the older boys and figured the three of us would chum around together, but it didn't work out that way. I don't suppose you remember, Robert, but there's one hell of a gap between nineteen and sixteen when—"

"I remember," Forsythe said drily. "I may not look like a golden youth but I'm not much older than you. To Levi and John you would have been a mere kid, a pest, a nuisance."

"A tiresome brat. If it had been only Levi, I think I'd have been accepted. He was a nice, easygoing chap. But John was ruddy possessive. He wanted Levi to himself and made that frightfully clear. John told both Meg and me to push off. Meg was thick-skinned and paid no attention, but I was hurt and stayed out of their way."

Forsythe reached for his pipe and started to load it. "Did you and Meg chum around?"

Teddy smiled and even white teeth gleamed. "With Meg I pulled a John Josephson. She was three years younger and a girl. Not that Meg gave a damn about me. She was obsessed with the older chaps. But I was bored stiff and started hanging around the Owen farm. Gareth was about my age and a decent lad. Not all frozen and grim like he is now, but cheerful and outgoing. Trouble was the amount of work his father piled on him. What a complete monster that Walter Owen was! I detested him. He was such a snide sort of chap. He never came right out

103

and told me to clear off, but he'd make remarks to Gareth as though I wasn't there. Things like, 'You mustn't bother the young gentleman, me boy, young gentry has better things to do than hang around with the likes of you.' "

Teddy paused, one hand idly toying with the gold chains on his chest, his eyes abstracted. "Regardless of those remarks I kept on going to the farm. A few times Gareth managed to sneak off with me and we had a swim or kicked a soccer ball around or did some fishing. I kept a wary eye out for old Walter and if he wasn't around, I'd sneak into the kitchen of the farmhouse and spend some time with Emmy. I kept assuring myself I was going to the farm to visit Gareth, but it wasn't the truth. It was Emmy I was interested in and I had one hell of a crush on the girl. Then something happened . . ."

His hand fell away from the glittering chains and grasped one knee. Forsythe puffed on his pipe, sipped coffee, and waited. He had a feeling any effort to prod the other man would close him up like a clam. Finally, his patience was rewarded.

"I wasn't trying to be a peeping Tom," Teddy muttered. "The reason I crept up to the kitchen window and peered in was to see if the coast was clear, if old Walter was elsewhere. It was early in the morning, before seven. That farmhouse was pretty primitive, w.c. in the rear yard and washing facilities set up on a bench near the scullery wall." He took a deep breath. "Emmy was having a sponge bath from a basin. She was standing there with her little bare feet on that stone floor and she was starkers. Not wearing a stitch. Generally she wore her hair in plaits but that morning it was loose, falling around her shoulders like a curtain of gold. She was slender but her breasts were quite large and the nipples were petal pink—" Teddy broke off and shook his head. "I better stop that. Get a bit too lyrical. Anyway, I knew I should

104

get the hell out of there, but I seemed unable to move, glued to the spot. I stood staring at those marvelous breasts and rounded hips and I was literally gasping. Emmy started washing between her legs and I swear I had an erection like a battering ram."

Teddy was breathing rapidly, as though he was still standing, a passionate sixteen year old, staring through the window of a farmhouse, at his first naked woman. "Then someone grabbed my arm and my heart nearly stopped. I figured it was Walter Owen and he'd give me a beating like he did Gareth, but when I was yanked around I was looking into my father's face. He gestured me to silence and hauled me away from the window. It wasn't until we'd reached the gates of Harry's estate that Dad let go of my arm and spoke. I expected him to flay me alive with words, but he didn't. He seemed . . . understanding. Told me he knew how I felt, once he'd been my age, too. Warned that if I got carried away, Walter Owen would be in a perfect position to blackmail our family for years. At that point I broke in and told Dad I loved Emmy and wanted to marry her. He lost control and grabbed my shoulders and shook me. He shouted I didn't know the difference between love and lust and asked how I'd enjoy being tied to a wife who couldn't write her own name, who couldn't count to a hundred. Finally he got himself under control and lowered his voice. He put an arm around my shoulders and said he wanted my solemn word I'd stay away from the Owen farm and Emmy."

"Did you give it?"

"No. I knew I couldn't keep it. I'd have to see Emmy again."

"Did you go back to the farm again?"

"I didn't have a chance. Dad grounded me for a week and the following day . . . that was when they were poisoned."

Forsythe opened his mouth but a brisk knock

sounded on the corridor door and Perce appeared at the bedroom doorway. "If you've finished your breakfast, sir?"

"All done." The barrister threw the napkin on the tray and the orderly lifted the tray off the bed.

Perce glanced at his watch. "I'll be back shortly to take you to therapy, sir. Will you need help getting ready?"

"I'll manage." Forsythe waited until the orderly had left the suite and then he said slowly. "I understand your parents had an argument the morning of that day. Did it concern Kate Kapiche?"

"Hardly. At that time Kate and Dad hardly knew the other one existed. Kate was newly married to Kevin Travis and she couldn't see anyone but her brawny Aussie. They couldn't keep their hands off each other. The quarrel my parents had that morning was over money. We were really indigent and Dad was trying to persuade Mother to appeal to her family for funds to tide us over. Usually Mother was putty in Dad's hands and would do anything he asked, but she balked at that. She said her family had disowned her and she'd rather starve than take a shilling from them. Dad fired back and they had a hectic row. I was completely shocked. Never before and never after did I hear my parents quarrel."

"Not even about Kate?"

"No. That took everyone, including Mother, by surprise. When the police finally agreed we could leave Harry's estate, we were all relieved to get back to London. Mother got a bit part on a television series, enough to tide us over, and then Kate Kapiche asked Dad to do a commercial for a male line of toiletries she was planning to market. It paid well and Dad agreed. It was quite a tasteful ad with Dad in tails with a gorgeous woman on his arm. You've probably seen much the same sort of ad. She's discreetly but madly lustful because of the odor of the after-shave he's wearing. Anyway, Kate and Dad started spending a lot of time together and suddenly the bomb dropped. Dad simply packed his clothes, told us he was in love with Kate and as soon as both of them had divorces they'd—Kate and Dad—be married. Then he took off.''

The barrister reached out and knocked the dottle of his pipe into an ashtray. ''Teddy, if you rather not talk about this . . .''

''It doesn't bother me much now. Ancient history. At the time I was as shattered as Mother was. I begged her not to give Dad a divorce, told her he'd come to his senses but . . .''

''She did divorce him?''

''Mother's proud. Said she'd hold no man against his will. Yes, she gave him his divorce. All of this happened in early November. I suppose if Kevin had cooperated, my father and Kate would have been married. But Kevin dragged his feet and by the time he agreed to a divorce—about April of the following year—fickle Kate had fallen for another man. This one was unattached and they were married at once. Dad made rather a dramatic exit. Went up to the roof of Kate's apartment house and jumped off.''

It was Forsythe's turn to shake a baffled head. ''Your father must have been deeply in love with Kate.''

''Oddly enough I've a hunch he wasn't. Oh, there was no doubt a strong physical attraction, but I believe it was Kate's money that Dad really fell for. He hated being poor. Another strange thing. When I look back to that time, it's Emmy I mourn for, not my father. He chose his own death, but she didn't. And Emmy should have lived. She was so gentle and so lovely.'' Teddy walked toward the sitting room, paused, and, without turning, said, ''A couple of things have disturbed me through all these intervening years.''

Again the barrister didn't prod. He stared at the other man's back, at the wide shoulders, narrow waist, slender hips, wondering if Teddy Chimes looked like his father. Then Teddy spoke and he had to strain to hear. "Probably it doesn't matter, but I've never understood what brought my father to the Owen farmhouse that morning. I didn't know he ever went there. And when he wrenched me around to face him . . . I'd swear he was lusting for Emmy as much as I was."

Teddy stepped into the sitting room and his voice drifted back. "I must have had a sheltered childhood. I know I was more innocent than most boys of sixteen. But that innocence and my childhood died that morning on the Owen farm, outside their kitchen, looking into my father's eyes." He added, "See you later. Tata for now."

Forsythe waited until he heard the hall door thud closed and then he threw back the duvet, gathered up fresh underwear and an exercise suit, and crutched into the bathroom. With the aid of the metal bar installed in the shower stall, he was able to shower and then, with an electric razor, he managed to shave. He noticed he was some stronger and, as both Athena and Geraldo had suggested, put a little weight on his bad leg.

When he swung open the bathroom door, he heard the roar of a Hoover competing with a vigorous contralto caroling a hymn. He smiled broadly and eagerly crutched to the sitting room door. As he gazed fondly at his favorite employee of the Damien Day he found himself wishing that Rosie the cleaning woman came in for longer than a couple of hours a morning. In the short time since he'd arrived, he'd found that Rosie was the best antidote to depression that he'd yet found. He bellowed a greeting and Rosie switched off the vacuum. She was short, enormously fat, and draped in a pink smock about the size of a pup tent. She had a round, highly colored face and bleached hair cut like a Dutch boy's. That round face split into a smile as she returned his greeting. "How's the gimp this morning, Mr. F?"

"Greatly improved. I'm able to put some weight on the leg now."

"Before long you'll be dancing like a gazelle."

"How are things at home, Rosie?"

"Gawd awful. Me old man's still out of work and me daughter left her hubby and came home dragging her two brats with her. And our cottage with only one bedroom. Guess who's sleeping on shakedowns in the parlor? Ah well, never so bad it couldn't be worse. She mighta bought that hubby of hers and then me old man and me would've been sleeping in the kitchen." Rosie patted a fold of the pink smock. "Notice I've put on some weight, Mr. F?"

Forsythe searched for something tactful to say. "That smock is cut so full you really can't tell."

"That's what I like about you. Always the gent. Turn your back for a sec like a good boy."

He wheeled around and heard sounds of cloth rustling and then a triumphant, "Got it! You can have a look now." Rosie waved a tall green bottle. "A pint of the best! Perce says you got a terrible thirst for bitters, so I smuggled this past that dragon, Miss Holly. Go good with your lunch and Perce can stand guard in the corridor so's Miss Holly don't sneak up on you."

"If she'd caught you . . ."

Rosie bellowed a laugh. "Sure and me old man and me would *both* be on the dole. But not to worry, luv. Picked a foolproof place to carry it. Between me girdle and me belly. Here, I'll hide it down here and none the wiser." Rosie bent, pulled a couple of books off a shelf and pushed the bottle behind them. "Don't look upset, Mr. F, the way I'm built the dragon hasn't a clue."

"You still took an awful chance and it could have cost your job. Do you do this sort of thing often?"

"First time and probably the last. Most people in this posh place don't give the time of day to a char. But you're different."

Forsythe considered offering a tip and discarded the idea. Money wasn't the answer for this type of service. He made a mental note to ask Miss Sanderson to select a feminine and frivolous gift for Rosie. For the present . . . he bent and brushed a kiss over her warm cheek. "And you're the best, Rosie."

The feeling of warmth lingered as he hobbled down the corridor. He passed the supply room and another pink-smocked cleaning woman stepped out of it. This one was nothing like his Rosie. She was scrawny and had shifty eyes and a sour mouth. Behind her he caught a glimpse of long shelves lined with bottles and tins and along the rear wall a row of pink smocks. Then his attention jerked back to the corridor. Perce was careening a wheelchair along, making straight for him.

"What's the hurry, Perce? Watch it!"

"Sorry, sir. Nearly banged your leg. We're a bit late for—"

"Orderly! No time for idle chitchat," Miss Holly bayed. "You've exactly three minutes to take Mr. Forsythe to therapy."

As the lift door closed behind them, Perce panted, "Honest to Gawd, I'm going to take up a collection and buy that blasted woman a stopwatch. Come to think of it, she don't need one. Hey, did Rosie get the beer to you?"

"That she did. I'd like to have it with luncheon. Think you could run interference with Miss Holly?"

"Put your money on it! Nothing suit me better than putting one over on that . . . *that* matron."

The beer that Forsythe drank with his luncheon was the best he'd ever tasted. Of course it had taken two people, risking their jobs, and a precarious ride against the bulging belly of Rosie to bring that treat to him. This

110

humble pint, he mused, had every right to taste like nectar and ambrosia.

Dinner that evening, cooked by a French chef and served at a table fragrant with a centerpiece of hot house roses and sparkling with fine crystal and silver, should have tasted like nectar and ambrosia. Instead it might as well have been ashes.

Darla served dinner and she made an eye-catching waitress. Her jeans looked sprayed on and she wore an Indian cotton shirt so thin that the dark smudges of nipples showed against it.

John Josephson's eyes were following the aide. "You know, Darla, you really are very deft at this sort of thing. Have you ever considered working in the food service industry?"

"Guess that's what I'm doing now. Came here thinking I'd be looking after sick folks and end up waiting table."

Her face was sullen and her voice dangerously close to insolent. Forsythe's eyes flashed to Kate Kapiche, but that lady was ignoring the aide. She was inspecting her geranium-colored lips in the mirror of one of her tortoiseshell compacts. A dress matching her lips clung to her breasts and hips, and that color should have clashed with her dark red hair, but didn't.

Carolyn Chimes, as she had once remarked, was Kate's direct opposite. Her thin body was draped in a severely tailored, dark gray dress relieved only by twisted ropes of crystal, coral, and pearl. The third woman at the table, Meg Eleven, was incredibly dowdy in a shabby twin set and a baggy tweed skirt. Forsythe wondered why she didn't make the slightest effort to look attractive and then his lips twisted in a self-mocking smile. He was a great one to criticize. His dinner garb was yet another exercise suit, this one burgundy and white. The other

111

men had made an attempt at dressing. Teddy looked remarkably young and handsome in his jeans and ruffled shirt. John Josephson was wearing what looked like an Armani suit, and Oglethorpe had decided to emulate Teddy. On him the low-slung jeans and gaping shirt were a complete disaster. The numerous gold chains almost disappeared in the matt of hair and fleshy rolls on his torso.

The artist's bulging eyes were fixed on Darla's Indian shirt. "You know if you ever get fed up with this area, you can look me up in London. I'm certain my house-keeper can find a place for you on my staff."

Darla ignored him, but Kate closed her compact and said lazily, "Harry, darling, you're getting past seduction. At one time you'd have been offering to paint the girl."

Oglethorpe was not to be diverted. Darla had finished serving the entrée and was pushing the serving cart across the room toward the gaping dumbwaiter. Apparently he found her rear view as enticing as her front, as his eyes were fixed on her clenching buttocks.

Carolyn Chimes cut into a slice of lamb and said thoughtfully, "Funny, Harry, I just remembered witnessing one of your attempts to persuade a young girl to let you paint her. Emmy Owen."

"Nonsense, my dear, your memory's playing tricks."

"No, I remember clearly. I'd walked up to the manor to speak with you about our rent money. We were going to be late paying and I was horribly embarrassed and nervous. One of your maids told me she thought you were in Levi's studio, so I walked around the house and you were in the rear garden. You had Emmy backed up against the studio wall and were waving a handful of notes at her. The child was bewildered and frightened. I asked what you thought you were doing and you said you'd offered her money to pose and the daft creature had become hysterical. At that moment Levi leaned out of a window and called you. You threw up your hands and went into the studio, leaving me to calm the girl.''

Oglethorpe nodded his head. "That's right. I'd completely forgotten that incident. Emmy couldn't seem to understand what I wanted.''

"Knowing you, I'm not surprised," Kate murmured. After a moment she added, "Carolyn, the eternal Good Samaritan.''

"You'd have felt sorry for the child too, Kate," Carolyn told her. "Emmy was incoherent. She even forgot that cart of produce and bread she pulled around and we had to go back later and retrieve it from behind the studio. But, at the time, I took her back to our cottage and gave her a cup of tea. I remember how attractive she looked. She didn't wear a speck of makeup and her dress was a cheap cotton thing she'd stitched herself, but she had a skin like silk and the heat glued that dress to her body like a second skin.''

Oglethorpe turned his head and the fringe of reddish hair brushed his shoulders. "It's no wonder every man who saw her wanted to get into her knickers.''

"Not every man," Josephson said stoutly. "Dad certainly paid no attention to her. That summer he was only down to the cottage a few times and he was so worried about his business he wouldn't have noticed the Venus de Milo if he'd tripped over her.''

"That's where you're mistaken, John. Take my word for it, Gib *noticed* Emmy. As I said, every man on my estate was hot for her.''

Kate reached for her water glass. "I can name one man who had no interest in bedding the wench. Kevin!''

Oglethorpe bellowed with laughter. "That I can't refute, Kate. I stand corrected. You had that poor devil so exhausted there was nothing left for another woman. By the by, whatever happened to Kevin?''

Kate shrugged a white shoulder. ''I've no idea.''

Her stepdaughter raised her gleaming head and, for the first time since they'd been seated, spoke. ''You should remember. You paid for his sheep ranch or station or whatever the Aussies call those places.''

''So I did. That was Kevin's price for the divorce. I keep confusing him with that other Aussie. Eddie?''

''Alfie. And he came from New Zealand. Poor Kate, so many men, such a short memory.''

Kate's teeth gleamed between her lips. ''Nothing like poor Meg. No men, and a long memory.''

Color flooded into Meg's face and Forsythe winced. It was Carolyn who rebutted. ''A cheap shot, Kate. But let's discuss Emmy and that summer. I understand both John and Harry are hoping that Robert can find a solution to our puzzle, but there's no harm in pooling our memories and seeing what we can come up with.''

''I wouldn't do that, Mother,'' Teddy said. ''Too dangerous. We could dig up things that have no bearing on the murders but might still hurt.''

Josephson was looking interested. ''I cast my vote with Carolyn. Why not try?''

''An excellent idea!'' Oglethorpe pushed his plate away. ''Now, we're all agreed that Emmy was a temptation to every male on my estate—''

''With the exception of Kevin,'' Kate said.

''And one woman.'' All heads turned toward Meg. The color had drained from her features, leaving her skin an ivory color. ''Didn't any of you tumble to the fact that Alice Constantine was a lesbian?'' she asked.

Forsythe realized he'd barely touched the food on his plate and now had completely lost his appetite. He also realized he was virtually invisible to the other diners. Some were exchanging glances, others avoiding eyes,

114

and Oglethorpe was staring at Meg. "Impossible!" he blurted.

"How well did you know Alice?" Meg demanded. "Was she a friend?"

"Not even an acquaintance," Oglethorpe admitted. "But she seemed a pleasant and respectable woman."

"I can't even recall what the woman looked like," Kate said.

"A big-boned woman," Carolyn said. "With a kind of gypsy good looks. I remember thinking she would have made a wonderful Carmen. A great deal of long black hair and bold eyes and tawny skin. Really quite striking. But I find, Meg, I must agree with Harry and think you're mistaken. Alice was a widow and she had the twin babies."

Meg smiled and the dimples flickered. "Her 'husband''s name was Marie and she was killed in a gay bar in a fight over Alice's favors. Stabbed, as a matter of fact. The babies belonged to Alice's sister who deserted them shortly after they were born."

"Meg," her stepmother said coldly. "Are you hallucinating?"

"I had an encounter with Alice, dear Kate, so I speak from first-hand experience."

"Why didn't you tell *me?*"

"What would have been the use? You were so wrapped up in your latest boy-toy, I can imagine your response. I can picture me telling you that our neighbor had been groping me and trying to pull down my bloomers. You wouldn't have heard a word. You'd have told me that was nice, be a good girl and go play, and tossed me a couple of pounds to buy something."

Kate seemed speechless and it was Carolyn who asked, "Did Alice actually make that approach?"

"No. She was more subtle than that."

115

"Then how can you be so sure? You were only a child."

"I may have been young but I wasn't stupid. But you want proof and here it is." Meg leaned forward, looking from Carolyn to Harry. "About five years after that dreadful summer I read an article in a London newspaper detailing the death of an Alice Constantine, her female companion, and two five-year-old twin girls. It mentioned the children were Alice's nieces. I did some checking and found out about Marie and the sister who deserted the children. If you don't believe me, you can check it yourselves."

Reaching across the table, Forsythe touched her hand. "Why didn't you tell me this last evening?"

"Quite frankly, I didn't consider it any of your business. I hardly think the fact that Alice was a lesbian has a bearing on the poisonings."

"And that's where you may be wrong, my girl." Oglethorpe's color was high and his eyes seemed to be bulging even more. Rather like a rock cod, the barrister thought. "When we mate that fact up with another fact we—"

"Babysitting," Teddy cried. "Alice Constantine kept hiring Emmy to babysit the twins. Said she needed to get some undisturbed sleep."

This was one time Josephson wasn't lounging back, looking drowsy. "We could be on to something. Emmy may well have appealed to the Constantine woman. Young, pretty, docile . . . Alice could have been forcing the girl into an affair."

Kate tapped her oval nails on the tabletop. "One thing I'll remind all you amateur sleuths is that Alice might have had the hots for Emmy, but she sure as hell didn't get her with child."

"This is all incredibly sordid," Carolyn said with

distaste. One hand idly twisted her necklace and Forsythe noticed how exquisite that hand was.

"Mother, I should imagine the motive for murder quite often is as disgusting as the crime itself." Turning back to Oglethorpe, Teddy said eagerly, "Let's play *what if*. What if Alice was mad about Emmy Owen and found the girl was pregnant? In a jealous rage she might have decided to kill the girl."

"Two flaws in your reasoning, my boy. As I told Robert the other day, Alice was the only person on my estate who didn't know about the red ants and the tin of arsenic in the shed."

Teddy seemed hot on the trail. "Alice had a couple of window boxes she was always fussing with. She had quite a nice showing of carnations and pansies and so on. One morning when I was passing her cottage, she hailed me and asked if I knew where she could get some fertilizer. I told her Mother got her gardening stuff from the shed behind the manor. Harry, I assume your tin of arsenic was labeled."

"Clearly." Oglethorpe nodded and Forsythe decided the older man also resembled a Buddha, the huge head majestically nodding over the obese body. The barrister also decided he was being unkind and knew why. These people had the bit in their teeth and had forgotten his existence. I'm miffed, he thought, I feel passed over and ignored. I'm also acting like a spoiled child, which is what Sandy would tell me if she were here.

"So," Josephson drawled. "We've established that Alice had a motive and she knew the location of the poison. Harry, you said there's another flaw in Teddy's theory."

Oglethorpe's eyes circled the table and brushed each face. "If Alice Constantine had decided to kill Emmy, do any of you think the woman, even wild with jealousy, would poison three other people, two of them small children? If Alice was clever enough to conceal her past from us, surely she was clever enough to plan a way of killing only Emmy Owen.''

Rather neatly reasoned, Forsythe thought, and waited for the other people to respond. Josephson was chewing his lower lip, Teddy was drumming his fingers against his water glass, and, at the end of the room, Darla was clattering dishes into the dumbwaiter.

It was Kate's rich voice that broke the silence. ''I've a thought. What if Alice forced the girl to reveal the identity of her seducer?''

''So?'' Carolyn said.

Kate's ripe mouth twisted. ''What if the villagers were right?''

''Incest!'' Teddy cried. ''Either her father or brother!''

Oglethorpe held up a pudgy hand. ''We could be on to something! This could provide the missing piece and give us the reason that Alice Constantine would poison the food for the entire family. As though she were wiping out a nest of . . .''

''Rats,'' Meg said flatly.

Reaching into a pocket, Oglethorpe extracted a flat leather case. He opened it and offered it around to the men. Teddy and Forsythe declined, but Josephson accepted a cigar and sniffed it appreciatively. ''Havana,'' Oglethorpe said. ''Not supposed to smoke now, but this calls for a celebration. Be nice to have a nip of cognac to go with it. My friends, do you realize after all these years, after the police investigation, and the famous Robert Forsythe giving it his best shot, that we've solved this case?'' He puffed out a burst of gray smoke and turned to the barrister. ''I don't like to sound pettish, Robert, but why couldn't you have used the same deductive methods that we just did? Come to the same conclusion.''

The barrister was conscious of the barrage of eyes

turning in his direction and also conscious of the wave of hot color flooding into his face. He was about to mention he'd not been in possession of one key fact when Kate Kapiche said lazily, "I suppose it might be the anesthetic they used on Robert for that knee operation."

Josephson said, "Huh?"; Teddy Chimes laughed; and Carolyn said testily, "Darling, you're making even less sense than usual."

"That's because you can't follow my thought patterns. Too complicated for your simple mind. What I'm saying is that when I had my appendectomy the anesthetic made me feel queer for days. Dopey and dizzy. Probably our Robert is madly clever but we've caught him at a bad time."

"When I was dopey and dizzy from anesthetic," Forsythe snapped. "Good as any other explanation to account for disappointing you with an instant solution." He reached for his crutches and struggled to his feet.

Oglethorpe glanced at his watch. "Leaving us so soon? It's barely seven."

"It's been a long day."

"One moment," Josephson said. "Do you think that's the correct solution?"

Forsythe glanced down at the man's haggard face and shadowed eyes. "It's a possible solution but impossible to prove or disprove. Emmy and Walter Owen are dead. So is Alice Constantine."

"Gareth Owen is very much alive," Kate said. "I vote we grill him."

Forsythe left them briskly arguing whether to grill Gareth or not. As he approached the doorway he caught a flicker of motion, but by the time he reached the corridor it stretched out long and shadowy and deserted.

8

As Forsythe passed the nurses' desk, Mrs. Elser poked her head out of the office. "Ah, Mr. Forsythe, I was hoping to catch you. Have you a moment? I'd like to show you the snaps we took this afternoon. Carolyn and Teddy and me." She simpered. "Laura borrowed one of those instant cameras from another teacher and the pictures turned out ever so nice."

Mrs. Elser had dressed for the occasion. The white organdy dress patterned with flowers that looked like purple orchids would have been suitable at a garden party and so would the purple suede sandals and jangling white bangles on both wrists. Her improbably brown hair had been tortured into a pyramid of rigid-looking curls.

She swept him into the office, pointed at the chintz-covered sofa, and turned to the desk. For a change, that piece of furniture was fairly neat. A number of schoolbooks sat on one corner of it, the blue-covered guest book and another with a brown cover was on another, and a pile of snaps and an ornate silver dagger were on the green blotter.

Sweeping up the snaps, the nurse handed them to

Forsythe. "Carolyn and Teddy were so accommodating," she gushed. "I asked Mr. Oglethorpe to handle the camera, him being an artist, you see. All those snaps are autographed on the back and Laura is going to take them to school with her just to prove her old mum really knows these people."

Forsythe looked through the pile. The Chimeses had indeed been patient. Carolyn and Teddy had been photographed in this room, in the corridor, several times in the Art Deco lounge, and in what possibly was a sitting room in a suite. In all of them Mrs. Elser was in the middle, clinging to Teddy and his mother's arms. Carolyn and her son photographed as one would expect people who almost daily face cameras to photograph. Nancy Elser, on the other hand, looked self-conscious, a touch smug, and in one shot close to imbecilic.

"What do you think?" Mrs. Elser asked.

Forsythe chose his words carefully. "Wonderful mementos." He pointed at the silver dagger. "That's a fine old dagger. Is it yours?"

"It is now." She picked it up gingerly and handed it to him. "I asked Mr. Oglethorpe if he would pose for a couple of snaps with me, but he said he loathes being photographed. Funny for a man in his position, isn't it? But he insisted I have this thing for a souvenir. Says he used it as a letter opener. It's terrible sharp and I guess what I'd better do is put it on the mantel with the snaps and that compact Ms. Kapiche gave me. What do you think?"

What the barrister was thinking was that Oglethorpe, as well as Carolyn and Teddy Chimes, was being quite generous. The dagger was obviously an antique and had a finely engraved hilt and a blade as sharp as a razor. Aloud, he said, "I should do exactly that. This is much too sharp to leave lying about." He handed it back to the nurse. "You seem to thoroughly enjoy working here, Mrs. Elser."

"Oh, I do! I most certainly do. But . . ."

"But what?"

"As my mum used to say, Nancy, there's always a fly in the ointment and isn't that the truth."

Wondering if that fly was named Kate Kapiche, the barrister struggled to his feet. "Ms. Kapiche hasn't been, er, temperamental again, has she?"

"Heavens, no. Sweet as honey, is Ms. Kapiche. And her clothes! I keep telling my daughter, Laura, you should just see the style of those clothes!"

Forsythe wasn't interested in Kate's outrageous wardrobe. He was thinking of that flicker of movement as he'd left the dinner table. "Have you seen Owen around this evening?"

She'd been staring down at one of the snaps. Without lifting her head, she said, "He came along a little while before you did and I told him to turn down the beds and get the suites ready for the night. It's Darla's turn to help the kitchen maid, so Owen may have gone down to the staff lounge on the main floor." She lifted her head. "If you need his services . . ."

Forsythe shook his head and hobbled to the door and down the corridor to his suite. He had a hunch that Gareth Owen had been standing in the shadowed doorway of the lounge while the murders of his sisters and father had been discussed.

The Flower Wing was so quiet that all he could hear was his own breathing and the muted thud of the rubber tips on his crutches. As he opened the door to his suite, he noticed that the door opposite, the one leading to the sitting room of the Iris, was ajar and a ribbon of light fell across the oaken floorboards.

He touched the switch that controlled the lights in the suite, and table lamps beamed in the sitting room and bedroom. Forsythe glanced down at the volume of Shakespeare and then shook his head. First things first. In the green-and-yellow bedroom was evidence that Owen had made his nightly rounds. The bed was turned down, pajamas and a robe were neatly draped across it, and on one pillow, as in a fine hotel, was a silver-wrapped truffle. He wondered what patients like Kate and Oglethorpe found on their pillows at night. Perhaps silver-wrapped dried fruit?

The evening regimen in the lavish bathroom went faster and more smoothly than usual, partially because he was becoming more adept at swinging around on the metal bars, partially because he seemed stronger. His shoulder muscles, which the night before had been aching, weren't bothering him and he was able to flex his bad knee without pain flashing down his calf.

He pulled on his pajamas and robe, brushed his hair, and returned to the sitting room for a well-deserved reward. Holding a glass containing a generous portion of Laphroaig, he made himself comfortable in a corner of the leather divan and reached for the phone. As his hand touched it, it shrilled and he jumped, sloshing whiskey over his robe. "I was just about to ring *you*," he told Miss Sanderson.

"Two minds with one thought. More news from the Saudi front."

She proceeded to pass on the details that Jennifer had given her and finally said, "So . . . your lass will be with you in three to four days. She'll alert me. I'll meet her at Heathrow, we'll drive down to the Damien Day, pick you up, and—"

"Wonderful! But why doesn't *Jennifer* ring me up?"

"Yesterday she tried but got a brush-off from a nurse with a voice Jennifer said sounded like chips of ice."

"That would be Miss Holly."

"That's what I thought. Blimey, but that woman's a

caution. She told Jennifer you were in the therapy room and she refused to take a message. Said she wasn't hired as a receptionist. Where the devil is Hielkje Visser?''

Forsythe smiled broadly. ''That's what I asked Miss Holly and she told me Hielkje had had a row with the receptionist, a Gerry something, and the woman quit. Hielkje promptly had a collapse and has gone to stay with some relative in London until Fran gets back. Miss Holly was prepared to contact Fran for instructions, but she didn't leave a forwarding number.''

''For that I don't blame Fran. If she had left a number, Hielkje would have driven her wild. It looks like Miss Holly is going to have to cope until Fran gets back.''

''Don't worry about Miss Holly. She's an expert at coping.''

There was a slight change in Miss Sanderson's voice. ''And how are you coping, Robby?''

''Fairly well. Time passes rather quickly here. Although at dinner tonight something weird happened.''

''Weird?''

''Make that odd. A couple of fellow patients had asked me to look into a poisoning that happened years ago and during dinner they solved the mystery themselves.''

''Sounds fascinating. Tell me more.''

Forsythe quickly gave her details and when he'd finished, she asked, ''This solution—does it hold water?''

''Hard to say. Most of the people involved are now dead.'' He laughed. ''Possibly what's wrong is my ego has been hit and I feel . . . pushed aside.''

''That suits me fine. Blimey, Robby, you're at the Damien Day to convalesce, not to race around acting like a sleuth. One thing you shouldn't be brooding about is murder. Bad for the morale.''

''Speaking of morale, Sandy, would you do an errand for me? Pick up something extravagant and daring in the lingerie line?"

"Wait until I tell Jennifer she has a rival!"

"If our Rosie wasn't a grandmother, Jennifer might have to worry. Whatever Rosie has should be bottled as an antidepressant. She's a cleaning lady and smuggled me in a bottle of beer hidden in her girdle. Brought it right past Miss Holly."

"Wow! Now that takes intestinal fortitude. I'd be delighted to select a peignoir for Rosie. Coloring?"

"Bleached blond, China blue eyes, high color."

"Size?"

Forsythe thought for a moment and then said slowly, "She reaches my shoulder and is as wide as she is tall. Better make it for a full-sized figure."

Miss Sanderson chuckled, agreed a full size it would be, and said good night. Forsythe drained the last drop of scotch in his glass, considered a second drink, decided against it, and took the glass into the bathroom to rinse. He turned off the lamps in the sitting room, but he left a bedside lamp burning and the lights in the bathroom blazing. Mrs. Elser, he thought drowsily, should be along shortly.

When she made her rounds, the nurse found Forsythe was sound asleep. For moments she stood by the bed, frowning down at him. Her hand hovered over his shoulder and then she shook her head. Leaving the lights on in the Primrose, she walked down the corridor toward the nurses' station. That corridor seemed very long and very empty.

9

The sound seemed part of his dream, part of the nightmare world he was struggling to get free of, part of the horror that was gluing his eyelids shut. He struggled to escape that world and, with an immense effort, managed to pry open his eyelids. Light from the bathroom fell in a long rectangle across the carpet; light from the bedside lamp fell across his face. Sweat was soaking his pajamas, and the duvet and sheet were twisting around his body.

He fumbled with the bedclothes and pulled them free. Sitting up, he dangled his legs over the edge of the bed and glanced at the traveling clock in its green leather case. Only ten . . . interminable hours to get through before daybreak.

Then the sound came again and this was no part of nightmare land. A scream, shrill and piercing. Without conscious thought, he responded. Luckily his right foot hit the floor first and he had time to bend his bad knee to keep from hitting with his left foot. He swore and clung to the bed with both hands. The wheelchair was across the room but the crutches were propped against the bedside table.

He started crutching toward the doorway and then turned back to the chair. This was as foolish as jumping off the bed. He was shaking and might take a fall. He reached the chair, discarded the crutches, and steered into the sitting room. Finally he was in the corridor. A couple of open doors were spilling light across the floor. Further down the hall were two figures, apparently grappling. One was John Josephson and the other was Darla.

"What's going on?" Forsythe demanded.

"Thank God!" Josephson grunted. "She's hysterical and there's blood . . ."

There was blood. Josephson was wearing a white undershirt and white silk boxer shorts ornamented with tiny red hearts. On the undershirt were several smears as bright a red as the hearts on the boxer shorts. "What should I do with her?" Josephson panted.

"Give her to me." Carolyn Chimes grasped the aide by both shoulders and shook her. "Stop it! Darla, get a grip on yourself."

Sobbing, the girl collapsed against the older woman. Forsythe could now see smears of blood on Darla's hands, down one cheek, on the Indian cotton smock. "Carolyn, where's she hurt? Darla, try to tell us."

"Not me," the girl wailed, waving one hand.

The barrister followed the direction of that hand. *"Kate!"*

He wheeled his chair toward the Iris, nearly collided with Josephson, and was in the garish sitting room. Lamps were glowing in that room and the bedroom. Nothing seemed amiss. The bed was turned down and on a desk near one of the windows was a tray with a steaming mug and a side dish containing two digestive biscuits. Josephson was right behind Forsythe's chair and he was joined by Teddy Chimes.

"Will someone explain what the hell is wrong?" Teddy asked. "Mother comes into my suite lugging Darla and rips me out of bed. Orders me to get in here and help. Help what or who?''

"We don't know any more than you," Josephson said. "The girl woke me up caterwauling and she's got blood all over—"

"Darla's hurt?" Teddy asked.

"I don't think so . . . Forsythe, what is it?''

The bathroom doorway was ajar and Forsythe was staring through the crack. He could see the curve of the tub, a plump white shoulder, a fall of damp, reddish hair. "Kate," he whispered.

Neither of the other men seemed able to move or speak. Taking a deep breath, Forsythe edged the chair into the bathroom. He took a long look at the tub's occupant and then reached out a hand to touch the base of the throat. "I think he's . . . he's dead.''

"He?" Josephson asked.

"Harry Oglethorpe.''

Death and the manner of it had stripped Oglethorpe of all dignity. Pink-tinged water drifted over his short obese body. Every bulge and unsightly fold of skin was exposed, the short legs were slightly bowed and marbled with ugly varicose veins, the left knee and the left elbow were reddened and swollen. To complete the indignity, his body shared the tub with various objects. A pink garment wound around one ankle; near that foot was a silvery glint on the tub's bottom; another object made of tortoiseshell and shaped like a huge revolver nestled on Oglethorpe's abdomen, covering his navel. There were gold initials on the handle of this and a dark cord wound from it, curled around the doorjamb, and snaked into the bedroom.

Teddy gulped and said, "I can't see any wounds.''

Forsythe pointed at the cord. "He could have been electrocuted. That looks like a hair blower.''

Josephson peered around the door, his eyes tracing

128

the cord. "It's still plugged into an outlet beside the dressing table. But what's Harry doing in Kate's bathtub?"

"He kept after me until I let him have the suite," a rich and silky voice said. "Has the damn fool gone to sleep in the tub? Meg, let go of me! Let me have a look." Kate pushed by Josephson and rammed Forsythe's chair against the side of the tub. She bent over his shoulder, made a choking sound, and then gave a shriek that was reminiscent of Darla. Forsythe could feel her weight falling limply against the back of the chair.

"She had to look, didn't she?" Meg said. "Give me a hand, John. We'd better take her into my suite. Carolyn's there, trying to calm Darla. We need help. Where are Mrs. Elser and Owen?"

Mumbling he knew nothing, Josephson helped her carry Kate out of the bathroom. Breathing a sigh of relief, Forsythe backed the chair away from the tub and its grotesque occupant, managed to turn the chair, and waved Teddy out of the way. For the first time he noticed that Teddy was wearing only a pajamas bottom. Without the glitter of gold chains, his chest look bare. Forsythe told Teddy, "We'd better find that nurse."

Teddy trailed along behind. "With this uproar you'd think the woman would be on deck. Can she be sleeping?" When Forsythe didn't reply, he trotted to catch up. "If the blood on Darla didn't come from Harry . . ."

"Exactly," Forsythe said grimly.

The nurses' desk looked the same as usual. On the desktop sat a black telephone flanked by a row of pens and a spiral notebook with a black cover. The overhead lights in the corridor were dimmed but brighter light fell from the doorway of the office. Forsythe glanced up at Teddy's ashen face. "Sorry, but you'd best come in with me."

"Wouldn't have it any other way," Teddy said with forced bravado.

Forsythe steered his chair around the corner of the desk, misjudged, hit a doorjamb, and allowed his companion to seize the handles and push it through the doorway. Teddy pulled the chair to an abrupt stop and swore softly, as though fearing to waken the figure in the desk chair.

Nancy Elser's chiffon dress was no longer bicolored. It was soaked with scarlet, a warmer, more vibrant shade than any dyer could create. Scarlet soaked the bodice, dripped into the lap, and then trickled into a puddle over the left sandal. It was as though a dam had blown and the fluids held in check had madly raced through the breech.

"Her throat," Teddy whispered and backed out of the room.

Forsythe would have liked nothing better than to have followed, but he forced himself to sit, fighting back nausea, and took a long and comprehensive look at the nurse and the office. The guest book and the other ledger still sat on a corner of the desk, but the Spanish textbooks and some notebooks were scattered over the cushions of the chintz sofa. The snapshots taken earlier that day had been pushed to one side of the green blotter.

There was little blood on the desktop, only a few drops near the woman's right hand, which lay across the blotter. Forsythe bent closer. Her index finger was coated with red at the tip and . . . Gingerly he lifted the hand. On the blotter were four printed letters. He studied them. Sprawling, formless letters making no sense. The flaccid hand he was holding still retained some warmth. She hadn't been dead for long. The killer . . .

He gently replaced the hand on the blotter, pushed the wheelchair backward out of the office and into the narrow aisle behind the counter. This time he had to jockey the chair clear by himself. He looked around for

Teddy Chimes, decided the man had bolted, and then saw him slumped in the chair near the lift. Teddy had buried his face in both hands and didn't raise his head as the barrister approached.

"Sorry," Teddy muttered. "No good at this sort of thing. Can't stand blood. Can't even stand that artificial goo they use in fight scenes in films. Turns my stomach." He shuddered. "Her throat . . . ripped from ear to ear . . ."

Forsythe decided that the other man wasn't far from hysterics. Surely he couldn't be the killer . . . but Teddy Chimes was a professional actor. "You'd better snap out of it and lend a hand. We need help."

"Little late for Harry and that poor nurse."

"But not too late for the rest of us. Unless, of course, you'd like to meet the person who slit Mrs. Elser's throat."

Forsythe's method was brutal but effective. Teddy's head jerked up. "Right! Better get onto the police. Where in hell is Owen?"

"Possibly down in the staff lounge." Or dead, or perhaps lurking behind a door with the knife that had killed the nurse. "Teddy, hand me that book beside the telephone."

The notebook contained the numbers of various areas in the building as well as the home numbers of its staff. The first call the barrister made was to the former matron's home. Miss Holly's voice was crisp and clear. "What is the problem, Mr. Forsythe?"

Forsythe outlined the problem. Miss Holly came directly to the point, giving him the number of the guardhouse. "Reilly is on duty. Have him bring another guard and come up immediately. Tell Reilly to leave the other guard on duty in the foyer to admit the police. Reilly is to take charge in the Flower Wing until I arrive. I'll be with you as soon as possible. Keep calm, Mr. Forsythe."

131

Forsythe delivered the message to the gatehouse and then rang up the police station in Hundarby. A voice as crisp and clear as Miss Holly's, but this one male, also took details, promised speedy assistance, and rang off. Forsythe leafed through the notebook, found the number of the staff lounge, debated about summoning Gareth Owen, and decided against it. Best to wait for help.

The security guard arrived first. Forsythe remembered him from his own arrival at the Damien Day. Reilly was the big, ruddy-faced chap he'd glimpsed through the window of the ambulance. He was warmly dressed in a sheepskin coat and a Russian-style fur hat. Both coat and hat were dusted with snow. His wide face was even redder from the cold and his lips were chapped. His eyes moved from the barrister to Teddy Chimes. Teddy was propped against the counter, his back turned to the lighted doorway to the office. His bare chest and shoulders were bumpy with gooseflesh and he was shaking.

"Better get a robe on, sir, you could catch your death," Reilly advised. Pushing away from the counter, Teddy wandered down the corridor, both arms tightly wrapped around his chest. "Is he all right?" the guard asked Forsythe.

"Probably in shock." The barrister jerked his head toward the office. "Pretty grisly in there."

Reilly's eyes flickered uneasily in the same direction. "Better not disturb anything till the police get here. Unless . . . any chance Mrs. Elser could . . . she is dead, is she?"

The memory of the figure propped in the desk chair brushed Forsythe's mind and he winced, feeling bile at the back of his throat. He swallowed and said huskily, "She's dead."

"You said there was also a patient—"

"Harry Oglethorpe. In the Iris Suite."

132

"Jes-sus! What's going on here? And where is Gareth Owen? Is he . . . he isn't dead too?"

"I've no idea." Tiredly, Forsythe leaned his head back. "Earlier this evening Mrs. Elser told me that Owen might have gone down to the staff lounge but—"

"We'll soon find out." Reilly grabbed the telephone. He waited, one booted foot beating impatiently against the carpet. "Owen! What the hell you doing down there? For God's sake, man, you're on duty and there's been two murders . . . that's what I said . . . Get up here on the double!" He slammed down the receiver. "That bleeding idiot! Down there sound asleep. Wait till Miss Holly hears about this. She'll rip his flipping head off."

"Hears about *what?*" a familiar voice demanded.

Never had Forsythe been so glad to see someone in his life. As Miss Holly stepped off the lift, he decided she was better than a company of commandos. He felt limp with relief and she shot a look at his pallid face. "Mr. Forsythe, I'll see to you in one moment. Now, Reilly, you were saying?"

Reilly yanked off his fur hat and stuttered, "O-O-Owens, ma'am. Just rang up the staff lounge and he says he's been having a kip. All hell's broke loose here and—"

He broke off and watched as the lift door slid back and Owen stepped out. His thick dark hair was rumpled and he was combing it with his fingers. When he saw the nurse, he stopped abruptly. Miss Holly swung around and Forsythe noticed she was wearing a heavy, navy-blue cape over the tartan skirt. There was a sifting of snow across her gray hair and the shoulders of the cape, and her voice was as icy as that snow looked. "Well, Owen, been getting some beauty sleep? I'll speak to you later about that. Right now you take Mr. Forsythe—" She swung around to the barrister. "Are the other patients out of their beds too?"

"All of them. In Meg Eleven's suite with Darla. The

133

aide found Mrs. Elser and then Harry . . . or perhaps it was the reverse. Miss Holly, the girl's in bad shape."

She turned back to the orderly. "Miss Eleven is in the Foxglove. First you take Mr. Forsythe to the Foxglove and then get brandy from the cupboard in the lounge. All the patients and Darla are to have a drink. Move!"

Owen moved as though he'd been shot from a cannon. The chair sped down the corridor and into the sitting room of the Foxglove. Owen pulled it to a stop just short of a collision with a sofa and left the room at a run. Taking a deep breath, Forsythe looked around.

Meg's suite was decorated in pale gray and plum. On the hearth a gas fire blazed. On the long sofa Kate Kapiche stretched, wrapped in a fluffy blanket, her head cradled in Teddy Chimes's lap. Teddy's shoulders and chest were draped in what looked like a woman's dressing gown. In a plum-colored armchair, Josephson, also wrapped in a blanket, not only slept but snored in short frenzied gusts. It was the only sound in the room.

"Where are Meg and Carolyn?" Forsythe asked.

Kate's rumpled head jerked up. "In the bedroom. With Darla. Where's Mrs. Elser? Why isn't she looking after us? What kind of nurse is that woman? For God's sake, all she's interested in is autographs and photo ops! Just wait until I get a chance to give Fran Hornblower a piece of my mind—"

"Shut up!" Meg stood in the bedroom doorway. She was wearing jeans, a heavy cable-stitch sweater, and moccasins. Her head turned and gaslight gleamed on the metallic-looking cap of black hair. "Thank God you're here, Robert. Kate keeps erupting like a volcano, John is sound asleep, Teddy is useless, and Carolyn has her hands full with that aide."

Forsythe managed a reassuring smile. "Miss Holly is now aboard and the situation is well in hand. Owen is bringing drinks for all of us."

134

Looking calmer and suddenly interested, Kate pushed herself up until her head rested against Teddy's shoulder. "That's the first sensible thing I've heard since Meg shook me awake." She looked past Forsythe's shoulder. "Ah, Gunga Din! Make mine a double and skip the soda."

Owen set a tray on a sidetable and poured. The man's hands were steady as rocks.

10

As Kate sipped brandy a faint tinge of color crept back into her face. She sat, braced against Teddy's shoulder, her eyes fixed covetously on the untouched glass on a table beside Josephson. Oblivious to everything around him, he slept on. Meg followed the direction of her stepmother's eyes and told the orderly, "Owen, Mr. Josephson shouldn't have alcohol. He's on heavy doses of antibiotics."

Gareth Owen shrugged heavy shoulders. "Miss Holly's orders, miss. A drink for all the patients. Take it up with her."

He gathered up the tray, ignored Kate's mutely extended glass, and strode out of the room. Kate looked down at the empty glass, her face twisted, and she tossed the glass at the hearth. It splintered, fragile crystal flying in gleaming shards in all directions. Part of the stem landed in Josephson's lap, but he didn't stir. Teddy continued to stare into space and Forsythe sat quietly, but Meg swore and Carolyn stepped into the room. "What was that noise?" she asked.

"Kate. Expressing displeasure at not wheedling another brandy out of Owen. There's one male who seems impervious to her overblown charms."

"You ungrateful brat!" Kate burst into tears.

"Here." Carolyn pressed her brandy glass into Kate's hand and dropped a crisp handkerchief into her lap. "Dry your eyes and drink that."

Kate mopped at her eyes. "Saint Carolyn. Working at her martyr's badge."

Her stepdaughter gave Forsythe a twisted grin. "Guess where I learned gratitude from."

Carolyn threw up both hands. "Will you two stop that! Meg, Kate, this isn't the time or the place, so sheathe your claws. Can't you understand that Harry's *dead?*"

Forsythe nodded. "I second the motion." He glanced up at Carolyn. "How's Darla?"

"She seems calmer since I got some brandy into her, but she's still incoherent. Odd way for a girl who works in a hospital to act. We're all shocked about Harry, but even Kate seems to be handling it better than Darla."

Forsythe glanced at Teddy, but he avoided Robert's eyes. Evidently Teddy hadn't told the others about Mrs. Elser. Should he tell them about the nurse or not? Forsythe's eyes wandered back to Carolyn. The dressing gown around Teddy's shoulders must belong to his mother. Carolyn was wearing only a peach-colored nightgown, full, long sleeved, with a wide yolk trimmed with lace. Her honey-colored hair fell loosely to her shoulders and was held back by a velvet Alice band. Oddly enough, with the wide blue eyes and straight blond hair, she did look a bit like a grown-up Alice in Wonderland, but the barrister had a hunch she was much tougher than she looked. Carolyn Chimes could handle the news of Mrs. Elser's death and probably so could Meg Eleven, but Kate . . .

At that moment the necessity of making a decision

137

was taken out of his hands. Miss Holly, followed by two men, stepped into the room. Both men were tall and had heavy builds. One was wearing a gray flannel suit, the other a suit of pin-striped navy blue. The one in the pin-striped suit had unbuttoned his shirt collar and loosened the knot in his tie.

Miss Holly wasted no time on unnecessary words. She gestured at pinstripe. "Detective-Inspector Creighton." Her hand moved to gray suit. "Detective-Sergeant Wood." In turn she called the names of the people in the room and then glanced around. "Darla McCormick?"

Forsythe made a gesture with his own hand. "In the bedroom."

As Miss Holly headed toward the bedroom, Sergeant Wood, who had been staring at John Josephson, walked over and stood over his chair. "Inspector, here's what I'd call a cool customer. Two murders and he's sleeping like a baby—"

"*Two?*" Meg said. "Harry and who—"

"Who?" Kate shrieked.

"Mrs. Nancy Elser," the inspector told her. "Didn't you know?"

"No," Forsythe said flatly. "Nice going. I was just trying to think of some way to break it gently."

Kate Kapiche threw back her head and started to howl, sounding remarkably like a timber wolf. Both her stepdaughter and Carolyn moved toward her, but Miss Holly was out of the bedroom and to the sofa first. Leaning over its back, she casually slapped Kate across the face. Kate looked at the nurse with absolute disbelief, gulped, and shut her mouth. She collapsed and buried her face in Teddy's lap. Absently, he patted the dark red hair.

"And that is quite enough," Miss Holly said. "Now, I want all of you in your suites and back in bed. I mean the patients. Miss Eleven, Mr. Chimes, you will take your

138

mothers to their suites and stay with them. Mr. Forsythe—"

"One moment," the inspector interrupted. "I'm in
charge here. I need some place for interviews and—"

"I'll ring for Owen. The orderly can show you to the
patient lounge. You may use that. There's a dining table
and chairs that will serve."

"Sounds fine." The inspector glanced around.
"We'll take these people in alphabetical order and—"

Miss Holly made a sound, not quite a word, not quite
a snort. She took two long strides and faced the policeman. "You will *not* take these people in *any* order. Not
tonight. In the morning you may question them, but I
must be present when you do. Do you understand?"

"No. And I doubt you do either, nurse. These people
happen to be murder suspects."

"First and foremost, they're *patients. My* patients.
They've been subjected to intolerable strain and stress.
Ms. Kapiche suffers from hypertension and could easily
have a stroke or heart attack. Mrs. Chimes is recovering
from pneumonia. Mr. Forsythe is convalescing from
major surgery. Now, do *you* understand?"

The inspector made a last gesture of defiance. He
pointed at Josephson. "Another patient in delicate
health, Miss Holly?"

"Yes. Mr. Josephson has Lyme disease. Fatigue is
one of the symptoms."

Sergeant Wood, who had been bending over the
sleeping man, stepped hastily back. "What kind of disease did you say, ma'am?"

"Lyme. Don't worry, it isn't contagious. It's con-
tracted from the bite of a wood tick." Miss Holly touched
Meg's arm. "Take your mother to her suite. Mr. Chimes,
I must insist you attend to your mother. Ah, Owen, there
you are. Please take Mr. Josephson to his suite and see

he's bedded down. Mr. Forsythe, I'll attend to you myself."

"Nurse," the inspector said. "We'll have to interview the aide. Darla . . ."

"McCormick. For that you must also wait until morning."

"Now see here—"

"The girl was completely unnerved. Incapable of making sense." Miss Holly patted a capacious skirt pocket. "I gave her a hypo. She'll be out for hours. However, after Owen has tucked in Mr. Josephson, you may interview him."

The inspector was glaring at his adversary. "I find you very high-handed, Miss Holly."

She gave him an icy smile. "You're a professional and so am I. Your job is to find a murderer. Mine is to keep the remainder of my patients alive. And that I intend to do." She glanced at her watch. "In precisely fifteen minutes the next shift comes on. Mrs. Frome is in charge and will answer any questions you may have. I must attend my patients."

Her instructions were obeyed. Meg extended a hand and Kate pushed aside the blanket and got to her feet. The sergeant's eyes goggled. She was wearing a nightgown the same shade of peach as Carolyn's, but that was the only resemblance. Carolyn's gown was modest, swathing her tall thin frame in flannelette. Kate's was chiffon, flowing airily around her body, casting a rosy glow over every swelling curve and delicious hollow. Quickly, Meg twitched the blanket from Teddy's lap and draped it over her stepmother. She led the other woman from the room. With the Chimeses it was the reverse. It was Carolyn who helped her son up and guided him to the door. Josephson had finally roused, but he seemed dazed and went docilely with Owen.

Inspector Creighton was now showing more interest

140

in Forsythe than he had in Kate's transparent gown. As Miss Holly turned the wheelchair, he stepped in front of it. "Your name is Forsythe?" he asked.

"Robert Forsythe," the barrister told him.

"I thought you looked familiar. We've met before. A number of years ago in Chester—"

"Tomorrow, inspector," Miss Holly told him. "Kindly step aside."

The lights in the corridor had been turned up and through the doorway of the Iris, Forsythe glimpsed a number of men moving around. Scene of the crime squad, he thought. An armchair had been moved to the right of the door of his own suite and Reilly was sitting on it. He jumped up and opened the door to the sitting room. "Do you want Marks and me to go back to the gatehouse, ma'am?"

"No. For the balance of the night I want Marks down in the foyer and I want you right here. From this point you can see all the doors of the suites. No one is to enter or leave any of them without my permission. Is that clear?"

Reilly nodded and Miss Holly wheeled the chair through the suite into the bedroom. The lights were still on in the bathroom and the bedside lamp still threw a circle of light over the rumpled bed. The nurse deftly straightened the bedclothes and plumped up the pillows. "In you go, Mr. Forsythe."

She pulled the duvet up to his throat and stepped into the bathroom. When she returned she held a glass of water in one hand, a vial of pills in the other. Josephson's words echoed in his ears. A nice lady in a white uniform . . . two pills . . . murder. Miss Holly said briskly, "I know you don't care for sleeping capsules, but you're taking these and I don't want any nonsense."

141

"I'd rather not. These things make me feel hungover the next morning."

"You have a choice. Either swallow these or I'll use a hypo."

Forsythe conceded. There was no withstanding this nurse. If her capable hand was offering belladonna, so be it. She rewarded him with a faint smile. "These pills work quickly and soon you'll drop off. I promise there'll be no ill effects in the morning." She tucked the vial back in a skirt pocket that the barrister decided was roomy enough to accommodate a dispensary. "Now, I'm about to tell you a bedtime story. My father was a giant of a man, weighing at least fifteen stone and considerably taller than you. My mother was small and dainty and fragile. In my memory my father was hospitalized three times. Twice my mother accompanied him and slept on a cot by his bed. The third time my dear mother was gone and it was my duty. I took time off from my job and stayed by his side. Father was a brigadier general and the bravest man I've ever known, but he had one fear. Hospitals turned this valiant warrior into a quivering mass of fear."

Forsythe stared up at her thinking she bore a resemblance to a brigadier general herself. Perhaps in the Cold Stream Guards. "When did you discover that Robert Forsythe is also a quivering mass of fear?"

This time her smile was not only wide but warm. "You do a good job of covering up, but the signs are there. I should imagine you're ashamed of this fear, consider it a sign of weakness. But I assure you that you're in good company. You'd be amazed at the number of otherwise courageous people who share this phobia. Right now I want you to understand that Reilly will be right outside your door." She swung around smartly and made for the sitting room. Over her shoulder, she called, "Sleep well, Mr. Forsythe."

142

"Is that an order?"

"It is."

"Then I obey," he said, and did.

To his surprise and a slight feeling of chagrin, all of her predictions came true. Not only was his sleep undisturbed but he awoke well rested and alert. He opened his eyes, saw something yellow bobbing around the window, and identified Perce drawing back the curtains. Reaching for the steaming cup on his bedside table, Forsythe took a cautious sip of tea. "Good morning. No need to wait around. I can look after myself."

This morning the orderly had lost his bounce and was a subdued man. He blinked his eyes at Forsythe and then mumbled, "Can't. Gotta stay around till you're up, sir. Miss Holly's orders. Case you slip in the shower stall or something. She says to tell you you're to use the chair today. I'd do what she says, Mr. F."

"I've every intention of obeying Miss Holly. Do you know how Darla is?"

"No idea. Mrs. Frome says they sent her home early this morning before I got here. She's got parents in Hundarby who got a cottage not far from me and the wife. Can't figure what's going on in this place. Miss Holly called for more security guards and there's one guy down in the foyer and another up here in this wing. They're carrying guns too."

"I should have thought the police would have posted their own people here."

"Heard there's an outbreak of Asian flu and they're undermanned." Perce shuffled his feet and then blurted, "What *did* happen to Mr. Oglethorpe and Nancy Elser, sir?"

"Surely Miss Holly told you?"

"All the aide and me were told when we come is that they both are dead. Miss Holly said to keep our traps shut

143

in town and not to gossip. Mr. Forsythe, how did they die?''

The barrister silently debated and then decided Perce had a right to know. ''They were both murdered.''

''But . . . why? And who did it?''

''That's what the police are trying to discover.'' Forsythe threw the bedclothes back and sat up. ''Are they interviewing yet?''

''Inspector Creighton and that sergeant are set up in the lounge. Right now Mrs. Chimes and her son are with them.''

As the barrister showered, shaved, and slipped into a fresh exercise suit, he decided that if the police were interviewing in alphabetical order, his turn would be next. In this he was mistaken. He had finished his breakfast and smoked a pipe before information in the person of Miss Holly arrived. She looked as fresh as a daisy and was wearing a full uniform. Not for the former matron were the soft, comfortable fabrics of the modern uniforms. She wore a calf-length, starched, white dress, a tall cap shaped like a bonnet, and white cotton hose.

She noticed the barrister's expression and said, ''Don't look so shocked, Mr. Forsythe. I sent home for this uniform. Regardless of Miss Hornblower's views, what is needed here now is a symbol of authority.''

''Have you been on duty all night?''

''No. After the patients were settled down, Mrs. Frome took over the wing. I stayed in Miss Eleven's suite with Darla McCormick until the police had questioned her and sent her home to her parents. I managed a few hours sleep on the couch in the sitting room. Until this matter is settled, both Mrs. Frome and I will be remaining in the building. There are sleeping rooms in the kitchen wing we can use.''

''You must be very short staffed.''

''We are. We've lost Darla and, of course, poor Mrs.

144

Elser and the aide on my shift is ill with influenza. The police are also short staffed and I had to use my own initiative and call in extra security guards—"

"Armed."

"Percival is really a deplorable gossip. Yes, Mr. Forsythe, I requested they have side arms. Desperate times call for desperate measures. And, until Miss Hornblower returns, I'm responsible for the safety of every person in this building."

"Has Fran been located yet?"

"I understand Inspector Creighton rang up Mr. Knight, so he probably does know where she is by now." Miss Holly looked toward the window. Snow was gusting against the panes. "I don't like the looks of this weather. I remember a similar storm a number of years ago and . . . Anyway, there is Miss Visser but I fear she is completely useless in a time of emergency."

If Miss Sanderson was here, Forsythe thought, she would not only agree but would also add that Hielkje Visser was completely useless at *any* time. The nurse was consulting a massive gold watch pinned to the stiff bodice of her gown. "I'm as bad as Percival! Here I am chattering away when I should be delivering a message. Inspector Creighton would like to speak with you in one hour. For some reason he's leaving you until last. He did mention last evening he had met you in Chester."

The last remark wasn't phrased as a question, but Miss Holly paused as though expecting an answer and Forsythe obliged. "Yes, the inspector did say that, but I don't recall meeting him before. A few years ago I was involved in a case near Chester, but the local inspector's name was Fitzgerald and he was a man in his fifties."

"Possibly our inspector was one of this man's subordinates." She moved toward the door and swung around in a rustle of starched material. "The inspector and his sergeant are in the lounge. You may make your own way there and you must use your wheelchair."

"I thought you were sitting in on the interviews."

"With the other patients I did. But I feel that you are quite able to handle yourself. After all, one could say it's your natural habitat, couldn't one?"

My natural habitat, the barrister told her silently, is in a courtroom at the old Bailey, but he couldn't deny the fact he was well acquainted with policemen and police procedures. The nurse stepped into the corridor but neglected to close the door and he could hear raised voices that indicated an argument was going on. Finally Miss Holly poked her head around the door. "It would appear you have a visitor, Mr. Forsythe. Go right in and remember, fifteen minutes and not a second longer."

His visitor proved to be Rosie. Forsythe blinked. It was the first time he'd seen Rosie divested of her smock. She was wearing a lavender-colored cardigan buttoned to the throat and a pleated fawn skirt that swung coquettishly around her dimpled knees. In one fat hand she clutched what looked like a man's handkerchief and her China blue eyes were puffy and reddened. He pointed at the leather divan. "Do be seated, Rosie. I hardly expected to see you this morning."

"We didn't know, Lila or me, about what happened here last night and drove up in our minivan as usual. One of those guards passed us through the gate, but when we got to the house that new chap in the foyer said we couldn't come in and wouldn't say why. I didn't back down a bit, no siree. Told him we had to hear from someone who counts and he rang up Mrs. Frome and she told him to let me come up. Lila's still down in the foyer." Rosie sniffed and swabbed at her nose. "Couldn't take it in when Mrs. Frome told me. I *had* to see *you* so I ran down the corridor and that guard wouldn't let me in and then Miss Holly come out and—"

146

"Slow down, Rosie." He leaned over and patted her hand.

"Thought you were dead too, Mr. F." She gulped. "It is true, innit? Nancy Elser's *dead*, is she?"

"I'm sorry, but, yes, she is. Was she a friend of yours?"

"That she was. Nancy come to live with her daughter about six months ago. Laura has the cottage right next to me and my old man. Reason Nancy's dead is because of me. I . . . I killed her!"

Rosie broke into a storm of weeping and the barrister rolled his chair closer and touched her heaving shoulder. The handkerchief she was plying seemed to be reaching the saturation point and he offered her a fresh one. The combination of silent sympathy and fresh linen seemed to be working. Her sobs trailed off and finally she was mopping at her face and blowing her nose. "Making a right idiot of meself, ain't I? But I feel so terrible guilty."

"Rosie, you had nothing to do with Mrs. Elser's death."

"If it hadn't been for me and my big mouth, Nancy wouldn't have been working in this place. When I heard Miss Hornblower was looking for some good nurses to work here this month, I went right over to Laura Elser's and told Nancy. Told her what a nice place this was and how all the people who come here are nobs and I talked her into seeing Miss Hornblower and she got the job and if I'd left Nancy alone she'd still be alive and—"

"Stop that right now!" He squeezed her arm and said sternly, "You are *not* responsible for what happened here last night. Pull yourself together and try and help me. We must find the person who killed your friend and Harry Oglethorpe. Tell me, can you think of any connection between the two of them?"

She shook her head and the flaxen hair bounced around her face. "I'd swear Nancy never even knew about Mr. Oglethorpe till she come here. She was thrilled about all these rich people and raved on about Mrs. Chimes and Ms. Kapiche and the rest till me old man and me got kind of tired of listening.''

"Tell me about Nancy and her daughter.''

Rosie settled back against leather and drew a long, quivering breath. "Laura Elser's a teacher at the girl's school in Hundarby. Teaches history. Moved into the cottage next door about six . . . no, make that seven years ago. Awful nice woman, Laura is. Her mum came to see her a couple of times each year, but Nancy was still working and it wasn't until last summer that she retired and came to stay permanent. Laura told me all the time her mum was raising her—her dad died when she was a baby—they moved all over the country. Laura laughed and said she had a patchwork-quilt education, a year in one town, a couple of years in another. Said her mum waited until Laura was raised and out on her own before Nancy settled down for any length of time. Seems before Nancy retired she worked in some hospital in Yorkshire for ten years. Nancy and Laura and me got along famous and was always having a cuppa together. Laura thought the world of her mum, don't know how she'll get along alone. Nancy was all the family the poor lass has.''

Tears flooded into the swollen eyes and trickled down the plump cheeks. Forsythe told her, "Rosie, best you get along home now.''

"Better see what I can do for Laura.'' She pushed her bulk up. "And Lila's down there, waiting and wondering. Miss Holly says as soon as the police say it's all right, we can come back to work. In the meantime the aides and orderlies have to do what they can. Couldn't even get into the supply room where we keep our stuff. Police got it locked up and tape across the door. Why's that, Mr. F?''

He shook his head, but he had a sudden vision of a

pink mass of cotton cloth floating in Harry Oglethorpe's bath. Rosie squeezed his hand, gave him a tremulous smile, enjoined him not to get killed in his bed, and took her leave.

11

etective-Inspector Creighton was obviously disappointed when Forsythe couldn't recall their previous meeting. He prodded the barrister's memory. "You'd asked Inspector Fitzgerald for photocopies of some newspaper clippings and came into the Chester station to pick them up. I got them together and handed them over to you." He looked hopefully at the barrister, but Forsythe shook his head. "Of course, that was a number of years ago and I was a sergeant. I've put on weight and have grown this." Creighton ran a finger fondly over a bold, bandito-style mustache.

"I must have been more interested in the clippings than anything else. I can't recall you. How is Fitzgerald? I do remember going to lunch with him. He kept talking about the diet he was on and eating everything in sight."

"That's the lad." Creighton grinned. "Last time I saw him he was acting much the same. Battling weight and nibbling diet food his wife gave him at home and sneaking out to pubs to gulp beer and nosh pork pie. Good officer, he's a superintendent now. Still raving on about how you solved the Dancer case. Claims you have

150

a mind like a steel trap. Said you broke the case by noticing a couple of tiny items no one else did. Couldn't believe my luck when I saw you here last evening and realized you were right on the spot when those people were murdered."

Forsythe glanced around the Art Deco lounge. The weather was still wretched and snow puffed steadily against the long windows behind the inspector's chair. The policemen had spread folders, notebooks, a portable typewriter, and a couple of small cassette machines higgledy-piggledy the length of the oval dining table. Sergeant Wood was in shirtsleeves and was studying a file folder at one end of the table. Forsythe had rolled his chair between two dining chairs and was facing the inspector. Both men were younger than he, appearing to be in their late twenties; both badly needed a shave; and both were haggard. But the inspector not only looked exhausted, he looked flushed and ill.

Creighton had paused, as though inviting comment, and when the barrister didn't speak, he continued, "Wood and I were shocked when Miss Holly let us talk with you alone. With the other patients she hung over us as though figuring we were going to whip out rubber hoses. Wood is scared green of her."

"Look who's talking! She's got you on the run too." Wood laughed and put aside the folder.

The inspector rubbed a hand over his chin and the stubble made a rasping sound. "Miss Holly's a terror but in some ways she's quite a woman. She said the chef would send lunch up for us and suggested you have yours with us. Is that all right, Mr. Forsythe?"

"Fine. Yes, I agree with you about our Miss Holly. Last evening when she arrived I felt as though the Marines had landed and everything was well in hand."

"Wish we had a few officers like her. The crime rate

in the Hundarby area would plummet. Oh, Wood, how about checking on lunch?"

The other policeman reached for the phone and shortly afterward he was lifting trays from the dumbwaiter. While they ate, conversation languished. Forsythe made a mental note that if Sergeant Wood ate this much habitually, he, like Fitzgerald, would be fighting the battle of the bulge. Creighton only picked at his food and by the time coffee was handed around, he was back to business. "I'm going to make a direct appeal, sir. Half my staff are off with that ruddy flu and I simply can't come up with more manpower. If Miss Holly hadn't arranged to have security guards look after this wing, I don't know what we'd do."

Forsythe had been eyeing the younger man warily. "Perhaps you should consider appealing to the Yard."

"My suggestion when I rang up the chief constable last night," Creighton said sourly. "Told him with this class of people and us so shorthanded, it was the only logical solution. He turned me down flat. He's a stubborn old goat—this is strictly *entre nous,* Mr. Forsythe—and can't be budged. Hate to ask this when you're in here as a patient, but could you see your way clear to giving Wood and me a hand?"

The barrister braced his elbows on the arms of the chair, templed his fingers, and regarded them. "I understand your situation and I sympathize, but I must be blunt. It's entirely different from being called in on a case and viewing it objectively and from being completely involved in it. There are a number of reasons that will prevent me from being of much assistance."

"Care to tell us what you're thinking?"

Forsythe touched his bad knee. "It's my own fault for delaying having an operation for so long, but this wasn't a simple patch job. It was a long, complicated

152

operation and I've been told convalescence will be just as tiresome. As a result I'm certainly not at my best."

"You said a number of reasons."

One of the reasons Forsythe had no intention of mentioning. Miss Holly had been on target and he was ashamed of his morbid fear of hospitals. He wasn't about to admit that his thinking processes were dulled through sheer senseless terror. But he could tell the truth about another reason. "Arrangements have been made to have the rest of my convalescing done in my home in Sussex. My secretary and fiancée will be picking me up in a few days and I have no desire to stay on here. My fiancée and I haven't seen each other since last August."

Creighton and his sergeant exchanged glances. Then the inspector shrugged. "Well, it certainly was worth a try. But surely you can listen to what we have thus far and perhaps make some comments."

The barrister glanced at his watch. "I'm due for a therapy session in about half an hour. I missed one this morning."

"No therapy today, sir," Wood told him. "Miss Holly nearly did her nut but this was one the inspector won."

"We hope to have the routine back to something near normal by tomorrow," the inspector elaborated. "So, what do you say to listening while we give you a rundown?"

One of my weaknesses, Forsythe thought, is an avid curiosity; it isn't so much that I love a mystery; I must hate them because I work so hard to unravel clues. He settled back in his chair, and dug out his pipe and tobacco pouch. Creighton correctly interpreted this as a silent assent and threw a triumphant look at the sergeant.

Wood shuffled the file folders into a pile and folded his big hands across them. Forsythe noted that the sergeant was quite an ordinary-looking chap, the type one

153

could meet, talk with, and later not recall the appearance of. Yet he had sharply intelligent eyes and a strong chin. Another thing Forsythe noticed was that the policemen worked like part of a well-oiled team. Creighton settled back in his chair and Wood took over. "If you'd like to read through these interviews, Mr. Forsythe, you certainly may. But it might go faster if I just give you an outline."

He waited, received the barrister's nod, and continued, "I'll begin at dinnertime last evening—"

"One moment," Forsythe said. "I've a couple of questions before you begin. How did Harry Oglethorpe die?"

"Mr. Chimes and Mr. Josephson said you'd made a guess that he'd been electrocuted. You were right. Ms. Kapiche says she left her hair dryer, a custom-made job, in its usual place—plugged in to an outlet above the dressing table. Apparently the murderer simply flipped the switch and beaned it around the door into the tub, and Mr. Oglethorpe died, probably instantly."

"But wouldn't that have knocked the lights out?"

Wood looked around the elegant room. "This is quite a place, sir. Even the wiring must have cost a mint. A circuit did go out in the Iris Suite but it controlled only a small number of outlets—the dressing table lamps, the ones on either side of the bed, a couple over the mantel in the sitting room of the suite. Not enough to really count. I take it you didn't notice those were off?"

Forsythe shook his head. "I didn't. The whole place seemed well lit. Now, my next question—have any of the other patients mentioned the deaths of the Owen family?"

"Several of them. Ms. Kapiche seems obsessed about it. She tells us the police can do nothing, that the murders last night were done by an evil spirit or ghost connected with those earlier deaths. The inspector tried to tell her he'd never heard of a ghost ripping someone's throat open, but she had an answer to that too. Said the evil spirit's inhabiting someone's body. Bunch of rot, but I don't mind telling you she had me looking over my shoulder for a time. What do you think, sir? Think there could be a connection with those murders done seventeen years ago?''

"If only Harry had died . . . yes, I'd consider the possibility. But carry on, sergeant.''

"Right. According to the testimony, you left the dining table about seven. Correct?'' Forsythe nodded again and held a kitchen match to the bowl of his pipe. He was rewarded with a mouthful of smoke and coughed. Wood had flipped open a folder and was running a stubby finger down a page. "The others stayed at the table for roughly an hour. Seems they were excited over the solution they'd come up with about the Owen murders and discussed it from all angles. I gather they felt they'd put something over on you, sir. By the by, do you think they really solved those murders?''

"Is this really germane now, sergeant?''

It was Creighton who said quickly, "Certainly not. Stick to the facts, Wood.''

The sergeant didn't seem even slightly abashed. He'd dug out a crumpled pack of cigarettes and was lighting one. "The next people who left the lounge were Ms. Kapiche and Mr. Oglethorpe. She says they parted in front of her suite.'' He dug through a pile of loose papers, found what he wanted, and handed the sheet to the barrister. "Care to look this over, sir? Sketch I made of this wing. Here's where we are—the patients' lounge. Here's the corridor leading to the nurses' station and the lift. I've put in the corridor that runs at right angles to this one. From the nurses' desk there's a clear view of all the doors to the suites. Okay so far?''

"Absolutely. But I've seldom seen a nurse at that

desk. Generally they're in the office behind it. Mrs. Elser, in the evenings, spent nearly all her time in there. She was taking a course in Spanish and did her homework there."

Creighton coughed and cleared his throat, but his voice was still husky. "Strange way for a nurse in charge to act. Sounds pretty negligent."

Forsythe had finished with his pipe and was cleaning the dottle out in an ashtray. He gave it one last thump and set it aside. "This place really isn't much like a hospital. All the patients are mobile and don't need constant nursing. The orderlies and aides do most of the work and the nurse simply fills out charts and dispenses medication. Miss Holly is very much on the job, but Mrs. Elser was quite casual. I received the impression she wasn't overly fond of work. Now, let's have a look at this." Picking up the sketch, he studied it. "Eight suites and the supply room. The suite on the left-hand side of the corridor, the one closest to the nurses' station, unoccupied—"

"*Was* unoccupied," the sergeant said. "Now Miss Holly and Mrs. Frome are using it as the nurses' office. We locked and sealed their office as well as the Iris Suite and the supply room. Didn't bother Miss Holly, but Ms. Kapiche is hopping mad. Seems all she took out of the Iris when she handed it over to Mr. Oglethorpe was her night clothes and sponge bag and cosmetic case. She wants to get her clothes out of the sealed suite, but we can't let her do it. Last I heard Mrs. Chimes was offering to lend her some duds but Ms. Kapiche was still breathing fire."

Forsythe grinned and bent his head over the sketch again. "So . . . we have the Jasmine Suite, previously unoccupied, then my suite, the Primrose. Harry Oglethorpe was next to me in the Orchid. Then, at the end of the corridor, Meg in the Foxglove. Right-hand side of the

156

corridor—Teddy Chimes opposite Meg in the Lilac. Then John Josephson in the Pansy—"

"My God!" Creighton blurted. "Those names! Sounds like a meeting of a village horticultural society."

Forsythe finished the list. "Kate was in the Iris and Carolyn in the Lily. And that's the only flower name that seemed to fit. Carolyn Chimes strikes me as being much like those lovely white-and-gold lilies. Yes, sergeant, this sketch is accurate. Even the dimensions seem accurate. You'd have made an excellent draftsman."

Wood looked pleased. "That's what my teachers kept telling me, sir."

"Should have listened to them," Creighton said. "Probably be a better life than a policeman has. Easier on your family too." He sighed and pulled himself to his feet. "I'm going to rustle up coffee or preferably a pot of tea. Think I'll drop into the Jasmine and see if Miss Holly will give me a couple of aspirin. Continue, sergeant."

The sergeant watched as his superior officer made a beeline for the door. "He looks awful, doesn't he?"

Forsythe nodded. "I've a hunch he's running a temperature."

"I agree. Miss Holly will probably stick a thermometer in his mouth and order him to bed. He's coming down with that dratted flu and that'll leave me and a few constables to hold the fort in Hundarby."

"In that event your chief constable will have to listen to reason and call in the Yard."

"Too late for that. I take it you haven't been paying attention to the news. Even if the chief did agree, there's no chance of the boys from London getting to us now." He waved a hand at the snow-shrouded windows. "Worst storm we've had in years. Not just in this country either, all over the Continent, too."

The barrister was aware of a sinking feeling in the pit of his stomach. "You mean . . ."

157

"I mean power and phone lines are down and roads are impassable all over the country. Thus far we've been pretty lucky around here and the phones and power are still working, but the roads are getting bad and we haven't the machines to clear them."

"Just why didn't Inspector Creighton mention this when I was telling him about my secretary and fiancée driving me to Sussex?"

"Wondered about that myself. Guess he figured you'd think he was exaggerating, putting on pressure to get you to help with this case. Or maybe he didn't want to upset you."

The barrister was fighting a feeling of wild panic. "Then to all intents and purposes we're marooned here."

"Not quite that bad, sir. Still can get back and forth from Hundarby." The sergeant shot a dubious look at the window. "Way that snow's coming down could change that too."

Get your mind off this, Forsythe thought, or you'll be gibbering like an idiot. Reaching for his pipe, he started stuffing dark tobacco into the carved bowl. "You were telling me about the events of last evening."

"Right you are. Shortly after eight last night everyone was in his or her quarters. All of them said they hadn't seen Mrs. Elser as they passed the nurses' station but she made her rounds later. We understand she generally made her rounds around nine or after. Last evening she was early and Mr. Josephson said she entered his suite about a quarter to nine. She worked up the corridor and the last suite she visited was Mrs. Chimes's. Mrs. Chimes told us that the nurse seemed a bit different than she usually was. Seems Mrs. Elser was always questioning Mrs. Chimes about her life and her work in television but last evening"—Sergeant Wood bent his head over a file folder—"Mrs. Chimes's exact words are, 'I was quite surprised when Mrs. Elser didn't strike up a conversation

158

about my professional life. She seemed abstracted and finally I asked if there was something amiss. Mrs. Elser said she'd hoped to speak with Mr. Forsythe, but when she got to his suite, he was asleep and she hadn't wanted to waken him. I asked if I could help and she said no, she'd leave it until the next day. I must admit I was curious and asked questions, but all Mrs. Elser would say was that Owen had stopped in her office after preparing the rooms for the night and he was threatening to quit—' ''

"Owens? Quit?''

Wood bobbed his head and shuffled folders until he found the one he wanted. He flipped it open. ''In his interview Gareth Owen told us he would never have taken this job had he known that many of the people from his past were going to be patients here. He said he did his best to cope, but he overheard a conversation in the lounge last night that slandered his family. Seems he brooded for a time and then he went to the nurses' office and told Mrs. Elser he'd have to quit. She asked his reason and he told her. She said he must speak to Miss Holly, as she was the nurse in charge. I suppose you know what Gareth Owen overheard.''

Yes, Forsythe thought, and I can see why the man was furious. Nothing like having a group of people decide your sister was killed by a lesbian lover because that sister was carrying a child conceived by either your father or yourself. "Sergeant, I can understand Owen's outrage. After he left Mrs. Elser, what were his movements?''

''He said he spoke to the nurse around eight. Then he went down to the staff lounge on the main floor to cool off. He watched television for a time and then he dozed off. He was there when Reilly rang down and told him about the murders.''

"Any one to back that up? Say Darla McCormick?''

Wood shook his head. ''They're running a skeleton

staff this month and either the orderly or aide on that shift has to help out in the kitchen. Seems the chef and his assistant go home as soon as dinner has been cooked. They leave one kitchen maid to finish up. Owen and Miss McCormick took turns helping the kitchen maid clear away and last night it was the aide's turn. Miss McCormick told us they had the work done around nine and the kitchen maid and she sat having tea and chatting until nearly ten. Then Miss McCormick realized the time and hopped up to make up the nightly tray for Ms. Kapiche—''

''Kate? She's on a strict diet.''

The policeman smiled broadly. ''Doubt this grub would put on weight. All Ms. Kapiche was allowed was a cup of hot Ovaltine made with skim milk and two digestive biscuits. Apparently Ms. Kapiche insisted on having it each night and most often never touched it. Anyway, Miss McCormick said good night to the kitchen maid who was going home, took the lift up to this wing, and went directly to the Iris Suite. She tapped on the door, opened it, and went in. There was no sign of Ms. Kapiche in either the sitting room or bedroom so the aide put the tray down on a desk in the bedroom and was about to leave when she noticed the bathroom door was ajar and the light was on.''

''I can guess what Darla did then,'' Forsythe said. ''She glanced around the door and assumed the person in the tub was Kate.''

''Exactly. All she could see from that angle was a shoulder and some wet reddish hair. She said she didn't know what to do, whether to go into the bathroom or not. Seems Ms. Kapiche can be a bit testy at times. But then Miss McCormick decided maybe Ms. Kapiche had dozed off in the tub and she stepped into the bathroom.''

''And panicked?''

''Not at that point. Says she was quite cool and

160

checked for signs of life. When she couldn't find any, she left the suite to summon the nurse on duty. When she got to the nurses' office she . . . well, it seems no lights were on. She could make out a figure sitting at the desk—"

"With the lights off . . . how?"

"From the reflected glow of the corridor lights. She called Mrs. Elser's name, but there was no response. Miss McCormick decided the nurse was sleeping, got angry about that, and put out her hands to shake the woman awake."

Forsythe winced. "Which accounts for the amount of blood the aide had on her."

Wood was lighting another cigarette. "I can see why the girl went completely to pieces. She must have stuck her hand in that wound in the murdered woman's throat."

The thought of that wound, gaping like an obscene second mouth, brushed across the barrister's mind. "When Teddy Chimes and I got to that room, all the lights were on there."

"The aide snapped the switch on. She couldn't figure what she had all over her hands and . . . Good Lord, what a hell of an experience for a kid of seventeen! That's when she ran down the corridor screaming." Wood flipped pages. "Mr. Josephson heard her and went to her aid. Then you arrived on the scene, and Mrs. Chimes was the next one. Miss Eleven said she was sleeping soundly and Mrs. Chimes woke her to help with the aide."

"What about Kate Kapiche?"

The policeman grinned. "Seems at night she wears those eye shields and ear plugs to help her sleep. Claims she knew nothing about the disturbance until her stepdaughter shook her awake."

"About the change of suites. Did anyone know about—oh, here's Inspector Creighton and he has refreshments."

161

"Courtesy of Miss Holly." Creighton slid the tray down the table to his sergeant. "You be mother and pour. This tea tray cost me, so enjoy. Miss Holly offered it as a bribe if I'd let her take my vital signs and temperature—what are you two laughing about?"

Wood handed around steaming cups and offered a plate of biscuits. "Told Mr. Forsythe Miss Holly would be taking your temp when you asked for aspirin. Do you remember last year when I was in hospital after that villain bent a chunk of lead pipe over my noggin? Miss Holly reminds me of the matron. Her name was Baker and she was about half this nurse's size, but what a Tartar! When Miss Baker said jump, every man on the ward asked how high."

Creighton took a sip of tea and shook his head at the offer of biscuits. "Better not. I just upchucked for the third time today. And here's some news, Wood, that will wipe that grin off your face. Seems I've got the bloody flu and my temp's hitting the stratosphere. Miss Holly ordered me home and I guess you'll have to drive me. On top of everything else, I'm dizzy as a bat."

The news did wipe the smile off his sergeant's face. Glumly, Wood asked, "What in the devil are we going to do, inspector?"

"Exactly what I asked Miss Holly. She told me if I killed myself, I'd be away from work permanently and pointed out this flu has resulted in a number of deaths. In turn I pointed out there was a murderer in this building, but Miss Holly said that couldn't be helped and I was to get home, take lots of aspirin, and go to bed." Creighton rubbed his brow. "Mr. Forsythe, I suppose Wood has told you about the weather conditions. We can't even call for help from another area. Has Wood filled you in on what we've learned thus far?"

"He's given me some details. If you feel up to it, I've some questions."

"Fire away."

"Tell me about the change of suites."

The inspector made a visible effort to concentrate. "Seems Mr. Oglethorpe wanted the suite Ms. Kapiche had. For the light, she said. He kept after her and she kept refusing until last evening. After Mrs. Elser made her rounds, Mr. Oglethorpe dropped into Ms. Kapiche's suite and asked her again if she'd switch suites with him. Wood, what was the time?"

"Ms. Kapiche said he came into her suite a few minutes after nine, sir."

"Apparently Ms. Kapiche had been trying to persuade the artist to paint her portrait and he offered her a bribe. Promised he'd paint her if she let him have the Iris. So she agreed. He wanted to ring for the orderly and the aide and have all their possessions moved, but she said she was too tired. So they took their nightclothes; by the by, Ms. Kapiche already was wearing that see-through nightie, and he took some shaving gear and she took a sponge bag and a cosmetic case and each moved into the other one's suite."

"Sounds like the way Kate and Harry would operate. Not even bother telling the staff about the move. As dodos—"

"Dodos?" Creighton asked.

As Forsythe explained the term, he was wondering how he'd ever forgotten this man. Creighton was as memorable as his sergeant was forgettable. His hair was receding, but his eyebrows and bold mustache were dark and luxuriant. His nose looked as though it had once been broken and set badly and was slightly lopsided. Far from an ordinary chap, the barrister thought. "Anyway, inspector, both Harry and Kate seemed to feel they could do much as they wished. Rather arrogant people. Did they tell anyone else about the change of suites?"

"Not a soul. And Ms. Kapiche said when they went

across the corridor to their new quarters, she saw no one. The other patients told us they knew nothing about it until after the murders." Creighton passed his cup to the sergeant, who tipped the pot over it. "Anything else?"

"So . . . if no one else knew about the switch, the murderer could have been trying to murder Kate and not Harry."

"It's possible. It's also possible the murderer knew about the switch and entered the bathroom knowing quite well who was to be electrocuted. You could argue it either way."

"I take your point," Forsythe said. "Have you been able to tell whether Harry died first or if Mrs. Elser did?"

Creighton started to answer and then broke into a storm of coughing. As he reached for the handkerchief in his coat pocket, his elbow caught his teacup and sent it careening across the table. Wood deftly caught the cup and righted it. A trail of tea dribbled across the polished surface and the sergeant grabbed a linen napkin from the tray and mopped it up. He shot an anxious look at his inspector. Creighton had pressed the handkerchief to his mouth and he was sagging back in the chair. He said thickly, "Carry on, Wood."

The sergeant's eyes moved to Forsythe. "That's indefinite too, sir. Our medical officer says they died so close together it's impossible to tell. The killer must have polished off one of them and, almost immediately, killed the other." He held up a large hand. "I know what you're going to ask. About those items in the tub with Mr. Oglethorpe's body."

"Which were?"

"One pink smock, large size, used by a cleaning woman and stored in the supply room. Thin plastic gloves, ditto. One antique silver dagger formerly owned by Mr. Oglethorpe but given to Mrs. Elser as a keepsake. And the murder weapon—the hair blower belonging to

Ms. Kapiche. The smock and gloves had been used to protect the murderer's clothes from Mrs. Elser's blood and the bath water was tinged with a pale pink from those blood-soaked objects.

"So, Mr. Forsythe, we have two possibilities. One—the killer donned the smock and gloves, went to the nurses' office, cut Mrs. Elser's throat, and then walked to the Iris Suite, tossed the hair blower in the tub, electrocuted Mr. Oglethorpe, peeled off the blood-soaked smock and gloves and threw them into the tub."

"As well as the silver dagger."

"That too." Wood's wide mouth twisted. "Kind of used the tub as a wastepaper basket. Number two possibility—it could have happened in reverse, with Oglethorpe killed first."

The barrister stared across the table at Wood. "I can hardly credit the murderer electrocuting Harry, donning the smock and gloves, and virtually butchering the nurse. That would have meant the killer would have had to return to the Iris to get rid of the knife and smock and gloves."

"It does sound insane," Wood admitted. "But that may be exactly what we're dealing with here."

Wood, his worried eyes fixed on the inspector, moved restlessly and Forsythe said, "The blotter on the desk in the nurses' office . . . it looked as though Mrs. Elser had tried to write something with her own blood."

Creighton straightened his sagging shoulders. "Weird! Four letters. Could you make them out, Mr. Forsythe?"

"I only had a quick look but I thought they might be o-n-c-e."

"The lab boys took the blotter with them, but that's what Wood and I figured they were." He leaned forward. "Here we had a woman more dead than alive who makes an unbelievable effort to leave a message and she prints

165

four letters that sound as though she's starting to write a fairy tale."

"Inspector," Wood said. "I think I'd better get you home before you pass out and Miss Holly has another patient on her hands."

"I hate to admit it, but you're right. If I'm going to be laid up, I'd prefer to be at home."

Wood had pulled on his gray flannel jacket and now he stuck his arms in the sleeves of a topcoat. He helped his inspector don a heavy tweed coat and wound a muffler around his neck so tightly that Creighton sputtered, "For God's sake, man, you're strangling me! Anyone ever tell you that you make a bloody rough nanny?"

As they left the lounge, Creighton was leaning heavily on the other man's arm. Wood called back, "See you in a little while, Mr. Forsythe."

The barrister muttered, "I devotedly hope so, sergeant."

12

lthough it was only a few minutes after four, the lounge was already darkening. Forsythe wheeled around the table and pulled his chair in beside one of the long windows overlooking the driveway.

A late-model sedan, with Wood at the wheel and the huddled form of Creighton at his side, pulled away from the manor. An effort to clear the driveway had been made but abandoned after a few yards. When the sedan reached the unshoveled area, it slewed sideways and Forsythe held his breath. Wood managed to right the car and it plowed slowly along through the gateway. As Wood tried to turn onto the road leading to Hundarby, the car skidded again and drove deep into a snowbank. A security guard, wearing a greatcoat over his uniform and a tartan cap with earflaps, came out of the guardhouse and leaned his weight on the rear bumper. After a number of false starts, the car lurched clear and made the turn successfully. Forsythe found he'd been holding his breath and expelled it.

He wondered if they'd make it into Hundarby safely. He also wished that, sick or not, Creighton had stayed on in the Damien Day. Was there anyone in this place to be trusted? Even the nurses or Perce the orderly could have lingered in this huge building and killed both Harry and Mrs. Elser. He caught himself up sharply. This was sheer paranoia.

Wheeling his chair around, he piloted it into the corridor. As he drew level with the nurses' station, he noticed tape stretched across the office door. He shivered and turned down the corridor leading to the suites. The door of the first suite, the Jasmine, was open and as he wheeled past it, he heard Miss Holly's stentorian voice bellowing his name. "I hear and obey," he muttered and turned the chair into the sitting room.

Miss Holly, in white-starched glory, was seated at a refectory table. Beside her stood another nurse. This woman was about half the former matron's age, dressed in a pant suit of silky white synthetic, and with short, sandy hair and sharp features.

"Mrs. Frome." Miss Holly waved a hand at her colleague. "Robert Forsythe. You haven't met before as Mrs. Frome had the late shift and didn't come on until all of you were asleep."

Mrs. Frome nodded and asked how he was. Her voice was low and husky and pleasant, but her expression was much like Miss Holly's. Forsythe had a feeling that in time Mrs. Frome might be a matron herself.

Miss Holly's sharp eyes brushed across the barrister's face. "I presume you know that Inspector Creighton is being taken home by his sergeant?" She waited for Forsythe's nod and then said, "In view of the weather conditions I've taken certain precautions for the patients' welfare. Another security guard, Amos Tiptree, is now on duty in this corridor. Dinner will be served in the suites and this evening you may read or watch television, but you must not socialize. If you wish to speak with any of the other patients, you may do so now. Tiptree will

168

keep track of who goes into which suite. Is that clear, Mr. Forsythe?''

He nodded again. It was crystal clear. If another dead body was found, Miss Holly was making quite certain she'd know who last had been with that person. A reasonable precaution, he thought, and one that did give a measure of security.

Miss Holly signaled that the interview was finished by bending her neatly capped head over a file. Taking the hint, the barrister turned his chair and propelled it from the room. The chair that Reilly had used the evening before was occupied by another uniformed guard. As the wheelchair approached, the guard sprang to his feet. "Mr. Forsythe?"

"Yes, and you must be Mr. Tiptree."

Amos Tiptree was young, looking as though he should still be in school. He was a gangling chap with an undershot chin and a trace of acne on his cheeks. The leather holster attached to his belt seemed to pull that side of his thin body down. The holster flap was unfastened and the boy had a nervous habit of drumming his fingers on the revolver handle as though to assure himself the weapon was still there. The barrister wondered briefly if arming this lad was a good idea.

Tiptree was consulting a clipboard. "You're in this suite?" He jerked his head. "The Primrose?"

The boy was making a notation on his clipboard when Forsythe heard his name called. John Josephson had stepped into the corridor. "Could I speak with you for a moment, Robert?" The guard had swung toward Josephson, his hand grasping the holster of his weapon. "Take it easy, son," Josephson said quickly. "I don't plan to throttle Robert and stick his body in my wardrobe. Anyway, we'll be well chaperoned. As you noted down, Mrs. Chimes and her son are already in my suite."

Carolyn, seated on the white velvet love seat, was

gazing down at the hearth. Wordlessly, she pointed a thin finger. Shards of porcelain were scattered over the hearth rug and the polished floorboards. She bent, picked up a scrap, and handed it to the barrister. It was a delicately painted head, the golden hair garlanded with minuscule flowers. "The Dresden shepherdess," he muttered. "The one you said looked like Emmy Owen, John."

"Yes." Josephson stooped and picked up another shard. This piece looked like part of a skirt. "This is the way I found it; someone picked it up and beaned it against the hearth. Nasty! It was a lovely thing."

"And valuable," Carolyn agreed. "When was it done?"

Josephson gazed at the shard as though searching for an answer. "The only time I was out of this suite was when the police summoned me to the lounge for an interview. That was around ten o'clock. When I got back, I found this mess."

Teddy Chimes had been looking out of a window. Now he swung around and said impatiently, "Completely senseless and I think you two are reading too much into it. One of the cleaning staff could have knocked it off the mantel and been afraid to own up."

"The cleaning women weren't allowed to work this morning," Josephson reminded him. "That orderly with the yellow sweater—what's his name?"

"Perce," Forsythe said.

"Perce made my bed and tidied up a bit, but I was sitting right where you are, Carolyn, all the time he was in the suite. At that time the figurine was all right."

"But the guard in the corridor—" Teddy broke off and said slowly, "Reilly must have taken off before I was out of bed and this kid with the spots didn't take over until around lunchtime."

Josephson was still holding the shard of porcelain.

170

"While I was with the police, someone came in here and smashed this figurine."

Or perhaps *you* did, Forsythe thought cynically. He rolled his chair in beside the love seat. "John, Teddy, would you mind sitting down? My neck gets stiff from peering up at people." Josephson sank into an armchair and Teddy took a seat beside his mother. He was wearing dark slacks and a Black Watch jacket, which he was hugging around him as though he were chilled. "I think we should talk. Try to find a solution to this affair."

Teddy shook his head and a lock of blond hair fell forward over his brow. "Robert, I'd suggest we let the police handle this. I've had quite enough of being an amateur criminologist. Look where digging around got Harry."

"I'd like to agree but I fear we may not be able to depend on the police."

"Why not?"

"Asian flu. Most of the Hundarby force are off sick and Miss Holly had to send Inspector Creighton home with it. Sergeant Wood had to drive him to the village and with the weather conditions Wood may not be able to get back here. The roads—"

"We know," Carolyn said. "Teddy and I have been following the reports. In some areas they've declared a state of emergency. The Midlands have been hit particularly hard." Carolyn glanced at Josephson and then turned to look at her son. "I agree with Robert. We'd better be prepared to help ourselves." Her eyes fastened on the barrister's face. "What do you want from us?"

"How did you people stand on the solution to the Owen poisonings that Harry proposed at dinner last evening?"

"A split decision. Teddy and John and Harry thought they'd solved the mystery. Kate wavered back and forth and Meg argued it was all flimsy and circum-

171

stantial evidence and I was neutral. We argued for nearly an hour after you left and then decided we'd better go to our suites. Kate and Harry walked down to this wing and the rest of us tagged along behind them. We didn't see Mrs. Elser but the lights were on in the office and I'm afraid we more or less tiptoed past for fear she'd buttonhole us and start chatting about show biz again. I hate saying this, Robert, but she was a bit of a bore at times."

"Carolyn, you seemed to spend more time with Mrs. Elser than any of the rest of us. What was your opinion of her?"

She frowned thoughtfully. "A pleasant enough woman but shallow and somewhat scatterbrained. Yet . . . she was also one of those not terribly bright people who can be stubborn and tenacious."

"Tenacious is the right word," Teddy chimed in. "I'd no intention of posing with Mrs. Elser for about forty snaps, but she kept at you until she wore you down. The famous bulldog perseverance."

Forsythe said, "She certainly didn't wear either Harry or Kate down."

Teddy smiled. "Mother and I are too soft for our own good. Find it hard to say no. Kate certainly doesn't suffer from an overdose of niceness and Harry gave Mrs. Elser that dagger to get her off his back."

Josephson turned his head toward the barrister. "I wasn't famous enough to warrant Mrs. Elser's attention so I know little about the woman. She did ask me if I knew Robert Redford and when I said no she lost interest."

"Carolyn," Forsythe said. "I understand that when Mrs. Elser came into your suite last evening, she was different than usual."

"She was still fluttery, but she seemed . . . I don't know what word to use to describe her. Worried? Perturbed? No, too strong. I suppose I'd say she was disturbed. I asked her if something was wrong and she told me that Gareth Owen—"

"Yes. Sergeant Wood told me about Owen. Later you heard Darla screaming in the corridor and you came to John's aid."

She nodded her sleek head. "I sleep soundly, Robert, but that shrieking did wake me. I tried to calm Darla, but she was hysterical and so I went for help."

"And routed me out of bed," her son said feelingly.

"That's right, darling, and you sleep even sounder than I do. Then I dragged Darla into Meg's suite. I had to shake her awake. Meg is cool and as soon as she saw the state Darla was in, she jumped out of bed. I told Meg I had no idea what was wrong but she'd better go to Kate. Meg ran out and I remained in her suite until the rest of you came straggling in." Carolyn spread her lovely hands. "That's all I know."

"You know all about my movements. I must have been spacey because I remember Reilly telling me to get some clothes on and I went looking for Mother. I found her in Meg's suite and she took off her robe and put it around me."

"Teddy was in shock," Carolyn said gently.

Josephson finally put the shard of porcelain on the table at his elbow. "You know my movements too, Robert."

"Robert," Carolyn said hesitantly. "Do you think Mrs. Elser and Harry's deaths are connected with the Owen murders?"

"At this point I don't know what to think. We could argue that Harry was murdered first and Mrs. Elser saw or heard something that would have posed a threat to the killer. But we don't know which one died first. It might have been the nurse, and that would blow that theory out of the water. On the other hand the killer's target could

173

have been Kate Kapiche and Harry's murder could have been an error."

"Some error," Josephson said morosely. "Just *what* in hell can we do?"

Forsythe gave the other man a long, level look. "For openers you can start telling the truth."

"What are you talking about? Truth about what?"

"About the father of Emmy Owen's baby." Carolyn's mouth opened and Forsythe shook his head. "Kindly hear me out. I've listened to all your versions of that August so long ago. All of you agree on one fact. Every male on Harry's estate, with the possible exception of Kevin Travis, was infatuated with the girl. Names were bandied about. Both Teddy and John admitted they were strongly attracted to Emmy. There's evidence that even solid family men—Gibson Josephson and Cliff Chimes—had Emmy very much on their minds. Harry, who obviously liked young girls, was panting after the girl. And yet the one name that is never mentioned in connection with Emmy Owen is Levi Oglethorpe. Was he immune to the girl's beauty and physical attraction? John describes his friend as an ordinary nineteen-year-old boy. Any boy that age would have been attracted to Emmy. Was Levi somehow immune? I think not.

"And consider this. Levi was the one person who had an area all to himself. He had a renovated stable that he used as a studio. We also know that Emmy Owen left her cart of dairy goods and bread behind that studio on at least one occasion. It's probable that Emmy left her cart there on other occasions and crept into the studio to be with Levi." Forsythe's eyes drilled into Josephson's. "You knew all about that love affair, didn't you?"

The other man threw both hands up. "You win! Yes, when Levi found the girl was pregnant, he told me. They'd been intimate for months. Levi asked for my advice and then totally disregarded it."

174

"What advice did you give him?"

"Not to be a damn fool and ruin his life. To tell Harry and let his brother handle it. We both knew what Harry would do. He'd haul Levi over the coals, but he'd end up buying old Walter off. Good advice, but Levi wouldn't take it. Insisted he was in love with the girl and intended to marry her. He knew Harry wouldn't hear of it, so Levi was making plans to elope with Emmy. I knew his inheritance from his father's estate wouldn't be his until he reached thirty, so I asked him what they'd live on. Levi said he'd a legacy from his mother that would tide them over." Josephson shook his head. "I argued with Levi until I was exhausted. I pointed out Emmy's mental condition and warned him that after the physical attraction waned, he'd be stuck with a wife who would be an eternal child and with Walter Owen as a father-in-law. But Levi wouldn't budge an inch and finally I threatened to tell Harry."

Forsythe leaned forward. "But you didn't do it."

"I couldn't betray Levi and he knew it. He was ruining his life and my hands were tied. I was worried sick. Then, about a week after Levi confessed to me, the Owens were poisoned and the problem was resolved."

"A convenient but drastic solution. John, are you positive that Harry didn't find out about Emmy and his brother?"

It was Carolyn who spoke. "You'd have had to have known Harry longer than you did to answer that question, Robert. If Harry had found out about Levi and Emmy, every person on the estate would have heard about it. Harry was the type of man who was incapable of keeping a secret. You also must remember it was Harry who asked you to investigate those murders. Would he have done that if he'd known his beloved younger brother had been the father of Emmy's baby?"

"John asked me to investigate too and he knew all about Levi."

"Hey! That's right," Teddy said. "John, you sat there last night at dinner and acted as though you were convinced that Alice Constantine had murdered the Owen family. And that the father of Emmy's baby was definitely either Walter or Gareth Owen. And Mother and I are supposed to be actors!"

Forsythe smiled. "You could both take lessons from John, who is supposed to be a businessman. As a matter of interest, John, why *did* you ask me to look into the murders?"

"When Harry told me he'd asked you to investigate, I decided I'd better get into a position where I could wave a red herring in front of your quivering nostrils. You see, I thought you'd claim the man who got Emmy pregnant was the person who killed her and that just isn't so. I can't have Levi's memory defiled like that." Josephson looked earnestly at Carolyn and her son. "Levi wasn't capable of hurting anyone, was he?"

Teddy shrugged. "I really didn't know him well enough to answer that question."

His mother hesitated and then said slowly, "I didn't know Levi well myself, but from what I saw of him, I'd agree with you, John. He seemed a gentle, creative boy."

Josephson took a deep breath. "Robert, one point I was honest about was how I feel about the person who killed the Owens. I still feel that monster ruined my life by killing my father and my best friend. And I can't forget the hell my mother lived in for years."

For a time no one spoke and then Teddy said, "So Alice Constantine wasn't involved at all. Was she even a lesbian?"

"I've no idea," Josephson said. "Meg said it's a matter of record, so Alice probably was but she certainly wasn't having an affair with Emmy Owen."

"So, now we have one answer, but are no closer to the vital one," Carolyn said. "Exactly who did put arsenic in that pot of chili? And, most important of all, was it the same person who killed Harry and Mrs. Elser?"

A tap sounded on the door and Carolyn jumped. Perce stepped into the room. "Dinner trays are on their way and Miss Holly says everyone has to be in their own suites and she says you're to stay right there."

Carolyn sighed. "Miss Holly missed her calling. She'd have made an excellent jailer. Teddy darling, I suppose this is good night. I'll see you in the morning."

As Forsythe wheeled the chair across the corridor to his suite, he noticed that Reilly was once again seated in the armchair near his door. His head was bent over a pocketbook and the flap on his holster was fastened. Forsythe found he was glad to see him.

Perce delivered the dinner tray and, at the barrister's direction, arranged the dishes on a low table in front of the gas fire. Forsythe was balancing on his crutches and looking out of a window. A strong wind was blowing in from the sea driving a curtain of snow before it. The barrister glimpsed white-topped breakers crashing up on the shingle and, although the double-glazed glass prevented him hearing the wind, he could see the yews bending nearly double. The snow was now so high that he could see only the heads of the statues in the Italian garden; the stone benches had disappeared under a blanket of white.

Turning away from the desolate scene, he watched Perce unload the tray. "Dinner's earlier than it usually is," he told the orderly.

"That's because the chef's in a rush to get home, sir. Raoul's scared stiff he'll get stuck here with a murderer running loose."

"I can't say I blame him. Perce, may I ask a personal question?"

Perce set down an insulated coffee jug. "Ask away."

"That sweater. You must be fond of it. You wear it constantly."

Perce laughed. "What you're wondering is how do I get away with wearing one sweater every shift with Miss Holly on deck. Answer is, I don't. Had to tell the woman what I'm going to tell you. I happen to have seven of these damn yellow things."

Forsythe was intrigued. Sitting down on the leather divan, he shook out a napkin. "Obviously you dislike that pullover. Why do you have seven?"

The orderly lifted a metal lid from a dining plate and set a dinner of Beef Richelieu before Forsythe. "It all started with the wife. She's a lovely lass and I call her Sweet Sue; that sure fits my Susie, but her mother! A ruddy storm trooper of a woman. Hates my you know what. Figures I'm not good enough for her daughter. I was foolish enough once to tell the old hag I don't like yellow and never wear pullovers. So, every blessed Christmas and birthday that lousy woman gives me a yellow pullover. She must have bought the stock out of a store because they're all the same. To please my Susie, I got to wear them, so I do it at work and soon as I'm home off they come and I stick on my blue cardigan."

"That's one mystery solved, Perce." The barrister picked up a fork. "Is Gareth Owen still in the building?"

"He's downstairs napping. None of us are going home tonight. Miss Holly's orders. There're a bunch of rooms in the kitchen wing we're using."

"When he wakes up, would you give him a message? Tell Owen I'd like to see him."

Perce promised to deliver the message and said, *"Bon appetit!"* He laughed at the barrister's expression. "Thought that would shake you."

"You speak French?"

"Picked up a few phrases from Susie. Nancy Elser

178

talked her into taking French lessons. Nancy was taking Spanish, you know. Kept talking about going to Spain next year with a friend and said that was the reason she came to work here. To get money to finance the trip." Perce's voice broke and his eyes were suddenly moist. "Can't figure why anyone would do that awful thing to Nancy. She was a real nice woman. When our youngest kid was born last December, Nancy came over and helped Susie for a week. Wouldn't take a penny for it either."

The orderly shook his head, wiped a sweater sleeve across his eyes, and left Forsythe to his dinner. The beef filet was tender, the Madeira sauce perfect, and the vegetables delicious, but Forsythe had no appetite. He forced himself to eat a little beef and a few mushrooms before pushing the plate away. He glanced at the dessert dish, didn't bother lifting the lid on it, and reached for the coffee jug.

As he spooned sugar into a cup, Owen arrived. The man stood inside the door and their eyes met. His expression was completely hostile. "Perce said you want me."

"Would you answer some questions for me?"

"No. With the police I had no choice, but I don't have to talk to you. Do I?"

"You're certainly under no obligation to answer my questions, but don't you want an end to it? Don't you want to know who killed your family?"

Owen's wide mouth twisted in a sneer. "Thought you people had that all figured out at dinner last night. I saw you sitting right there and I didn't hear you arguing against those other bastards." He swung around and reached for the doorknob.

Forsythe said softly, "Emmy . . . Elsbeth . . . Annie. Harry Oglethorpe told me you were fond of your sisters."

The man's back stiffened. "How I feel about my sisters is none of your business. But I'll tell you something." He swung around and said savagely, "My father

179

was rotten! From the time I can remember he booted and cuffed me around. Never a kind gesture, never a word of praise. I hated him then and I hate his memory now. But my father *never* laid a finger on Emmy! He was rotten but he wasn't *that* rotten. As for me doing that to Emmy—''

''Gareth. I know you and your father had nothing to do with your sister's pregnancy. I know who was the father of her child.''

Owen stared at the barrister. Then, as though his knees had weakened, he stumbled over to an armchair and sank into it. ''Who?'' he whispered.

''Levi Oglethorpe.''

''The artist? The young chap who painted pictures?''

''That's the boy. Did you know him well?''

''Didn't know him at all. Saw him walking with that other young chap . . . Josephson, a few times. Mr. Forsythe, why didn't you tell this to that bunch of vultures last night?''

''I only discovered this a short time ago.''

''Sorry I fired off at you. Tell me, this artist . . . did he poison my sisters and father?''

''I don't know, Gareth. All I have to go on is other people's memories. Both John Josephson and Carolyn Chimes feel Levi was incapable of harming anyone.'' He considered briefly and then asked, ''Gareth, did your sister Emmy not confide in you?''

''In a lot of things—yes. Like how her sewing was coming and maybe a show on television she saw when Mrs. Jarman invited her to visit. Emmy loved television and our father was too tight to buy one. But Emmy could be secretive too. I never knew she was pregnant until after . . .''

''Yes.'' Forsythe took a sip of coffee, found it was tepid, and set down the cup. ''Perhaps we've been going about this the wrong way. The police assumed, and so did I, that the murders were committed with either Emmy or your father as the prime victim. Is it possible the poisoning could have been directed at *you?* The only person who knew you wouldn't be eating dinner with your family that night was Mrs. Jarman. Can you think of any enemy you had?"

"I was only fifteen, Mr. Forsythe. Do kids of that age have enemies?" Owen's low brow wrinkled in thought. "I did have fights at school. About Emmy. Some of the boys called her dummy and poked fun at her. Said she was a boob with big boobs. That sort of thing. But those boys lived in Greater Eveline and never set foot on the Oglethorpe estate. No way they could have got that arsenic. Are you sure that Levi couldn't have wanted to get rid of Emmy?"

"I'm not sure of anything. But John Josephson told me that Levi loved your sister and intended to run away and marry her. I know what you're thinking. Harry Oglethorpe. It would appear he had no idea about his brother and Emmy." Owen shook a baffled head and Forsythe added, "Could you tell me what happened to you after the inquest?"

"The Jarmans took me in. Mr. Jarman saw to leasing the farm and I went into Greater Eveline and lived with them. They'd had a bunch of kids, but they were all grown and they had a big house. The Jarmans were awful good to me, but I knew it was hard on them in a town that size."

"I suppose there was gossip."

"An awful lot of loose talk. About Emmy and me and my father. Some people still figured I'd killed my family and there was a moving away from me and sidelong looks. People can be cruel, can't they?"

Forsythe agreed. He pictured the life this man, then a mere lad, had endured in that town. *Cruel* was the right word. Owen was silent for moments and then he said, "I stuck it out until I was eighteen and the farm was legally

181

mine. Then I sold up and left town. The Jarmans tried to talk me into staying on and letting Mr. Jarman teach me the butcher trade, but I knew they'd be better off without me. So I went to London and worked at different jobs—washing dishes and parking cars and working in a couple of factories. Then I decided if I was going to make a decent living, I better get a trade. So I went to work in a hospital to learn how to be an orderly."

"Did you find life easier in London?"

"Much easier. Nobody knew about my past or stared at me as though I was a freak. For the first time since I lost my family, I was just another chap. But I never was able to get friendly with anyone. By then I guess I was a loner. Scared stiff of getting to like a person and then having that person find out about what happened to my family and all. Then . . . I met Athena!"

Owen's rugged face glowed as he continued, "Athena's a wonderful woman. I asked her if she'd move in with me and she said no. Said she sensed there was something festering away inside me and she wouldn't have a more intimate relationship until I told her and we lanced it. I warned her that when she knew about my past, she'd shun me and she gave me that wonderful smile of hers and said, 'Try me.' I told her about Emmy and Elsbeth and little Annie and she started to cry. She understands how I feel and she *loves* me. Soon we're getting married and we're going to have a family. Athena loves kids. I'm a lucky man."

Yes, the barrister thought, it appeared that finally this poor devil had had a stroke of luck. "Gareth, I'm happy for you and I'm also glad that Athena is safely in Hundarby."

The other man's face darkened and he stared at the window. Ice crystals were driving against the panes. "That's what's worrying me sick. Athena's here. Miss Holly rang up Athena this morning and asked if she would come out here and stay until this storm is over. I went in to the village to talk her out of it, but she insisted on coming here."

"Couldn't Miss Holly have asked Geraldo?"

"He has that flu and is pretty sick. I'll tell you one thing, Mr. Forsythe. If Miss Holly thinks I'm going to spend all my time waiting on the patients, she's wrong. I'm keeping my eyes on Athena. If anything happened to her . . . well, life wouldn't be worth living."

"You do exactly that. Athena's a lovely woman and one to be cherished." Forsythe paused and then said, "You saw Mrs. Elser twice last evening. Could you tell me about it?"

"Not much to tell. After I overheard that conversation in the lounge—"

"Were you deliberately eavesdropping, Gareth?"

The other man flushed. "I'm not that kind of chap. I wasn't sneaking around! I went to the lounge to tell Darla, if she'd like, I'd help Edna—that's the kitchen maid—clean away after dinner. Earlier that afternoon Darla had told me she wasn't feeling so good and I felt sorry for the kid. Anyway, when I got to the lounge I heard that Mrs. Chimes say something about Mr. Oglethorpe trying to give my sister money and well . . . I stopped and listened. Do you blame me?"

"Not in the slightest. Carry on."

"I listened to all that garbage about my family and then you made a move to get up so I walked down to the nurses' station and went in. Mrs. Elser was sitting at the desk in the office, looking through a bunch of snaps. She wanted to show them to me, but my mind was swirling around with what I'd overheard and I said I wasn't interested. That seemed to make her sort of annoyed and she told me to get a move on and get the suites ready for the night. So I turned down the beds and so on and then I went into the supply room and had a smoke."

Owen was staring into space and Forsythe prodded, "And then?"

"I went back to the nurses' office and blurted out I was quitting—"

"Was Mrs. Elser still looking at the snapshots?"

"No. She was sitting on that chintz sofa with a notebook on her knees and a bunch of textbooks around her. She asked me why I wanted to leave and it ended up with me telling her the whole horrible story. She was kind of a silly-acting woman, but she was also one of the kindest people I've ever met. She told me she could see why it was impossible for me to stay on and asked me to give my notice to Miss Holly the next day because she's the nurse in charge."

"And that was all?"

Owen tapped huge fingers against a denim-covered knee. "She asked a bunch of questions. Where did we live . . . who rented cottages from Mr. Oglethorpe . . . what my sisters looked like . . . how the poison was given to my family. When I left her, she was standing by the desk, staring down at the pile of snaps. The last thing she said was that she was going to speak to you. Did she?"

"When she got to my suite, I was asleep. If she'd only wakened me . . ."

"Can't be helped, Mr. Forsythe. One thing we can't do is change the past. Is there anything else?"

"I can't think of anything, Gareth."

The orderly loaded the virtually untouched dinner on the tray and said good night. By then the room was quite dark, but the barrister sat on the divan, gazing at the gas fire. His talk with Gareth Owen had been unproductive and he remembered what Carolyn Chimes had said. The mystery of Emmy Owen's seducer was solved, but the identity of the poisoner was still concealed in

184

memories and time. He wondered if the murderer who had killed Nancy Elser and Harry Oglethorpe would also, at some future day, still be concealed in memories and time.

13

E ven the soft gray light of early morning couldn't steal the vibrant colors from the Art Deco lounge. On the oval table was a coffee urn, an assortment of cups, and a platter containing a few croissants. The platter was ornamented with a vivid ceramic picture of the present monarch and her prince consort.

Across the room on Kate Kapiche's favorite golden sofa Miss Holly perched, flanked by Mrs. Frome and a placid-faced woman wearing a striped uniform. To the right of the sofa were three chairs occupied by Owen and Perce and Athena Khalkis. The orderlies wore white, high-necked tunics and white cotton trousers. Athena's luscious curves were hidden under a white smock but her dark brown hair, generally braided, fell loosely around her face and cascaded to her waist. On the far side of the sofa three security guards sat twisting their caps in restless hands.

Facing the sofa was a row of six dining chairs occupied by the four patients and their two guests. Most wore robes over nightgowns or pajamas and the only one who had dressed, Teddy Chimes, hadn't had time to brush his blond hair. Kate, with Carolyn's tailored blue robe pulled over the froth of her peach nightie, was pouting and staring balefully at the former matron. Kate said hotly, "When that police chappie in that vulgar pin-striped suit said you were high-handed, he was dead on. How *dare* you order us out of bed in the middle of the night?"

Pulling out the massive watch from her starchy bosom, Miss Holly consulted it. "Ten after six. Hardly the middle of the night. Despite your life-style, Ms. Kapiche, there are some people who do rise at this hour."

"You just wait until Fran Hornblower gets here! After I talk to her she'll have you out on your ass before you can say *matron!*"

"Do control yourself. This sort of threat and silly behavior won't help. As for Miss Hornblower . . . it may be quite a while before she or anyone else can reach us. And I assure you, Ms. Kapiche, I should like nothing better than to leave this place."

Kate's lips parted, but Carolyn put a quieting hand on the other woman's wrist. "This storm?" Carolyn asked.

Miss Holly's glacial eyes flicked toward the actress. "Precisely. The local roads are now blocked and, as of an hour ago, the phone lines are down. The last phone conversation I had was with Sergeant Wood. As some of you may know, the sergeant had to escort Inspector Creighton back to Hundarby late yesterday afternoon. Both the sergeant and I were concerned about the weather conditions and the sergeant's plan was to take his inspector home and return here immediately."

Forsythe pulled his wool robe closer around his chest. "But Wood didn't get back, did he?"

The nurse's austere face turned toward the barrister. "He didn't. By the time they reached the inspector's home, the poor man was raving with delirium. Mrs. Creighton is seven months pregnant with her first child and the sergeant simply couldn't leave her to try and handle a man her husband's size when he was raving and thrashing about. By the time the sick man was settled and quiet, Sergeant Wood found the roads were impassable. He promised me he was doing everything in his power to get a machine to dig out a path to us. But—''

"This is ridiculous!" Josephson was on his feet. His robe flapped open, revealing brightly patterned pajamas, and his wiry hair stood up around his face. "Do you mean to tell me there's no snow-clearing machinery in this area?''

"That is correct, Mr. Josephson.''

Forsythe looked down at his hands. His knuckles were white from pressure. Fighting a flood of panic, he thrust both hands in his pockets. He wasn't the only one fighting panic. He could hear it in John Josephson's voice as he said, "*What* are we going to *do?*''

"Cope," Miss Holly told him. "I won't pretend I'm not perturbed by the situation, but we'll handle it. I had the foresight to ask Owen, Percival, and Mrs. Gunther''— Miss Holly waved a hand at the placid-faced aide—"to stay over last night. Also, Miss Khalkis joined us yesterday. Mr. Reilly, Mr. Tiptree, and Mr. Marks were on night shift and so are still with us. However, the other security guards I was counting on could not reach us in time. There is no sense in having men on gate duty under these weather conditions, so these three guards will take three shifts and at all times one of them will be on duty in this wing.''

Meg Eleven, huddled in a gray flannel robe, was looking down the line of faces opposite her. "No chef or kitchen staff?''

"No. Mr. Morceau and his assistants are not with us. Which may be as well. Raoul is highly strung and tends to be hysterical. But we shan't go hungry. Mrs. Fromes's aide, Mrs. Gunther, has worked as a cook. Right, Mrs. Gunther?''

188

The aide bobbed her head. "Yah," she said with a thick Teutonic accent. "Before I work at hospital in town I work at place called Bluebird Cafe. I like to cook but do only plain cooking, nothing like fancy things Raoul Morceau do."

Miss Holly gave her an approving glance. "And to assist Lisl Gunther we have Peter Percival, who has also worked at a restaurant."

Perce was fiddling with his sleeve, trying to fold back a yellow wool cuff under the white linen. He glanced up and said, "When I was going to school I helped out in me uncle's fish and chip shop. And I'm a fair grill cook. Bangers and bacon and tomatoes and stuff like that."

For the first time since they'd entered the lounge, Miss Holly smiled. "Don't look so hopeful, Ms. Kapiche. I assure you that you won't be receiving grill food. We have a plentiful supply of salad ingredients as well as other food." She looked from one patient's face to the next. "Despite our situation we mustn't let down. As much as possible, our regular routine will be followed. With only one physiotherapist, we can't hope to encompass the work done by two, so Miss Khalkis will concentrate on the one who needs her most—Mr. Forsythe. He'll continue to have his full session twice daily. The rest of you will have your massage times cut." She turned toward Meg and Teddy. "You young people are able bodied and must pitch in and help. Your own suites and your mothers' suites will be your responsibility. To neaten and change linens and so on. Also, Miss Eleven, as you are a nurse, you must be prepared to give Mrs. Frome or me a hand if we should require it. Any questions?"

"One remark," Teddy muttered. "I don't know where to start in making beds or doing housework. That wasn't part of my education."

"A pity. It should have been. Every boy should be taught at least the basics. Don't despair, Mr. Chimes. It's

189

never too late. Your mother can direct you and you can do the physical work. Mr. Forsythe's room and Mr. Josephson's will be cared for by Owen—"

"No way!" Josephson was on his feet again. "There's a good chance Gareth Owen killed both Harry and that nurse."

Miss Holly, amid the rustle of starched skirts, came to her feet. As though pulled by wires, every member of her small staff jumped up. "You also are a suspect, Mr. Josephson. So . . . who will be at risk when Owen enters your quarters—you or him?"

The patients were getting to their feet too and Kate was clinging to the man next to her who happened to be Forsythe. He swayed on his crutches and Miss Holly said sharply, "Ms. Kapiche, kindly watch what you're *doing*. Mr. Forsythe, you were told to use your chair when you leave your suite. Percival will see you back to the Primrose before he joins Mrs. Gunther in the kitchen. Don't let me see you on those crutches in the common areas again. Mr. Reilly and Mr. Tiptree, you had best go down to your quarters and get some sleep. Mr. Marks will be on duty in the corridor. The patients and their two guests will return to their suites and will stay in them. At lunchtime Mr. Tiptree will escort you back to this room."

Kate's jaw set. "I want my luncheon served in my suite!"

Color flooded into Mrs. Frome's thin face and her mouth snapped open, but Miss Holly touched the other nurse's sleeve and said crisply, "We don't have a large enough staff to deliver trays to your suites. Mrs. Gunther and Percival will cook the food and send it up on the dumbwaiter and Owen will set it up buffet style as he did breakfast—"

"Breakfast!" Kate said scathingly.

"Continental. The best we could manage. Ms. Kapiche, please try to act your age. Neither your wealth

190

nor your importance in the business or social world can assist you now. We're attempting to survive until help can reach us. I demand cooperation." Miss Holly beamed a wintry smile around the group of people. "Perhaps it would be easier if you could consider yourself a modern version of the Swiss Family Robinson."

Miss Holly, Mrs. Frome, and the aide-cum-cook were the first to exit the lounge. Closely following them were the rest of the staff and then the patients straggled out. Forsythe, with Perce pacing at his side, was the last. Perce seemed to like the new order no better than Kate Kapiche. He was muttering away and finally Forsythe said impatiently, "If you have something to say, kindly speak up."

"Swissfamilyflippingrobinson! That woman reminds me of the captain of the *Bounty*. What was his name?"

"Bligh."

"I can just see our Miss Bligh standing by the mizzenmast or something, opening her big yob, and yelling, 'Keel-haul the blighter!' "

Forsythe opened the door of the Primrose and gave the orderly a withering look. "If we're all in one piece when the police get the snowplows through to us, you'll have our Miss Bligh to thank for it." He slammed the door in Perce's startled face.

Miss Holly was hardly the captain of a ship in the midst of a mutiny, the barrister thought, she was more like her giant of a father—a general and a good one. He barely had time for that thought when the door creaked open and Kate hissed dramatically, "Half an hour. My suite. *Be there.*"

Mr. Christian, he thought, fomenting mutiny? There was no time to shower, but he managed to shave, pull on an exercise suit, and gather up his pipe and tobacco.

In the leather-and-paneled sitting room of the Or-

191

chid, other members of the modern Swiss Family Robinson were gathered. Kate was wearing an exercise suit the same color and cut as his own and her dark red hair was yanked back into a ponytail. She wore no makeup or jewelry and was a living example of that occasional rare woman who needs no enhancements for beauty. John Josephson, wearing a white silk roll top and a suede jacket, was leaning against the mantel. His face looked a trifle less gaunt and there was a trace of color in his cheeks. Carolyn and her son sat on the leather divan and Meg was gazing out of a window at the snow and the breakers pounding against the shingle.

Kate stepped aside so Forsythe could wheel his chair up beside the divan. "Being a good little boy, aren't we? Using our wheelchair just like nanny ordered."

Meg swung around and said wrathfully, "Robert happens to be showing good sense. The way you grabbed him in the lounge could have overbalanced him and injured that leg of his. Around you he's safer in a wheelchair. And, as far as Miss Holly's concerned, I agree it's time you grow up and stop acting like a spoiled brat!"

"Dear little Meg," Kate said with poisonous sweetness. "I keep forgetting you're kind of a nurse too. Sisters under the skin with Iron Pants Holly."

Carolyn was on her feet. "Please! That's quite enough! Kate, you insisted we come here. Why?"

Kate moved over near Josephson and stood on the hearth rug. Clasping her hands behind her, she said slowly and seriously, "One point that abominable nurse made was valid. We are trying to survive. And I don't mean from blizzard conditions. I feel every one in this room, with the possible exception of Robert, is in danger. I *know* the murderer is going to kill us before the police manage to get us out of here."

Forsythe blinked and said, "*Know*. Do you mean you have knowledge of the murderer?"

"I know what he's done and . . . I know what he means to do. I tried to talk about this with Harry and he laughed and called it superstition. Now Harry is *dead*."

Forsythe was frowning. "For a woman who couldn't even remember what happened to Gareth's family . . ."

"Robert, I know that made me look rather foolish but I assure you that was only a type of temporary memory block used by my mind to conceal a situation I just couldn't bear to face. Poor Harry. I keep wondering if he had time to look into his murderer's face and realize I'd been right all along."

Turning her back to the window, Meg said, "I think you'd better explain."

"When the Owens died, Meg, you were too young to realize what was going on. But surely the rest of you must know what I mean." She looked from Carolyn to Teddy to Josephson. "The Owen family died in August. Early the following year the people who'd been on Harry's estate started to die. Gibson Josephson—"

"My father died of a heart attack," Josephson said curtly. "And my mother died just recently."

Kate put a hand on his shoulder. "I was about to say your parents died natural deaths. But they were the only ones who did."

Josephson jerked away from her hand. "Levi died accidently. A small boat on the Seine. He was alone."

"How do you know he was alone?" Kate swung around to face him. "They found the boat overturned and his body was discovered several days later, washed ashore. Levi happened to be an excellent swimmer. Do you deny that?" The question must have been rhetorical as she raced on. "Suppose Levi wasn't alone? Suppose someone knocked him over the head and tossed him into the water? Suppose—"

"Kate darling, your imagination is running wild," Carolyn said gently.

193

"Exactly what *Harry* told me."

"She does have a point, Carolyn," Josephson said. "Levi *was* a good swimmer, far better than me. Let's hear her out."

Kate smiled at him. "Support from an unexpected source, John. Now, more wild imagination. Carolyn, suppose your husband didn't commit suicide?"

Both Teddy and his mother were sitting bolt upright. The color was draining from Carolyn's narrow face and Teddy put a protective arm around her thin shoulders. He said curtly, "Your supposing is getting cruel, Kate."

Carolyn's lips quivered. "You of all people should know that Cliff *did* take his own life and *why*. I gave him a divorce and suddenly you no longer wanted him. Cliff's career had been steadily going downhill while he danced attendance on you and he was desperate. The day before he . . . Cliff came to me and begged me to take him back. I still loved him and I wanted to, but pride . . . stupid blind pride. I told him I wouldn't take your leavings."

Meg turned back to the window and Josephson looked uncomfortable but Kate simply waited until Carolyn had finished and then she said, "Cliff didn't leave a suicide note. It would have been simple for someone to lure him up to the roof of my apartment house and push him off. Carolyn darling, please don't hate me for what I'm going to say. Everyone tells me how shallow I am, how superficial my emotions. Perhaps they're right, but it takes one to recognize one. Your husband wasn't able to fall in love. Oh, Cliff could be infatuated, love in a physical sense, but to kill himself for love—he was as incapable of that as I am."

Carolyn hid her face against her son's shoulder and Meg walked over and patted the older woman's shoulder. "You'd better get on with your supposing, Kate. Who's the next victim in your fairy tale?"

"Alice Constantine and the little girls."

"They died in a house fire and it certainly wasn't arson."

"It's possible that it was a clever case of arson, Meg. Possible that Alice and her woman companion and her nieces were murdered and the house set ablaze."

"I suppose it's possible," Meg admitted. "But your theory falls to pieces with Kevin Travis. He's still alive and well in Australia."

"Are you certain about that?"

"No. But I assume—"

"Assuming doesn't count. Kevin may be dead too. Now Harry's gone and that leaves the five of us. Can't any of you understand what I'm saying? If we don't do something and do it fast, we'll all be dead too."

As she finished speaking, an uneasy silence descended on the room. So quiet was it that all that could be heard was the tiny hiss of the gas jet, the muted tick of the Regency mantel clock, and the creak of leather as Teddy shifted on the divan. Finally John Josephson moved. He pushed a footstool aside and sat down heavily in one of the black leather chairs. He looked up at Kate.

"I'll admit I feel as though you've pulled a rug out from under me. Your reasoning makes a weird kind of sense and yet . . . Robert, you're our authority on criminology. What do you think of this?"

"An assassin who has killed over a period of seventeen years? Murdered a number of people without raising a breath of suspicion? Offhand, I'd say highly unlikely. A person who would do this would have to be unbalanced. Could anyone conceal that type of insanity?"

Josephson gave him a twisted grin. "I was hoping for answers, not more questions. Kate, you dreamt this theory up. Who do you have pegged for this monster? The person who murdered the Owen family?"

"No." Kate tugged at her ponytail and straightened her shoulders. Under the loose top her large breasts surged. "The person who is *avenging* the Owen family. The person who doesn't know the identity of the poisoner and so is killing us one by one—"

"Kate!" Meg was staring at her stepmother. "You're accusing Gareth Owen."

"I am. Gareth is the only person in this building with a motive. The only one capable of a twisted and obsessed love that would lead to murder."

Forsythe wheeled his chair back a few feet. "In that case I no longer have to answer questions with questions. Gareth Owen has *not* been killing off the former residents of the Oglethorpe estate one by one. At the time of the early deaths—Levi and Cliff's—Gareth was living in Greater Eveline with Rita and Carl Jarman. He was still in his teens and had neither the funds nor resources to travel to Paris and London and Birmingham to do murder. Gareth was a simple country lad only a couple of years older than Meg."

Meg smiled brightly at the barrister and her dimples flashed. "Good for you! That's certainly setting Kate's thinking processes straight. Now, I think we should ask the poor man's Miss Marple to rebut. Come on, Kate, drop some further gems of wisdom before us."

While the barrister had been speaking, Kate had looked like a thundercloud, but now she managed a small smile. "Meg darling, if you mean more pearls before swine, it seems a waste of time and effort. Perhaps I am wrong about Gareth, perhaps I am wrong about those early deaths, but I'm *not* wrong about Harry. His murder was connected with the Owen family—"

"Then explain Nancy Elser's murder," Teddy broke in.

"*Et tu,* Teddy? I don't know about Mrs. Elser. Perhaps she knew something about Harry's death. John, for God's sake, back me up!"

His head rested against the back of the Eames chair

196

and he gave her a weary smile. "Sorry, Kate, I'm afraid I can't. Your theory has as many holes as Harry's about Alice Constantine."

Forsythe fully expected Kate Kapiche to fly into a rage. She didn't. Her shoulders sagged and she dropped into the other leather chair and propped her chin on one hand. "I'm sorry, too. Sorry for all of us. My friends, you'll think *me* mad but I tell you I *feel* it. There's madness here somewhere and you won't believe me until you look into its face." Her voice dropped to a whisper. "By then it will be too late."

14

Gareth Owen swung the scarlet-painted door wide, pushed the wheelchair into the bright anteroom of the therapy section, and called, "Athena, I have Mr. Forsythe."

"I'll be right there," she called back.

When Athena Khalkis stepped into the anteroom, Forsythe noted that she'd taken off the smock and was in her working gear—zebra-striped leotard and white body stocking and, calling attention to the short but shapely legs, white-and-black–striped leg warmers and white Reeboks. Her ivory skin was glowing and her lustrous dark hair had been braided and pinned high on her head. Her appearance was a perfect foil for the colorful room. The walls consisted of panels of burnt orange, chrome yellow, turquoise, and electric blue and even the wooden furniture had been painted in garish colors. It was overpowering and Forsythe was glad to rest his eyes on Athena's pristine black and whiteness.

She greeted the barrister and shared a radiant smile between the two men. Forsythe glanced up at the orderly and glimpsed the adoration that briefly transformed the man's rugged face. "I'm going to bring you an early lunch," Gareth told the woman. "All you had for breakfast was coffee."

"That's all I *ever* have for breakfast," she pointed out.

"Then you'll have to change your eating habits." Owen looked down at Forsythe and told him proudly, "Athena's eating for two."

"Blabbermouth!" She reached up and put a hand over his mouth. "We aren't even sure yet, Mr. Forsythe, and already he's fussing over my diet."

"I'm sure." Owen pulled her hand away from his lips and tenderly kissed the palm.

"Talk about unprofessional conduct!" She tugged her hand away. "Wait until Miss Holly hears about this."

Forsythe smiled from Athena to the orderly. "In case Gareth's right, congratulations!"

Owen beamed down at him. "Put your money on it, sir. When Athena's done with you, I'll pick you up, Mr. Forsythe."

The scarlet door swung closed behind him and Athena guided the chair through an archway into the inner room. "Gareth likes you," she said and pulled the chair to a stop beside the massage table. "And that's quite a compliment. He doesn't take to many people."

She helped Forsythe stand and supported him as he hopped up on the table. Deftly, she peeled off his exercise top and then the baggy trousers. At first Forsythe had been embarrassed at wearing only briefs in such close contact with the beauteous Athena, but now he accepted it as matter-of-factly as she did.

"Gareth's a nice chap," Forsythe said and then added thoughtfully, "as a boy he must have lived a ghastly life."

"Over on your stomach. There, that's fine. Relax. Hm, the muscle tone in this leg is definitely improving."

Under her strong hands he found not only his bad leg but his entire body relaxing. "Yes, Gareth had a bad childhood with that awful father of his and after his family died his life must have been a nightmare. It drove him right away from people. He'd been hurt so badly it was a while before he'd even trust me, but since I persuaded him to tell me about his past it's been some easier for him. I was glad to hear that he'd talked to you about his family's deaths. That's a healthy sign." She touched his shoulder. "Turn over, please."

Forsythe rolled over and the therapist moved to the end of the table. She lifted the foot of his bad leg and placed it against her palm. "Press down as hard as you can. Yes . . . that's good. Relax. Did it hurt very much?"

He masked the pain with a smile. "Not as much as it did the last time." He gazed up at her. The lovely oval face, framed in thick braids, was warm with compassion. He said impulsively, "You shouldn't have come back here. Gareth was right. You'd be better in Hundarby."

"Please!" She threw both hands up. "Gareth did everything short of locking me up to keep me in our cottage yesterday. He was still emotionally raw after overhearing that dinner-table discussion about the deaths of his family. How could those people have been so cruel, so unfeeling?"

"To be fair, you must realize that they had no idea Gareth was listening."

"An eavesdropper rarely hears good about himself? Is that how you defend them?"

"Not quite." Forsythe stared past her shoulder at the ceiling. Light beamed down over the table. "I know Gareth had old wounds torn open, but those other people also have wounds—"

"They didn't have three sisters and a father die ghastly deaths! They didn't have a whole town wonder if

200

you'd got your own sister pregnant and then killed her! They didn't—"

"Whoa! I'm on your side."

"Sorry." She lowered his leg gently and smiled down at him. "Lioness firing off in defense of its cub. I suppose I am a bit overprotective and you may be right. Perhaps those murders did have an adverse effect on the people who are patients here now. One point I want to make. I know that Gareth had an opportunity to kill Mr. Oglethorpe and Mrs. Elser and I also know he has no alibi for that period of time but . . ."

"You don't think he did?"

"I *know* he didn't." Athena spoke with the same assurance that Owen had earlier. "He's huge and powerful but he's as gentle as a kitten unless . . ."

"Unless what?"

"Unless someone he values is threatened. Then . . . yes, he could kill."

He repeated something to Athena Khalkis that he once had said to Abigail Sanderson. "There isn't a being on this earth who is incapable of violence under the right circumstances."

"Roll over again. You've earned a back massage." Strong fingers kneaded the muscles at the base of his neck. "You're saying any of us could murder."

"Exactly. Luckily few of us ever meet those special circumstances."

The fingers moved slowly downwards, probing at the vertebrae, then sliding over to a shoulder blade. Forsythe was completely relaxed and his eyes closed. Athena spoke, but her voice was low and soft and sounded as though it came from a long distance.

By the time the barrister wheeled his chair into the lounge, most of the other people in the wing had eaten and left. A solitary figure perched on the golden sofa near the porcelain greyhound. Miss Holly waved. "Bring your lunch over here, Mr. Forsythe."

He inspected the buffet spread the length of the dining table. Lisl Gunther might be a plain cook, but the food looked appetizing. He selected a leek pasty, some vegetable salad, and a freshly baked apple tart. The nurse's lunch, arranged on the teak-and-ivory table, proved to be even more generous than his own and she was spooning up what looked like barley soup. "Delicious," she told him. "Thank heavens for a good appetite and a sound digestion. You're very late for your lunch, Mr. Forsythe. I was about to go looking for you."

"I dozed off on the massage table and Athena decided to leave me there while she lunched."

"Very wise. I should imagine you can use the rest." She put down the soup spoon and reached for a leek pasty. "Your record in criminology appears to be most impressive. I haven't followed the newspaper and magazine accounts myself but Mrs. Frome has and she told me about some of your cases. Both of us are wondering . . ."

This was the first time since he'd met this indomitable woman that she had showed hesitancy. He waited several moments and then prompted, "Yes?"

"One of our—Mrs. Frome's and my—great fears concerns patient safety. Mrs. Elser and Mr. Oglethorpe were killed in a very bold and rash way. When you consider so many people could have spotted the murderer in that blood-soaked smock in the corridor . . . we find it disturbing. Admittedly, we've posted an armed guard in the corridor, but Mrs. Frome and I are still uneasy."

He put aside his salad plate and reached for the tart. "What you're trying to say is that you fear the murderer might kill again."

"Precisely. And to be blunt, we feel the target might be you." She raised a commanding hand. "Do hear me

202

out. You're the person in this building most capable of uncovering the identity of this killer. As such, you're a source of danger to him or her."

Forsythe managed a slight smile. "And to be blunt with *you*, this murderer is safe from me. To date, I don't have a clue. This phobia you diagnosed—fear of hospitals—has slowed my mental processes to a crawl."

"Then you had better speed them up. The killer certainly isn't aware of your fear. You've done too good a job hiding it. I think you'll agree our only safety is in unmasking this person." She sipped tea and asked, "Is there any way I can help?"

"There is one thing. But I doubt you'd consider it."

"Try me."

"The nurses' office. I'd like to look around in there."

"It's locked and has a police seal on it."

"I knew you wouldn't consider it."

"That's where you're wrong." She rose, smoothed crisp cotton over her hips, and gave him a smile. "The only reason I hesitated is that it's better if none of the patients witness our breaking and entering. Ms. Kapiche has become increasingly insistent about reclaiming her peacock wardrobe from the Iris. But we may be in luck. After lunch Mr. Marks escorted all five of them down to the library for fresh supplies of books and videotapes. Come along, Mr. Forsythe, we're about to break the law."

Their luck held while the nurse peeled back the tape and unlocked the door with her master key. But, as she switched on the office lights, the lift door hissed open and a group of patients, shepherded by Marks, stepped into the corridor. Kate, still wearing the borrowed exercise suit, led the pack. She immediately gave tongue. "Will you look at *that*. Oh no, I couldn't step into the Iris to get a few clothes, but Miss Holly can open up another sealed area. Miss Holly! I *demand* that you—"

"Mr. Marks," the nurse said quietly. "You'll escort

Ms. Kapiche to her suite. Ms. Kapiche, you're obviously overwrought. Either go quietly or I shall be forced to use a sedative.''

Kate tossed her head and her gaze locked with the nurse's. Then her eyes fell away and she stalked down the hall, muttering something about the authorities and the medical society. The others followed her. Both Carolyn and her son were smiling. Miss Holly called, "Mr. Marks, Mr. Tiptree will be relieving you in twenty minutes. Be sure to stop in the kitchen and have lunch before you take your rest period.'' Quite unruffled, she stepped into the office.

Forsythe glanced around the room and decided that all that had been removed by the police had been the desk blotter and, of course, the pitiful figure propped in the desk chair. The ledgers balanced on a corner of the desk; the schoolbooks were scattered over the chintz-covered cushions of the sofa; the tin of herb tea, the brown pottery pot, and matching mugs sat beside the hotplate. Bloodstains, now dried a rusty brown color, splattered over the ivory-washed wall near the desk; blood had soaked into the beige-colored carpet under the chair; blood crusted on the chair back and the forward part of the seat.

He took a deep breath and immediately wished he hadn't. The last time he'd been in this room it had the hot brassy smell of fresh blood. Now the stale air had a lingering sweetish odor of decay, a fetid stench that reminded him of an autopsy he had once attended. Glancing up, he saw his companion was standing in the middle of the room, both arms folded over her starched bosom. He asked, "Should we touch anything?''

A tiny smile twitched at the corners of her lips. "We've already broken the law and I see no reason not to continue. Anyway, as you may have noticed, the police have already dusted for prints.''

Miss Holly, Forsythe told himself, was more alert than he was. There were traces of powder on many of the surfaces. He reached for the ledgers. "These are?"

"The one with the blue cover is the guest book. You must recall signing it. All the entries consist of is the patient's signature and current address. The other ledger, the brown-covered one, is a list kept by the nursing staff. In this case Mrs. Elser handled the entries. It's slightly more complicated, consisting of the name, full addresses, health reason for admission, physician, and a short medical history of each patient."

"What was your opinion of Nancy Elser?"

"Personal or professional?"

"Both."

"I have no personal opinion. Until we came to work here we'd seen each other only a few times. Passed on the street and attended a meeting of the Women's Institute of Hundarby. Our entire conversations consisted of remarks on the weather."

"Professional?"

Her brows drew together in thought. "She did what was required. No more, no less. Although she was somewhat untidy in this room, she was meticulous in keeping records and updating the patients' charts."

Forsythe flipped open the ledger with the brown cover and located the entries for January. All of them were made in Mrs. Elser's handwriting—small, crabbed, neat. He read them through. Not much he hadn't known here. Harry Oglethorpe gave two addresses, a town house in Mayfair and a pied-à-terre in Paris. He listed three physicians and suffered from gout and arthritis. Ms. Kate Kapiche apparently had no less than five residences, one in New York, and was afflicted with hypertension and a tendency toward obesity. The last entries were the two guests, Mr. Theodore Chimes and what had originally been Ms. Meg Eleven. The *Ms.* had been crossed out and *Miss* substituted.

After opening the ledger with the blue cover, he found the same list of names in the same order; only these were signatures. His signature was below Kate's, and Meg's was the last one on the page. Mrs. Elser had indeed been meticulous with records. After the scrawled Meg Eleven was an entry in Mrs. Elser's crabbed handwriting. In brackets—*Miss.*

He replaced both ledgers on the desk and wheeled over to the sofa. There were two textbooks and three spiral-ringed notebooks tossed on the cushions. He flipped through them. Each book was inscribed with Mrs. Elser's name and her address. He looked through the notebooks, which had only exercises one would expect a fledgling student of Spanish to write.

He was aware that Miss Holly had moved and was now standing behind him, reading over his shoulder. She spotted it before he did. A large hand reached out and an index finger pointed. He turned his head and their eyes met. "My congratulations, Miss Holly. You seem to have the makings of a detective."

He threw the notebook back on the sofa and reversed his chair so quickly that his companion barely had time to jump out of his path. After scooping up both ledgers, he opened the brown-covered one. His finger touched the entries, one by one. *Mr. John Josephson—Lyme disease. Mr. Robert Forsythe—operation on patella of left leg and a lot of medical jargon beyond his comprehension.* His eyes flickered down the rest of the column before he opened the blue-covered book and repeated the process.

He sighed heavily. "That's the answer then."

Miss Holly had been reading over his shoulder again. Now, she stepped around the chair and looked down at him. Her wide brow was furrowed. "I believe your congratulations on my detecting ability were premature. I must admit I don't follow your reasoning process with these guest books."

"You couldn't be expected to. You didn't hear that particular conversation. It took place the day that Carolyn Chimes and John Josephson arrived here. We were in the Art Deco lounge and . . ."

He explained in detail. When he had finished she nodded and said, "There were other witnesses?"

"All the other patients and their two guests were there."

"Hmm. Very well, I don't dispute the identity of this killer but . . . what possible motive could there be for Mrs. Elser's death?"

"To silence her. If my reasoning is correct she was a danger to the killer."

"But your reasoning, Mr. Forsythe, is, if I may be blunt, guesswork."

He said drily, "That's mainly what detective work is, Miss Holly. We've no way to verify this guesswork until the police can get to us."

"And we've no idea how soon that will be." She straightened her wide shoulders and thrust out her chin. "I do believe you're right. What course of action should I take? Citizen's arrest?"

"House arrest in a luxury suite with a private security guard at the door? Think! We've no proof we—"

"Surely Mrs. Elser's notebook constitutes sufficient evidence. And we have your testimony on that conversation in the lounge to back it up."

His mouth moved in an ironic smile. "As a barrister I don't think I've ever heard flimsier evidence." He snorted, a derisive sound similar to that made on occasion by his secretary, Abigail Sanderson. "A good defense attorney could rip that evidence to shreds in no time. And, I assure you, if we're wrong, the defendant would be in the catbird seat, in a position to sue both this hospital and *you* for an immense amount."

She gazed down at him, her eyes bleak. "But the alternative is to allow a possible psychotic to run loose. Shouldn't I, at least, alert the security guards?"

Forsythe twisted his hands together. "How good actors are they?"

"Mr. Reilly?"

"I was thinking of that young lad. Tiptree."

"I take your point. Mr. Tiptree is a bundle of nerves. He could well alert our psychotic."

"Exactly."

"In that case I suppose our only course of action is to carry on exactly as we've been doing. Do nothing that could precipitate further violence. Pray that Sergeant Wood can get to us soon." She pulled out her watch and examined it. "Time for your session with Miss Khalkis. Owen is busy putting linens through the washing machines, so best I take you down to the basement."

"No." He piloted his chair through the doorway, skirted the nurses' counter, and headed toward the lift. "You must have rest. There's really nothing to be done at present. Remember, act naturally."

She didn't argue but, as he drew level with the lift door, she called down the corridor, "Mr. Tiptree, is all in order?"

The boy jumped up, a magazine dangling from one hand, the other clasping his revolver butt. "Everyone in their suite, Miss Holly."

"Fine. As soon as I speak with Mrs. Frome I shall be going down to have a nap. Should you have a problem, kindly refer it to Mrs. Frome in the Jasmine." Lowering her voice, she asked Forsythe, "Should I tell Mrs. Frome?"

"That must be your decision. I've only seen her a few times. Can she handle it?"

"She's an excellent nurse but . . . perhaps she couldn't hide her revulsion. No, I think this is best known only to the two of us. After you've finished your therapy I'll see you, Mr. Forsythe. Perhaps by that time we can come up with a plan."

She waited until the lift arrived and Forsythe trundled his chair into it. Before the door swished shut, he had a glimpse of Miss Holly, erect, white clad, valiant.

Forsythe perched on the edge of the massage table watching Athena as she pushed his wheelchair out of her way. He'd had his leg exercises, his leg massage, and his back massage. Athena opened a door on a storage cabinet, took out a small leather harness, and carried it over to him. "This is what I was telling you about. Watch. I buckle it around your ankle like this. Then you lift your leg as high as you can. At first it will be difficult, but as the knee strengthens it will become easier."

He hefted the small object. "I shouldn't think it will be difficult. This is as light as a feather."

"It won't be for long." She laughed and he liked the sound. Her laugh, like her speaking voice, was low and melodious. "See this pouch on the side of it? When you use it, I'll put lead pellets into it. Just a few to start with but working up to—one moment, I'll show you." She took the harness and returned to the cabinet. Forsythe couldn't see what she was doing, but when she came back and handed him the harness it was heavy, and he told her so. She laughed again. "Not to worry. By the time we get to this weight your knee will be strong enough to take it. Now, best to get your exercise suit back on."

She set the harness down beside him and reached for his suit. He pulled the top on himself and lifted his bad leg while she tugged on the trousers. Bracing his weight on both arms, he pulled his body clear of the table long enough for her to pull the trousers up into place. Even

209

with that small exertion he found he was breathing heavily. Athena patted his shoulder. "Rest for a moment. Then we'll get you into the chair. Is Gareth going to pick you up?"

"I doubt it. Miss Holly said he was in charge of the laundry."

"So that's why he hasn't been popping in every few moments. Honestly, that man is like a hen with one chick. Would you care for a cup of coffee?"

"Please."

He watched Athena as she walked the length of the room. She had a dancer's walk, that coltish grace, those strongly muscled legs. His thoughts wandered to Gareth Owen. Fate had decided to finally award him with a woman like this, perhaps soon a child . . . a fortunate man and one who richly deserved to be.

She stepped into the anteroom and disappeared from sight. He picked up the harness and hefted it again, wondering if he would ever be able to lift his leg with this heavy thing attached to his ankle. From the anteroom came the clatter of china, the tinkle of silver, and then a dull thud. Had Athena dropped something? He glanced up and saw that the scarlet door to the corridor was now wide open and glimpsed the shadowy hall and part of the lift door.

Gareth? Deserting his laundry duties to check on his beloved? But no sounds came from the anteroom, no voices, no rustle of movement. A deep and ominous silence. And then, too late, Forsythe realized who was in that anteroom.

She stepped into the archway and stood, a heavy revolver in one hand, the other arm hugging her waist as though with glee. Strange, he thought, you expect madness to display some dreadful stigma for all to see. But, at first glance, she looked the same as always. Twin set and single strand of pearls, baggy skirt, and low-heeled brogues. Her cap of hair gleamed like metal under the strip lighting and there was that touch of hardness on her mouth.

There were two differences. One was her expression. Meg Eleven looked elated and fulfilled. The other was the blood. Blood matted the gray wool of the twin set, stained the tweed of the skirt, crusted the large, capable hands. There was a smear of scarlet on her ankle, another near her mouth.

Forsythe's mouth felt parched, but he managed to keep his voice steady. "Tiptree's revolver?"

"The *late* Mr. Tiptree. As in dead. As in with his throat cut in the bathroom of my suite. As in how you soon will be."

"But not by cutting my throat."

"I don't dare get that close to you. Mr. Tiptree obligingly turned his back so I could knock him out first."

"Athena?"

She shrugged, a careless little gesture. "The butt of my revolver over her skull. If she isn't dead, she will be before I leave here."

"You like killing?"

She smiled and deep dimples flickered in her cheeks. "Very much. When I finish here and go up to the Flower Wing, I'll kill to my heart's content. I've waited so long for those people."

Forsythe felt bile rise to the back of his throat. She planned a massacre. "This time you're not going to get away with it."

"Like I did with the Owens? Who cares? You know as well as I do, Mr. Barrister, that I'll be tucked away in a nice comfortable mental institution. Mad Meg!"

"Mad Meg from childhood."

The dimples flashed again and she lifted her arm until the revolver was in direct line with his face. "Clever, aren't we? Get Mad Meg to tell her life story and

211

wait for rescue. But no rescue for the renowned barrister and crime fighter. I made sure of that when I knocked Mrs. Frome out and took her keys. Patients and staff are all locked into their suites or the kitchen wing."

He said gently, "Meg, I've never hurt you."

"You've been looking for me. Searching back through the years trying to find me, to punish me. When Miss Holly took the tape off the office and let you in, I knew you found me. But I will tell you this. I watched them die. Elsbeth died first, then Annie. On that flagstone kitchen floor. Emmy was trying to help the younger girls and Walter was crawling toward the kitchen door. I'd been crouching by the kitchen window and I stood up. Emmy looked directly at me. She was clutching her stomach and there was foam around her mouth. I was laughing, watching the slut and her bastard baby dying. Emmy was afraid of me. Dying and still afraid. She backed toward the stairs to the loft and started crawling up them, trying to get away from me. I'd have liked to follow her. Liked to have ripped open her throat and her belly but . . . I knew I had to get back to the cottage . . ."

Now that the woman had started talking, she couldn't seem to stop. Her facade was cracking and he was beginning to see what was behind it. Her lips were moist and a worm of saliva crawled from a corner of her mouth.

He fought to keep his eyes on the horror of that face. From the corner of his eye he'd detected a flicker of movement, a white uniform and large noiseless feet in scarlet Reeboks slowly creeping up behind the madwoman. Forsythe was praying she wouldn't sense that stealthy approach, but his prayers weren't answered. She swung around, the revolver whipping toward Gareth. "Good!" she said. "Now you can die with your Greek whore!"

Without conscious thought, Forsythe's arm flew up and he threw the weighted harness with all his strength.

It hit her forearm and the revolver went spinning across the room.

Quick as a cat, she sprang after it. Gareth was faster. He kicked it into a corner and held out his arms. She backed away and he followed. Then Forsythe saw his face and he called urgently, "Gareth! Just restrain her. For God's sake, man, she's insane!"

The orderly didn't seem to hear. He reached out and gathered her into a dreadful embrace. One huge hand grasped her right wrist and he bent it over his left forearm. He said, "Elsbeth!" and snapped the bone in her arm. Forsythe watched helplessly, incredulous eyes following the struggle. There was another crisp snap, a moan from the woman. Gareth pushed her away. Her right arm dangled limply from the shoulder.

He smiled down at her and reached for her left arm. "Annie!"

"No! Gareth!" Forsythe shouted. "Enough!"

He might as well have shouted into the wind. Another snap. This time an agonized scream. He had to stop this. Forgetting everything but Gareth Owen and Meg Eleven, he jumped off the massage table. He landed heavily on both feet and his left leg buckled. Liquid fire exploded in his knee and lanced down the calf. He fell forward. He landed on his stomach and the wind was knocked out of him.

Gareth roared, "Emmy!" Meg shrieked and Forsythe pulled himself up on his sound knee. Dragging his bad leg he inched painfully across the floor.

He was too late. Gareth's voice was now cool and controlled. "Athena and my baby," he said. "Now I break your neck."

Her neck snapped with the same sound a tree branch makes in a heavy frost. Forsythe collapsed on the floor. Tears were blinding him and then, mercifully, he passed out.

15

A s though to make amends for the worst winter in recent history, spring came early. By April the lilac bush outside the long study windows in Forsythe's Sussex home was in full bloom. A window was open and the strong scent of the massed purple flowers perfumed the room.

Through another window the gaunt figure of Meeks could be discerned. He was checking the job his nephew, newly installed as gardener, was doing. Meeks had stopped the boy, was pointing a bony finger at a knot garden, and appeared to be giving stern advice. Beyond the two figures the velvety expanse of emerald lawn sloped down to the sunlit waters of the pool. Beyond was a glimpse of the plane trees that had been planted by Forsythe's grandfather.

It was a view that the barrister never tired of, but, conscious of the many eyes fixed on his back, he turned away from the window and limped back to the leather chair behind his massive desk. John Josephson said, "You really are moving well, Robert. Not even using a cane."

"Until recently I was forced to use two canes, but now I can move for short distances unaided. Feels wonderful after months of crutches and wheelchairs and canes."

Carolyn Chimes tugged down her trim suit jacket. "I'd hoped to meet your fiancée."

"Both Jennifer and I thought she might be here indefinitely, but on Monday she received an urgent summons and had to fly to Los Angeles. I feel lost without her, but that's simply selfishness. Actually Jennifer and I had longer together this time than we've ever had."

"I was looking forward to meeting Miss Sanderson," Miss Holly said.

He smiled at the nurse. In a pale green suit with a yellow silk blouse, Miss Holly was looking springlike and cheerful. "You'll definitely meet Sandy later, Miss Holly. Right now she's holding the fort in chambers, but I'll be returning to work shortly and Sandy should have more free time. She's anxious to meet you too and fully intends to look you up."

He glanced around at his guests. Both Teddy and Kate had lost weight and Josephson and Carolyn had gained a few pounds. All of them were looking much more fit. Josephson said abruptly, "I'm flying back to Los Angeles myself tomorrow and that's why I was so insistent that we see you. I suppose taking your time could be called selfish too, but, although we know the outlines of this terrible business, we're foggy on details. I . . . all of us thought you could fill them in for us. First, have you any news on Gareth?"

"He's undergoing treatment, of course. Gareth was right out of his mind when he killed Meg. He thought Athena was dead and he went berserk. She was only unconscious but she did have a fractured skull and later suffered a miscarriage. Athena is now fully recovered and

215

is spending most of her time at the sanatorium with Gareth. She's convinced in time Gareth will recover."

"Will he be prosecuted?" Carolyn asked.

"I doubt it. After what Meg Eleven did to the man, I can hardly see a jury handing down a sentence. But we'll have to wait and see on that one."

Kate's hands had clenched and her knuckles were white from pressure. She whispered, "He broke her to pieces. Literally broke—"

Forsythe made a muffled sound and Josephson said harshly, "That's enough, Kate! Robert was there when Gareth did it."

Her mouth twisted and tears filled her eyes. "I keep thinking this whole thing is my fault. As though I did or didn't do something that would have prevented it." Tears were running down her cheeks, but she didn't seem to notice them and made no effort to wipe her face. "If I'd been a more maternal sort of woman. Paid more attention to Meg when she was a child." She started to sob and Teddy walked over and perched on the arm of her chair. He pressed a crisp handkerchief into her hand and put a comforting arm around her shoulders.

"Hindsight, Kate." Carolyn spoke with unusual force. "What's done is done. Meg was a monster!"

Josephson made an impatient gesture. "Suppose we allow Robert to talk? That's what we're here for. Robert?"

Before the barrister had a chance to respond, Miss Holly said eagerly, "Do you want me to explain what we found in the nurses' office?"

"Later. This is a tangled web and best to start from the beginning." He braced his elbows on the arms of his chair, templed his fingers, and gazed down at them. "Meg Eleven may have developed into a monster, Carolyn, but in the beginning she was a lonely and probably frightened child. She also inherited a rather dreadful legacy. Shortly after I met Kate, she told me about her first husband. She said Roddy Eleven had been so jealous that he beat her if she even glanced at another man. It was clear Kate was terrified of him and was glad when he was killed. What she described was a man suffering from an insane form of jealousy. Whatever else his daughter inherited from Roddy Eleven, she also inherited this trait.

"And here we have a child, little more than an infant, left in the care of Kate Kapiche." Kate let out an anguished wail and Forsythe gazed at her with cold hazel eyes. "You made a terrible guardian for that child. You put her into the hands of servants and went merrily on with your own life. Meg did find one person who loved her. Your elderly cook, a woman named Grady. Grady was devoted to the child and Meg loved Grady. Perhaps if she'd lived . . . But she didn't and just as Meg was entering puberty, an unsettling time at best, she lost Grady. You'd think, Kate, you'd at least have tried to replace Grady with another warm motherly woman. But you were too involved with another love affair to care. So Meg, a child from an unstable father, bereaved of the only person who'd ever loved her, was put in the hands of a companion who was nicknamed, with good reason, Shoddy Toddy!"

One of Kate's hands clung to Teddy's arm. The other balled his handkerchief, now sodden, in a fist. "I thought Miss Todd was efficient. She had references—"

"Come off it," Carolyn said. "One look at that frowsy woman and you knew what she was. For once in your life be honest."

Josephson wrenched his eyes from the barrister and glared from one woman to the other. "For once in your lives be quiet! Robert, will you continue?"

"All of you sketched in that summer for me. Miss Todd couldn't have cared less about Meg and the girl chased around behind the two older boys. She certainly wasn't interested in John. Levi was the one who drew

217

her. He possessed an unusual beauty and we can understand why any lonely girl like Meg would be attracted to him. But it wasn't what we commonly term a crush. She was madly, and I use that word deliberately, in love with Levi and—"

"I much doubt," Teddy interrupted, "that a thirteen-year-old girl could be in love with anyone."

"Yet you were the one, Teddy, who claimed to be in love with Emmy Owen. And you were only sixteen at the time. As for Meg, she was an unusual adolescent. And she was completely obsessed with Levi Oglethorpe. John did his best to drive her away, but she sneaked after the boys, spying on them. Unknowingly, Levi encouraged her by talking with her occasionally and even sharing his lunch with her once in a while. We know this was only kindness, but Meg didn't. She must have considered these were signals that eventually Levi would love her—"

"Hate to break in again," Teddy said with a quick glance at Josephson's lowering expression. "But I think you're doing one hell of a lot of surmising."

Forsythe was packing dark, fragrant tobacco in his cherry-wood pipe. He didn't look up as he said, "At times all we can do is surmise. But a great deal of what I'm saying is based on your own memories of that summer. To continue. All was serene until Meg discovered not only had her beloved Levi been having an affair with Emmy Owen but had the girl with child and was making plans to run away and marry her.

"Again we must hazard a guess at how Meg discovered this. She might have heard a conversation about it, perhaps the one between Levi and Emmy or it might have been the one where Levi confessed to John. We know that Meg was a sly, sneaky type of girl who delighted in eavesdropping and spying. It's obvious she was also intelligent. There was no way she was going to allow Levi to marry Emmy Owen and she immediately began to plan to kill the girl. It's obvious Meg didn't care about having to kill the younger Owen children and Walter. Meg stole some arsenic from the tin in the gardening shed, crept up to the kitchen window at the farmhouse, and dropped it into the chili. At supper time she returned so she could watch them—" His voice broke and his fingers clenched his pipe. "She watched them die.

"When Emmy was dead Meg must have believed that everything would carry on as it had for years. She would be sent down each summer to stay in the cottage on Harry's estate and she'd be close to Levi. She was probably convinced in time Levi would love her. Imagine how she felt when Harry suddenly sold his estate and took his brother to Paris. Then, a few months later, Levi was drowned—"

"I'm sorry, Robert, but I *must* interrupt." Kate had regained her composure and her eyes were dry. "Was I completely wrong about those earlier deaths? Levi and Cliff and—"

"Completely. Levi died accidently, Cliff Chimes committed suicide, Alice Constantine and the children died in a house fire. One thing you were right about was the feeling of madness you sensed. As all of us now know, that came from your stepdaughter."

"You could be right. I was always uneasy around Meg. After that summer I saw little of her. First she went to boarding school, then she went on to nurses' training . . . dear Lord, how Meg must have *hated* Harry!"

Forsythe inclined his head. "I doubt Harry would have lived long if he'd returned to England after his brother's death. But he embarked on what he called a gypsy existence and spent most of his time wandering around the continent.

"In the meantime Meg was growing up and she took a nursing degree. I think we're all agreed she was a tragic

219

figure. Meg could have been attractive, but she didn't chose to be. She had no friends, either male or female. It's obvious she'd had her love, lost him, and fully intended to punish the world for taking Levi Oglethorpe from her. The next point I'm certain about is when she was working in a hospital in— But now, Miss Holly, it's your turn. Tell them about our breaking and entering and what we discovered in the guest ledgers—"

"And the Spanish textbooks." She slid sideways in her chair and faced the four survivors. "I feel rather guilty about being so keyed up but that was my first experience as a detective and I must admit I enjoyed it. As all of you know, I took the police tape off the nurses' office and unlocked the door. The first thing Mr. Forsythe did was look over both the guests' ledgers. I confess I couldn't see the point of that. Well, he finally put the books down and then he checked Nancy Elser's schoolbooks that were on the sofa. He was thumbing through one of her notebooks and had reached the page she'd been working on that evening. Mrs. Elser had been copying down Spanish numerals and I looked down the column. *Uno . . . dos . . . tres . . .*"

She looked enquiringly from one person to another, but Josephson was shaking his head and the others looked baffled. "The letters Nancy wrote on the desk blotter in her own blood. O-n-c-e! The Spanish word for *eleven!*"

Carolyn shivered and asked, "But . . . why didn't she write Meg's name in English?"

Miss Holly turned to the barrister and he said, "Perhaps Mrs. Elser feared that Meg might come back, see the message, and destroy the blotter if she did. You must remember the poor woman was dying when she scrawled those four letters."

"But *why* did Meg kill the nurse?" Teddy asked. "And who died first—Harry or Mrs. Elser?"

Miss Holly swung around to face him again. "One question at a time. As a matter of fact, Mr. Chimes, I was puzzled about the motive myself. What earthly reason would Meg have to kill Nancy Elser? But then Mr. Forsythe wheeled back to the desk again and looked through the guests books for the second time. He explained to me that in both books Meg was listed as Meg Eleven and yet—" She broke off and asked, "Do any of you remember when Mrs. Elser came to the patients' lounge to welcome the last batch of guests?"

"The day we all arrived?" Carolyn thought and then said, "Yes, I do remember. It was during dinner and Mrs. Elser was making quite a ceremony of it. Kate said something nasty about a welcome wagon and—"

"And that is what Mr. Forsythe had just remembered that day in the office," Miss Holly said. "He told me that Nancy Elser had greeted Miss Eleven as *Omega* Eleven. He thought Meg must have written her full name in the guest book but that wasn't the case. His very shrewd question was, 'How did Mrs. Elser know the woman's full name?' And the answer had to be that they'd met somewhere before."

Carolyn's fine blond brows pulled together in thought. "I agree they must have met before. No one could guess that *Meg* was a shortened form of *Omega*. But neither let on. Both Meg and Mrs. Elser acted as though they were strangers."

Miss Holly glanced at the barrister again and he took over. "There was an excellent reason for that. Meg certainly would never have let on where and how they met and as for Mrs. Elser . . . she was suddenly faced with a person she'd known under much different circumstances and that person was revealed as the stepdaughter of a wealthy, powerful woman. A woman whose name is practically a byword in this country and abroad. The famous Kate Kapiche. Admittedly, Nancy Elser wasn't terribly intelligent, but she did know revealing her knowledge of Meg Eleven's past wasn't to her advantage."

Teddy removed his arm from Kate's shapely shoulders and leaned forward. A glimmer of sunlight, slanting across the study, blazed in his fair hair and gleamed in the glass of the bookcase behind him. He said, "Let me guess where they met. One common factor—they were both nurses. That hospital you started to talk about a few moments ago, Robert?"

"Ah," Kate said. "I told Robert that Meg had last worked in a hospital in Leeds and had left because she had a nervous collapse caused by the death of some of her patients. Is that the connection?"

"That's it," Forsythe told her. "A cleaning woman in the Damien Day, a wonderful lady named Rosie, lives next door to Nancy's daughter. Laura Elser had told her that Nancy worked for ten years in a hospital in Devonshire—"

"One moment," Josephson broke in. "Are you still surmising?"

"No. Inspector Creighton checked this out and it's factual. Nancy and Meg both worked in a maternity hospital in Leeds. Meg was there only for a matter of months. During that time three women, all in their late teens, died on Meg Eleven's shift. One of these young women had a history of heart trouble, but the other two had appeared to be in robust health.

"The supervisor of this hospital initially was reluctant to disclose the details to Inspector Creighton, but after he was told that Meg was dead and had been responsible for several deaths, he finally opened up. It appears that Meg came under suspicion in the deaths but nothing could be proved. The hospital could only discharge Meg with the warning it would be best if she entered another profession."

Kate was nodding her head and a sheaf of dark red

hair brushed one cheek. She wasn't wearing one of her bird of paradise outfits but looked charming and somehow younger in a lilac linen gown with a Peter Pan collar. "Meg never told me the hospital had discharged her. All she said was that she had nervous problems and would have to find another line of work that would be easier on her emotions. It was then that she took a position at a clinic working with abused children and battered women—" Abruptly she broke off and then said, her voice suddenly shrill, "Dear God! Surely she didn't . . ."

"I'm afraid she did," Forsythe said grimly. "Shortly before she arrived at the Damien Day she was booted out of that clinic and again, she left under a cloud. It involved two young women in their late teens. Both had husbands who had been classified as potentially homicidal. As a counselor Meg Eleven urged those girls to return to their homes, to try and rescue their marriages. The girls were young and confused and easily influenced. Both returned to their brutish husbands. One girl was beaten to death, the other crippled. The one who died was six months pregnant."

All his listeners looked sick. Finally Josephson spoke. "Why in the name of mercy did Meg kill those poor women? In a strange and twisted way I can understand her poisoning Emmy, but I simply can't understand why she continued to murder helpless pregnant women."

"For a time neither could I," Forsythe said. He smiled at Josephson. "I didn't let on, but I was suffering from the same phobia you have. Terror of hospitals. Because of this my mind wasn't ticking along on all—"

"You certainly did a good job hiding it," Josephson told him. "I can tell you one fact, Robert. Next time I have to be hospitalized, they're going to have to hog-tie me. What about you?"

Forsythe stroked his long chin. "Oddly enough I

seem to have lost all fear. Although I have little memory of it, Miss Holly tells me that the police managed to get us dug out the day of Meg's death and they took us by ambulance to the hospital in Hundarby. When I really was taking notice again, I'd been transferred to one in London and, much to my surprise, felt no fear of the place at all. I've no idea why."

Miss Holly was smiling at him. "I have. That experience in the therapy room must have acted as a catharsis. I much doubt you'll ever suffer from that particular fear again. But do tell us how you discovered Meg's motive in those other women's deaths."

Forsythe leaned back in his chair and the soft old leather sighed. "Remember back to the night of Mrs. Elser's death. When Gareth Owen went to her, he told her he was forced to resign and why. He ended up telling her all about his family's deaths and Mrs. Elser asked a number of questions. One of these questions was rather odd. She asked what his sisters had looked like. When Creighton uncovered the deaths at the maternity hospital and the clinic in London he found one other similarity besides age and pregnancy between the young women who had died. All of them were pretty blue-eyed blondes." He turned to Josephson. "All of them must have looked a bit like your Dresden shepherdess."

"And like Emmy Owen. Meg must have smashed that little figurine because of the resemblance," Josephson said. "What about Teddy's other question. Did Harry die first or was it the nurse?"

"The police believe it had to be Nancy Elser and I agree with them. I have a hunch that after Mrs. Elser spoke with Gareth she did a very stupid thing. She must have either called Meg into the office or gone into the woman's suite while making her rounds. She probably told Meg that in the light of what she'd heard about the

224

Owen murders she must tell what she knew about Meg and the deaths in the maternity hospital.''

Josephson ran his fingers through his wiry brown hair. ''I still fail to see why that led to the nurse's death. Admittedly it would have thrown light on those poisonings, but Meg was only a child at the time and it would have been impossible to prove.''

Forsythe raised his brows. ''Why do you think Meg Eleven came to the Damien Day in the first place? To succor a stepmother she despised? Hardly. Meg was there because all the survivors of that summer were there. And her first target was Harry Oglethorpe. Again, we're forced to do some guesswork. Up to this point Meg had successfully got away with murder after murder. Harry might have been her only target and she was still sane enough to hope she could kill him and still not be detected. But if Nancy Elser started to babble about the murders of young blondes in a maternity hospital, the police would look directly at Meg. So the nurse had to be silenced.

''Meg acted quickly. She went to the supply room, donned a smock and plastic gloves, and returned to kill Nancy Elser. Then she switched off the lights in the office and went to kill Harry.''

''And that,'' Miss Holly said smugly, ''is where your reasoning is flawed, Mr. Forsythe. In my new role as detective I find a snag. How did Miss Eleven know about the change of suites? How did she know Mr. Oglethorpe was in the Iris? How did she know he was in the tub where she could electrocute him? Are we about to surmise again?''

The barrister smiled at her. ''To an extent. We do know that Meg, from the time she was a child, had spied on people. She must have seen the two dodos changing suites. We do know this. When Carolyn pulled Darla into Meg's suite that evening she told Meg to go to her mother. And Meg didn't go to the Iris, she went to

225

Harry's previous suite, the Orchid. Ergo, tyro investigator, Meg knew exactly where to find Harry.

"The second part of your question. Possibly Meg was going to try to kill Harry with the same knife she'd used on the nurse. But she found him dozing in the tub, Kate's hair dryer handy, and took advantage of this. She peeled off the smock and gloves and tossed those items and the knife into the tub with Harry's body. All she had to do then was scuttle back to her suite and pretend to be asleep."

Carolyn shook her sleek head. "What an actress Meg was!"

"Psychotics frequently are," Miss Holly told her. "I recall one private patient I had. A charming lad about fifteen. He had me convinced the horror stories his parents told me about him were garbage until one evening he came at me with a meat cleaver." She rubbed an upper arm. "I still have a scar from that encounter. But, Mr. Forsythe, Meg's sanity or the remains of it, must have given when she saw us going into the nurses' office."

"It did. After she butchered Mrs. Elser, I should imagine her sanity was hanging by a thread. In the therapy room she said I had to die because I'd been hunting her down, that I'd found some clue that would expose her. But, on the other hand, she no longer cared about being caught. She enticed young Tiptree into her suite on some pretense, got him to turn his back, knocked the boy out, and slit his throat with a knife she'd stolen from the lunch buffet. Then she went to the Jasmine, knocked out Mrs. Frome, took the master key, and locked the unconscious nurse in the suite. After she'd locked the doors of your suites, she went downstairs to the kitchen wing and locked in Lisl Gunther, Perce, the two security guards, and you, Miss Holly. But she made a mistake—"

"Gareth Owen," Miss Holly exclaimed.

"Either Meg forgot about him or thought he was in

the kitchen wing. But Gareth was in the basement, in the laundry room. He was keeping a close watch on Athena and— But you know the rest.''

For a time they sat silently and then Carolyn murmured, ''She was going to kill all of us. Why? I'd nothing to do with Levi. I barely knew the boy.''

''Mother's right,'' Teddy said. ''I can see Meg hating Harry and Kate and even you, John. You did your best to keep her away from Levi. But my mother and I . . . no, I don't understand.''

Forsythe rested his head against the chair back. He felt a breath of air stir his hair and smelled the combined odors of lilac and freshly mown grass. Such a peaceful setting for such a ghastly discussion. He heartily wished these people would go away, would allow the peace of the old house to comfort him again. Miss Holly bore a scar from a charming psychotic on her arm and he had a wound too. His didn't show but it was there and still raw and hurting. For the remainder of his life in nightmares he would hear bones snapping as Gareth Owen methodically broke Meg's sturdy body to pieces.

He sighed. These people had no intention of leaving until their question was answered. But he didn't have the answer and he told them so. ''I've no idea why Meg was going to massacre all of you. We could argue that she did blame John from keeping her away from Levi and we could say that Kate's disgraceful treatment of her as a child was enough to lead to murder. But there's no reason why she would hate Teddy or Carolyn.''

Miss Holly smoothed a wisp of gray hair back from her brow. She said crisply, ''How can we explore the motivations of a madwoman? But we do know this. Omega Eleven had been responsible for the deaths of many people. If I was going to hazard a professional opinion I'd say that when she witnessed the agonized death of Emmy Owen and her sisters and her father, Meg *enjoyed* it. She may have experienced her first orgasm. I feel that Meg Eleven continued killing, not only because of Levi Oglethorpe, but from simple delight in the act itself. Meg Eleven had many of the symptoms of a serial killer.''

The nurse glanced around the circle of attentive faces and added, ''It's also my professional opinion that we should leave now. Granted, Mr. Forsythe is stronger, but this is not only tiring but it's distressing for him. When we broke down the door of the kitchen wing at the Damien Day and found him sprawled on the floor of the therapy room I thought for moments he was dead. He wasn't, of course, but in going to Meg's aid he'd injured his bad knee and it's taken much longer to heal than it originally would have.'' Miss Holly picked up her handbag and took several steps toward the door.

''Please wait, Miss Holly,'' Kate called. ''I've an announcement to make. This is probably the last time all of us will be together because John's leaving tomorrow and I want you to know . . .'' Her voice trailed off and, amazingly, warm color rushed up her throat and suffused her face in a blush. ''I'm going to be married!''

''*Again?*'' Carolyn threw back her head and her graceful throat pulsed with laughter. ''It's been a long dry spell for you, hasn't it? Almost three years since your last divorce.''

''Two,'' Kate snapped. Then she relaxed and smiled widely at the other woman. ''Darling, best not to make fun. Soon we'll be related.''

Carolyn abruptly stopped laughing but her mouth remained ajar. For moments she seemed unable to speak, but then she stuttered. ''Wh-what are you talking about?''

Reaching up a shapely arm, Kate drew Teddy's face down and kissed him full on the lips. By now he was blushing as brightly as she was. "Mother," he blurted. "Kate and I . . . we're going to be married."

His mother sprang to her feet. Her eyes were blazing. "No! I won't allow it."

Kate drawled, "I hardly think you can prevent it."

Putting aside Kate's clinging arms, Teddy slowly rose. He faced his enraged parent. "I may play juve roles but I'm an adult, Mother."

"But she's old enough to be your *mother!*"

"Age has no bearing on how we feel about each other."

"But this woman . . . she'll use you and toss you aside like an orange peel."

"Not this time. This time it's until death do us part." Teddy patted his future wife's dark red hair and grinned. "We've signed a marriage contract and divorce will prove far too costly for my lovely Kate."

Josephson was smiling broadly and Miss Holly had a look of devilish glee. Forsythe smothered a laugh. He still had no idea whether Teddy Chimes resembled his father in a physical sense, but it would appear father and son shared one quality. Both of them liked money. It was also possible that Kate had finally met her match and had painted herself into a matrimonial corner.

Kate came lithely to her feet, slid an arm around Teddy's waist, and said sweetly. "Cheer up, Carolyn darling. Look at it this way. You haven't lost a son, you've gained a daughter. Soon you'll be my mummie-in-law."

For moments Carolyn looked wild with fury. Then the stiffness left her body and, without warning, she was B. D. Epps. Her eyes bulged, her mouth fell open, and she blurted, *"Cor blimey! Whatta flaming cockup!"*

The room virtually exploded with laughter and on the lawn outside the windows Meeks and his nephew turned bewildered faces toward the source of that wild glee. "Sounds like they're all hammered," the boy said.

"Shut your yob," his uncle told him sternly. "Does a body good to laugh like that."

Meeks was right. Laughter was doing Robert Forsythe nothing but good.